the Wish

# Books by Beverly Lewis

*The Wish*
*The Atonement*
*The Photograph*
*The Love Letters*
*The River*

### HOME TO HICKORY HOLLOW
*The Fiddler*
*The Bridesmaid*
*The Guardian*
*The Secret Keeper*
*The Last Bride*

### THE ROSE TRILOGY
*The Thorn*
*The Judgment*
*The Mercy*

### ABRAM'S DAUGHTERS
*The Covenant*
*The Betrayal*
*The Sacrifice*
*The Prodigal*
*The Revelation*

### THE HERITAGE OF LANCASTER COUNTY
*The Shunning*
*The Confession*
*The Reckoning*

### ANNIE'S PEOPLE
*The Preacher's Daughter*
*The Englisher*
*The Brethren*

### THE COURTSHIP OF NELLIE FISHER
*The Parting*
*The Forbidden*
*The Longing*

### SEASONS OF GRACE
*The Secret*
*The Missing*
*The Telling*

*The Postcard*
*The Crossroad*

*The Redemption of Sarah Cain*
*Sanctuary* (with David Lewis)
*Child of Mine* (with David Lewis)
*The Sunroom*
*October Song*

*Amish Prayers*

*The Beverly Lewis Amish Heritage Cookbook*

www.beverlylewis.com

# the Wish

BEVERLY
LEWIS

© 2016 by Beverly M. Lewis, Inc.

Published by Bethany House Publishers
11400 Hampshire Avenue South
Bloomington, Minnesota 55438
www.bethanyhouse.com

Bethany House Publishers is a division of
Baker Publishing Group, Grand Rapids, Michigan

Printed in the United States of America

Library of Congress Cataloging-in-Publication Data
Names: Lewis, Beverly, author.
Title: The wish / Beverly Lewis.
Description: Minneapolis, Minnesota : Bethany House, a division of Baker Publishing Group, [2016]
Identifiers: LCCN 2016017639| ISBN 9780764218897 (hardcover : acid-free paper) | ISBN 9780764212499 (softcover) | ISBN 9780764218903 (large print : softcover)
Subjects: LCSH: Amish—Pennsylvania—Lancaster County—Fiction. | Female friendship—Fiction. | GSAFD: Christian fiction. | Love stories.
Classification: LCC PS3562.E9383 W57 2016 | DDC 813/.54—dc23
LC record available at https://lccn.loc.gov/2016017639

Scripture quotations are from the King James Version of the Bible.

Cover design by Dan Thornberg, Design Source Creative Services
Art direction by Paul Higdon

16  17  18  19  20  21  22      7  6  5  4  3  2  1

For Barbara,
my sister
and
dearest friend.

There is nothing on this earth
to be prized more than true friendship.

—Thomas Aquinas

# Prologue

*Some people are simply born into the wrong family,* I thought, recalling my disappointing morning. My parents were older, and being the only child in the house since my sole sibling, Mahlon, married seven years ago, I'd come to believe that all the other families in our Plain community were more close-knit and interesting than my own.

Then, when the Gingeriches moved into the farmhouse near us, it seemed like an answer to prayer. Quickly, they became as close as any of my blood kin here in Lancaster County, Pennsylvania. Closer, really.

So I could hardly wait to visit them whenever possible. And this fine October afternoon—a Lord's Day set apart for reflection and visiting family—was no different.

The sky was the color of *Mammi* Speicher's Blue Willow plates and just as sparkling, too. No matter the weather or my circumstances, though, the divine peace of the Lord's Day reminded me to count my blessings. *Dawdi* Benuel, my father's father, had urged me to do the same.

Only this morning Dawdi had asked, "Do ya realize you spend more daylight hours over at the Gingeriches' than ya do round here, Leona?" We were feeding the livestock.

Neither my father nor mother had ever voiced this, not being ones to share their feelings much. But I supposed Dawdi Benuel was right and had every reason to say so. In that single look from him, standing there beside the feeding trough, I had witnessed a hint of frustration, perhaps even disapproval—not that it could change my affection for Gloria Gingerich and her family.

My mind jolted back to the present as, unexpectedly, I heard someone coming on the opposite side of the road. Nearing, I saw it was my lanky cousin, Orchard John, looking nearly like a large crow in his black broadfall trousers and *Mutze*—frock coat.

"Leona," he called, "if you're headed to see Gloria, she's not home." He crossed the road to me. "Seems odd 'cause they're all home 'cept her. How's that figure?" He grimaced and shook his head.

Since John had been courting my seventeen-year-old friend for nearly a year now, I assumed he had a right to wonder. "Did they say where she is? You could've waited for her to return, maybe."

"Not sure when she'll be back." John gave me a wave as he kept going, clearly peeved at coming all this way for naught. His father's one-hundred-and-fifty-acre orchard of fifteen varieties of apples, as well as cherries, prune plums, and peaches, was more than a mile away on Farmdale Road, so I couldn't fault him. Even so, it wondered me why he hadn't made plans with Gloria beforehand, like usual.

As for me, I would be content to visit with Gloria's mother for the time being. Jeannie Gingerich's big blue eyes always lit up when I knocked on the back door, and her warm greeting made me smile. Oh, such a *babblich* and vibrant woman, seemingly interested in whatever I had in mind to tell her. Still youthful and perty, too—no more than forty, surely. All the things my own *Mamma* wasn't.

And Gloria's father, Arkansas Joe, was charming in his own right, always making me feel comfortable in the house, drawing me into conversation—unlike my own *Dat*—joking with me, kidding me like he did his own children.

*The perfect family . . .*

Slowing my pace, I breathed in the damp, woodsy scent of autumn and savored the view of sugar maples aflame with deep crimson along the road where it dipped, then crossed over a creek.

I caught sight of the Gingeriches' redbrick house ahead and hurried my steps, anticipating the prospect of spending time there. This was the home where I'd played Dutch Blitz, baked apple dapple for dessert, and made faceless dolls out of leftover dress fabric. Oh, the many fun-filled days we'd shared together!

A family of five deer moved through a thicket of leaves in the woodland over yonder and then scampered out of sight. *Forever friends are sometimes closer than kinfolk,* I thought. *A blessing, for certain!*

And after these wonderfully happy years living side by side, I had every reason to believe the future with my dear sister-friend would be as bright as the afternoon sun.

## CHAPTER 1

The farmhouse that Arkansas Joe Gingerich had rented upon first coming to Colerain Township was one of only a handful of brick structures in the area, a rarity on Maple Shade Road. The plot of land was small compared to others on that stretch of country road, although there were plentiful outbuildings, all painted white—a solid corncrib and woodshed, a spacious separate stable, and a one-level barn. Like other Amish families, the Gingeriches had a pulley clothesline, the highest one Leona Speicher had ever seen. On *der Weschdaag*, when strong breezes blew, the clothes pinned to the line seemed to flap against the sky.

Leona headed up the paved lane, itching to set foot inside the gleaming house again. *A cheerful haven,* she often thought of it.

An arbor of grapevines was still green despite the arrival of fall, and on the back porch, golden mums lined up along the steps in large clay pots, some of them painted in stripes or polka dots.

Two pearly white barn kittens scampered away as Jeannie Gingerich greeted Leona with a welcoming embrace, as if she hadn't seen her in weeks. "*Wunnerbaar-gut* to see ya," she said, smiling and ushering Leona inside. "What would ya like to snack on till Gloria gets herself home—cookies, pumpkin bread . . . or both?"

"*Denki,* a cookie's fine."

"Just one?" Jeannie grinned as she scooted the plateful of cookies over next to Leona.

The sound of Adam's deep voice drifted from the front room. Orchard John had been right about everyone but Gloria being home.

"Is that Leona I hear?" Adam called warmly, momentarily ducking his head into the kitchen to greet her.

Leona smiled and blushed, cautious not to let her giddiness at his attention show. After all, Jeannie and her husband couldn't possibly know that Adam had seen her home last Singing for the first time. Even if they *did* know,

Adam likely wouldn't want to make much of it, young as they both were.

Leona chose a cookie and wished Adam had stayed put in the front room—she'd blushed in front of his mother, for goodness' sake!

Jeannie, however, gave no sign that she'd noticed anything unusual and quickly set Leona at ease by bringing up a sisters' day gathering—this one a quilting bee—Leona might enjoy attending next week with her and Gloria. "That is, if you're not workin' at Maggie's Country Store." Jeannie leaned her elbows on the table, her eyes intent on Leona. "I could drop by and pick you and your Mamma up, if you're both free."

"You know how my mother feels 'bout big doin's."

"Well, maybe *you* could go."

Leona could tell Jeannie really wanted her along and said she'd have to talk to her sister-in-law boss, the owner of the shop.

She realized anew how rarely she thought of spending time with her own small family in this same enthusiastic way. Did her parents feel the same toward her? Today, for instance, they'd talked of going to visit Leona's brother, Mahlon, and his family, not even asking if she wished to go along. She had mixed feelings about it—shouldn't she *want* to be with her real family?

*Shouldn't they want to be with* me?

Although, in their defense, they must have guessed where she'd rather be this afternoon.

Leona glanced up at the large kitchen calendar, with its photograph of a tall lighthouse on the edge of a cliff, white waves crashing below. Gloria's mother seemed to like lighthouses; there were three small statuettes on display in the hutch across the room from them.

"Have ya ever been inside a lighthouse?" Leona asked, suddenly curious.

"Only once—clear out in Oregon, if you can imagine that." Jeannie described in great detail traveling northwest in a twelve-passenger van, sharing the cost with other families. "This was before Adam and Gloria were born," added Jeannie. "My husband and I were newlyweds and decided to spend the night at Haceta Head Lighthouse Keeper's House. We could hear the waves beating against the cliff below . . . so different than hearing the mules brayin' in the barn."

Leona could scarcely relate to such an adventure, never having traveled away from the East Coast. Mahlon's wife, Maggie, was the only one she knew with travel aspirations, perhaps as far as Virginia for the Colonial Christmas tour of the Jamestown Settlement. Apparently, her sister-in-law had read about it in a travel book from the library.

*Maggie and her fancies,* thought Leona. Maggie certainly saw things differently than most area folk. She had an eye for pretty things, one that well served her boutique of home-crafted items. There, Maggie sold dozens of pretty candles in all different shapes, sizes, and scents, as well as gas lamps that looked so much like electric ones that even *Englischers* were fooled. For an Amishwoman, Maggie certainly had a knack for knowing what appealed to her customers. It was only in her shop that Maggie was able to indulge her tastes, Leona knew. Truly, Maggie was the closest thing to a sister she had, at least amongst relatives. They weren't close at all in age, but Leona enjoyed her company, especially at the shop, and looked up to her.

Going to the sink for some water, Leona noticed a gray carriage turning into the lane with Preacher Miller at the reins in his wide-brimmed black felt hat. Gloria, of all people, was sitting on the seat behind him, her dog, Brownie, a beagle–cocker spaniel mix, panting at the window. "Lookee who's here!" Leona said, and Jeannie rose to see, apparently surprised her daughter was being escorted home by the minister.

Jeannie called to her husband. "Joe! Preacher Miller's come to see ya."

Right quick, footsteps came from the

front room, and Arkansas Joe strode into the kitchen. He caught Leona's eye, giving her his usual winning smile. "There's our second girl," he said before putting on his shoes and dashing toward the back door, shoving it open. "Hullo, Preacher!" Joe announced, but Leona could detect a strange shakiness beneath his typically confident tone.

*"My father could prob'ly sell cars to the Amish,"* Gloria had once told her. *"Everyone likes him."* It had seemed like a strange comment at the time, one Leona didn't find all that complimentary. Still, she couldn't deny Joe's personality.

"I hope everything's all right," Leona said softly, wondering how Jeannie knew the minister had come particularly to visit Joe.

"Let's not borrow trouble." Jeannie sighed deeply and made her way to the back door to meet Gloria as she came up the steps. "Aren't *you* special, getting a ride with the preacher."

"Just happened to be going the same way," Gloria said, entering the kitchen. "He likes to help out when he can."

Overhearing this, Leona agreed silently, recalling a number of times the kindly man had offered her and Mamma a ride, as well. But there was a tension now between Gloria and her mother, and Leona sensed something lurking beneath their smiles.

Gloria hurried to Leona. "I was over at your place . . . wanted you to go walkin' with Brownie and me," she explained. "But not a soul was home."

"My parents went to visit Mahlon and Maggie and the children." Leona found it odd that she hadn't crossed paths with Gloria on the way here. Had Gloria run into her beau, Orchard John? *Maybe she cut through the back meadow. . . .*

Motioning for Leona to head upstairs with her, Gloria led the way to her room, which was situated at the far end of the narrow hall, past a spacious spare bedroom and a small sewing room. But it wasn't her afternoon walk she had on her mind. "*Kumme,*" Gloria whispered, leading Leona to the window. They peered down at her father and Preacher Miller standing at the base of the windmill.

"See that?" Gloria asked. She sounded frightened, as if watching something terrible unfold.

Leona squinted down and saw Brownie wag his tail at the minister, who absently reached to give him a pat. "Looks like a pleasant enough visit, ain't so?"

Gloria squeezed her hand. "If only that was all . . ." Her eyes were bright with tears.

"What's wrong, Gloria?"

She shook her head. "*Ach,* maybe I'm just tired, is all."

Her voice sounded so strangely flat, Leona was suddenly afraid to pry further . . . but she was certain Gloria wasn't saying all she knew.

## CHAPTER 2

*N*either Leona nor Gloria spoke that week of the preacher's visit, and Leona waved off her worries as the days rolled around to Preaching Sunday. As she talked outside with Gloria following the service, Leona noticed Arkansas Joe with Adam and the two younger Gingerich boys waiting near the horses. Jonas smiled up at his father as Joe stood shoulder to shoulder with Adam, both hands on towheaded James's shoulders. Their closeness seemed ever so appealing to Leona.

*The People here aren't openly affectionate, especially not in public.* She'd never seen any members of her own family act in such a way, yet she couldn't help wishing they did. Despite her own staid upbringing, the Gingeriches' displays of closeness warmed her heart.

She recalled the early fall day six years ago, when Gloria and her older brother, Adam, entered their one-room schoolhouse for the first time. That golden day had changed Leona's life. . . .

Ever so *freindlich*, Gloria was taller than any other girl in the sixth grade, her red-brown hair the color of Dat's Shetland ponies. Her sunny smile caught Leona's attention as she took a place in the desk one aisle over from her. Did she need a friend, too?

Sometimes on Leona's bluest days, Maggie would tell her, *"Loneliness is a choice, remember."* All the same, her sister-in-law couldn't have understood Leona's desperate yearning for a sister back then, having grown up with four of her own. To make matters worse, Leona's only sibling was ten years her senior, and a rather aloof brother to boot. Even most of her many cousins on both sides of the family were boys. The few girl cousins she *did* have were much older, some already married by the time Leona came along.

So she'd wasted no time that first recess welcoming Gloria, inviting her to jump rope. And later, during quiet reading time, Leona let her borrow a book of limericks. After school, they had walked home together, swinging their lunch thermoses in time.

The new girl was full of stories about her former home of Salem, in the foothills of the Arkansas Ozarks, where she was born. It was all Gloria talked about, like she'd left something very special behind.

Leona, on the other hand, told her what she knew of her father's Swiss Amish ancestors from Indiana, explaining that her grandfather Speicher had moved to Colerain with his parents when he was a boy. Later, she tried to describe the picturesque woodland beyond Dat's vast cornfield, with its mossy places where a girl could lose herself for hours.

"It's *gut* to have a special place," Gloria had said, her freckled face aglow. "Mine was our meadow back home. Ever so perty. My mother always hummed when she walked with me there."

Leona stuck her neck out and said that *her* mother was a woman of few words. "Always has been. Can't imagine her humming in a meadow or anyplace else."

The girls walked along the road in silence for a moment, following the ruts made by many horses' hooves. "Tell me more 'bout where ya used to live," Leona said. "Salem, you called it?"

"*Jah* . . . close to the Southfork River." Gloria went on to share adventures of canoeing and whatnot. "Adam and Daed liked to go rainbow trout fishin', too."

"My brother, Mahlon, likes to fish. Dat does, too."

"Well, White River's where all the big fish are in Arkansas," Gloria said, pushing her slightly wavy hair under her white head covering, a most unusual cup shape with many darts sewn in the sides. "And I mean *big*." She set down her thermos and stretched out her hands to show the size, and Leona noticed her cape dress had several long, pretty seams. "Don't tell my brother Adam I told ya, but once he got hooked when he went fishing with our younger cousin. Right in the head!"

"*Ach,* must've hurt!" Leona shivered at the thought.

Gloria nodded as her twelve-year-old brother darted past them to catch up with the other schoolboys. Adam's gray cloth suspenders did not make an X on the back of his cocoa-colored shirt like the boys' here, and the brim of his straw hat was narrower than any Leona had ever seen, with a yellow-gold band around it. *Awful fancy . . .*

Gloria mentioned her three-year-old brother, Jonas, who was already following their father around in the barn, and eighteen-month-old baby brother, James, who waddled around the house after *Mamm*. "Daed calls him our little penguin."

They giggled over that before Gloria returned to describing their former community—the bluegrass music at the old downtown square, the rodeo at the Fulton County Fair, and the giant fried turkey legs served there. Most of it sounded pretty foreign to Leona, yet Gloria talked so fondly of her beloved home, Leona asked why they'd left it behind.

She shook her head. "Not sure—but there must be reasons, knowin' my father." And that quick, she changed the subject to her butterfly collection and asked when Leona might drop by to see it.

"Tomorrow?" The word flew right out.

"*Des gut,* then." Gloria smiled and reached for Leona's hand. And from that day on, they were nearly inseparable.

Later, back home after Preaching, once Leona had rested in her room as her parents required, she sat at the kitchen table and read several psalms from her mother's large *Biewel* while Dawdi Benuel, who lived next door in their *Dawdi Haus*, sat in the rocking chair nearby, his head bobbing through his nap.

After she finished reading, she carefully

thumbed through the onionskin pages, noticing several bookmarks—one with tiny dried, pressed flowers from the Holy Land. *Purchased at Maggie's Country Store,* Leona thought, smiling.

There was also a get-well note, and when she examined it closer, she recognized the handwriting of a younger Gloria.

"She must've written this when I was staying with them," murmured Leona, noting the date. *When Mamma suffered with pneumonia . . .*

Gloria's sentiments, though childlike, were tender and caring.

> *Dear Millie Speicher,*
> *I'm awful sorry you are sick. Don't worry about Leona, 'cause she's all right. We're making sure of that! I hope you get well soon!*
> *From your neighbor,*
> *Gloria Gingerich*

Seeing the sweet gesture made Leona appreciate Gloria all the more—ever a reservoir of joy, it seemed. Mamma hadn't told Leona about the note, but that didn't surprise her. Mamma was typically reserved about most things. All the same, Leona was glad to see she had kept it.

Leona found herself waiting again for Gloria that evening, just outside the deacon's white two-story barn. It was Leona's ninth Singing since her sixteenth birthday, June 28, and the thrill of being old enough to be included with *die Youngie* still made her pinch herself. She especially liked sitting with Gloria to join their voices in song. Gloria had been coming for more than a year now, and Orchard John was mighty sweet on her.

Leona herself was being pursued by Gloria's brother Adam, a recent turn of events that tickled her friend. Gloria had even whispered, *"My brother's gonna fall for you, and then you'll be part of our family for real!"*

They had laughed at the notion, but Leona knew she would like nothing better. And Adam was awfully fun to be around. *Cute too!*

Searching now in all directions, Leona still saw no sign of Gloria, nor of Adam. *They said they were coming,* Leona recalled as she slipped silently inside the barn, purposely hanging back from the rest of the youth in hopes of waving the Gingeriches over if they arrived late.

One of the parent sponsors blew the pitch pipe to give the starting note, and the unison singing began. Not wanting to stand out,

Leona moved quietly to the far end of the long wooden bench and sat down.

Amidst the lilting strains of "Jesus, Lover of My Soul," her mind wandered back to the early months Gloria and her family had spent in Colerain.

---

The first time Leona went to Gloria's house and met her mother, she learned that, like her, Gloria was the only girl in her family. Jeannie Gingerich had made over Leona's pretty blond hair, then surprised her by giving her a gentle hug.

A few months later, following Christmas, Leona's Mamma became ill with pneumonia, so bad off that she was hospitalized for a while.

At school, Leona was startled to pieces when she was pulled aside by the teacher for her hair being all *strubblich* . . . and for wearing soiled clothing. She hadn't packed an adequate lunch, either, but the teacher's expression was sympathetic as Leona whispered that her mother was in the hospital, and Dat too busy to look after her properly. *"I haven't been able to keep up,"* she'd admitted.

When Gloria insisted during afternoon recess on knowing why their teacher had taken her aside, Leona told her. After school, Gloria had walked the whole way home with Leona, where she strode up to Dat, who was pitching hay to the livestock. Right then, she'd boldly asked if Leona might be looked after by *her* mother for the time being. "Leona's always *willkumm*," she said.

Leona held her breath, surprised Gloria would offer so much without first checking with her own parents.

Dat looked at Leona, his face serious, his cheeks ruddy. Leona wondered if he'd noticed her mussed-up hair and clothing, too, or how hard it was for Leona, having fallen behind on household chores while going to school. Even so, she felt sure he would mention that one of her many aunts could look after her instead. "Ain't necessary," he said. "She's fine here."

But Gloria's eyes were big and pleading, and she was not backing down.

For what seemed longer than a minute, Dat stared over their heads toward the Gingeriches' vast meadow, his profile stock-still. Then, thoughtfully, he looked back at Gloria before agreeing to her plea, provided the idea had her parents' blessing. "Well, I guess you folk are mighty handy, close by as you are. All the better for keeping Leona in school."

After her father had visited Gloria's parents to make arrangements, Leona packed up a few changes of clothing and went to stay with them, settling into their daily pattern of barn chores and kitchen duties.

During their free time, she and Gloria gathered pinecones and grapevines and acorns to make wreaths. Together, they had admired such decorations at the farmers market, and young though she was, Leona tried her own hand at it.

Leona was also present when Gloria asked her father for a puppy, saying it was all she'd ever dreamed of. Not long after that, Arkansas Joe took the two girls to choose a dog from a nearby farm family that had more puppies than they could manage. A light seemed to flicker across Joe's face as he knelt down with the girls and played with the puppy. *Was it joy at fulfilling his only daughter's wish?* Leona wondered.

Sweet Gloria had kindly insisted that Leona name the adorable beagle–cocker spaniel mix. Leona had taken a full day to decide on Brownie, which Jeannie had declared the perfect name for the bright-eyed puppy. Everyone had agreed.

Spending her time with the Gingeriches had sealed Leona's loyalties. Not only was she impressed by Gloria's parents' open affection for each other, but she appreciated them for taking her under their wing and including her in that same circle of love.

With all of her heart, Leona thanked the Lord above for bringing such wonderful-*gut* neighbors so unexpectedly into her life. And sometimes, while shaking rag rugs on the back stoop or feeding the chickens with Gloria, Leona caught herself imagining what it would be like to belong to *this* family, not just as a friend but for *real*.

## CHAPTER 3

Halfway through the two-hour Sunday Singing, refreshments were served: cookies and cake, and cups of hot cocoa. Leona again scanned the crowd for Adam and Gloria, yet there was still no sign of them.

*They must've changed their minds. . . .*

Not long after, Orchard John walked over and asked Leona, "Know anything 'bout Gloria and Adam?"

"Last I heard, they were comin'," she told her cousin.

Deacon Mose Ebersol's eldest son, nineteen-year-old Thomas, joined them, his light brown bangs cut straight across his forehead. "Are ya lookin' for the Gingerich girl?" he asked Orchard John.

John nodded right quick. "I thought for sure she'd be here."

Tom shook his head. "I doubt she's comin' tonight." He took a sip of his cocoa. "Not after . . . well, not now."

Neither of them questioned him. Being a minister's son, Tom had always been close-lipped, but something in his expression revealed concern.

*"I doubt she's comin',"* Tom had just said. What did he know?

Leona recalled Preacher Miller's unexpected visit last week to see Arkansas Joe, and Gloria's and Jeannie's peculiar reactions. And now, Adam had stood her up for their date tonight. She couldn't help wondering why.

Even after nearly all the fellows and girls had paired up and ridden away in courting buggies, Leona paced the cement barn floor, continuing to wait for Gloria and Adam. Tom had lingered as well with his deaf brother, eighteen-year-old Danny, the two of them standing outdoors for a time. Probably Danny had ridden with Tom tonight. Plenty of brothers liked to double-date in one buggy.

Eventually Tom stepped back inside and moved toward her as if wanting to say something. Partway there, though, he turned back and left without speaking, slipping out into the night to drive Danny home.

Alone now with only the sound of a horse neighing, Leona went to stand in the barn's wide doorway and stared out at the glimmering stars. She still hoped her dearest friend might yet arrive, if only to clear things up . . . to soothe Leona's worries as a dreadful feeling grew in her chest. *"It's nothing,"* Gloria might say. *"Nothing at all."*

Disheartened, Leona waited another half hour before heaving the barn door closed and trudging toward the dark road. Alone.

───◦❊◦───

Tom Ebersol arrived home early after the Singing, signaling once more that neither he nor Danny had invited a girl to go riding— something that had been the case for Tom for several months now. His father didn't come right out and inquire, but Tom presumed he was thinking, *No girls caught your eye . . . again?*

Of course that was far from the truth, though it was okay for Dat to think it as the two of them sat hunched over the kitchen table, chins on fists, playing a serious game of checkers and making short work of Mamma's pumpkin walnut bread. Danny had already headed for his room to read, not as interested in table games.

Tom strategized his next couple of moves,

trying to keep his focus on the wooden checkerboard instead of on pretty Leona Speicher. She had been even more pleasing to him without Adam Gingerich waiting on the sidelines.

"Ready to make your move?" Dat's question jolted Tom back to the game.

He sat there a minute, redirecting his thoughts, hard as it was. "*Es dut mir leed*— I'm sorry."

"Your mind must be elsewhere, son."

His father was right, but now wasn't the time to come clean. So Tom made the best move he could, given Dat's imposing line of black checkers, including two kings.

Dat reached for one of the kings, gripping it between his callused fingers while he murmured in *Deitsch*. Tom gave in to musing about Leona once more; anyone could see she was enamored with the Gingeriches, including, it seemed, Adam, which made it nearly impossible for Tom to get her attention. Tom recalled how very much like a loving father, and upstanding church member, Arkansas Joe had appeared to be today, after church. He wondered if she had any inkling that Joe wasn't always as pleasant and engaging as he appeared to be. The man could also be hotheaded. Joe had talked up to Preacher Miller here recently, which was unwise. Tom had long had a feeling about the man that he couldn't put his finger on. Over the years, he'd heard rumors that certain tools Joe had "borrowed" from fellow farmers sometimes had a way of disappearing. More recently, Joe had joked about the length of the second sermon. *"Too bad the seats are so hard—I could have taken a* gut *long nap!"*

Yet if trouble was brewing, Tom secretly hoped the Gingerich family might return to Arkansas, unlikely though that was. Church members who got themselves in hot water rarely held a defiant stance for long.

Truth be told, it wasn't Tom's place to sit in judgment of Arkansas Joe or anyone else, for that matter. But he couldn't forget that sitting across the checkerboard from him was his deacon father . . . a silent source of knowledge on any members who might be misbehaving.

He was worried for Leona, and for what might happen if she ever learned the truth about the family she so loved.

Dat won two out of three games before Tom called it a night and headed just around the corner of the kitchen to his room. In the stillness, he sat on his bed and bowed his head in prayer.

Later, he considered again the notion that Adam might not be such a good choice for Leona, considering his uneasiness about

Adam's father. After all, she'd grown up here in Colerain and was known to hold fast to the Old Ways, like the rest of her family.

He pulled on his pajamas and then raised the shade to see the moon rise. The stars seemed exceptionally bright against the ink-black sky. He recalled seeing Adam with Leona after the Singing two weeks ago, observing how she had responded with a smile when Adam spoke to her, and the way they sat close in his open carriage. *Am I wrong to care, when she's not mine to love?*

After a moment, he got into bed and reached for the quilt, wondering how long Leona had stayed around by herself after tonight's Singing before going home. He'd come close to offering her a lift, but he'd chosen to do the right thing and back away.

Still, as sleep eluded him, Tom wondered if he shouldn't have made an attempt.

*I'll keep biding my time.*

## CHAPTER 4

Gloria helped her mother with the washing the next morning, then began rummaging through the pantry with Mamm while the clothes hung on the line. Later, that afternoon, she asked to take the family buggy over to Maggie Speicher's little store in Bartville, several miles away. "All right with you, Mamm?"

"Be mindful not to make this hard on Leona." Her mother turned away, a tear in her eye as she announced she was going to start making supper.

"It's hard enough on *me*." Gloria followed her into the pantry. "Leona's my best friend."

Her mother's movements were quick and

jerky as she began reaching for various home-canned items. "I'm sorry, Gloria. I'm frustrated, too," she admitted. "This isn't the first time we've had to pull up stakes."

A look of sadness passed between them.

"Mamm?" Gloria wished there was something she could do to help her feel better.

Her mother blew out a long breath. "Best you be goin' to speak to your friend now, Gloria."

"I'll break it gently." The words caught in her throat. There was no easy way to do what her father had urged at the noon meal.

Heavyhearted, she left her mother and went to the utility room for her lightweight black jacket. She had no clue how to ease Mamm's obvious exasperation.

Outdoors, she reached down to pet Brownie, then hitched up the horse to the family carriage. Daed had been gone much of the morning to assist a nearby farmer with a big brush pile. They'd burned heaps of pruned branches and deadfall from various trees before he had gone over to Eden Valley to pay a visit to another farmer. He'd said nothing about why, though, and it made her nervous.

The smell of smoldering ash lingered in the air as Gloria climbed into the carriage and headed down the road, toward the narrow bridge, then west all the way to Farmdale Road.

*Daed's still workin' with neighboring farmers,* she thought, trying not to get her hopes up. *Maybe he doesn't want to send any signals.* This worried Gloria all the more. *What's he got up his sleeve?*

When she arrived at Maggie's inviting shop, with its yellow exterior and bold black door and shutters, she stepped down from the buggy and tied the mare to the hitching post. Walking toward the entrance, she offered up a silent prayer, more for Leona than for herself, though she needed wisdom, and that for certain. *How can I do this without falling apart?*

Opening the door, Gloria heard the bell jingle. Leona turned from the nearest display table, where she was arranging cloth placemats and other table linens, her eyes widening. "Gloria! Oh, am I ever glad to see ya here. What a *gut* surprise!" Leona hurried to greet her as Maggie made a sale at the cash register. Maggie smiled and waved at Gloria but kept talking to the customer.

Leona offered to show Gloria their new shipment of soy candles. "*Kumme,* you must have a look-see. You might like one for your Mamma's birthday next month."

Gloria held her breath, aware how pleased

Leona was at her dropping by. *And to think everything's on the verge of changing. . . .*

Try as she might, Gloria could not push aside Preacher Miller's—and then Deacon Ebersol's—visits here lately, and the ever-present look of aggravation on Daed's face. Or was it determination? And there was his insistence that she visit Leona today. *"'Tis only right that you're the one to break the news,"* he'd said, nodding his head, his bushy beard bumping his shirt.

"You okay?" Leona tilted her head like she sometimes did, eyeing her.

"Show me the new candles," Gloria said, trying to feign interest.

But Leona knew her too well. *"Ach, Schweschder,* you didn't come for a friendly visit, did ya?" Her face turned pale. "Something's the matter." She patted her chest. "I feel it in here."

"I . . ." Tears sprang to Gloria's eyes.

Quickly, Leona led her to an alcove displaying knickknacks and homemade soaps, as well as sachets of potpourri. "When ya didn't come to Singing last night, I was worried."

"Truth be told, Leona . . . I couldn't face the thought of goin'. Not when . . ." Gloria shook her head. If she let herself, she would crumple into a sorrowful heap on the floor. *"Nee,* I don't know how to begin. . . ."

"What's happened?" Leona nodded encouragingly, but her expression was all concern.

Not sure what else to say, Gloria decided to state it right out. "Daed's been put off church by our new bishop."

"What?" There was no mistaking the shock on Leona's face. "How can this be?"

Sighing, Gloria said, "Bishop Mast is older and much stricter. And . . . don't tell anyone, but he's concerned for my father's eternal destiny."

"The bishop *said* that?"

Nodding, Gloria fished out a hankie from her long sleeve and dried her tears.

"Careful, you'll wipe your freckles off." Leona gave her a smile as she repeated what she'd often said since their school days.

"Oh, I'm gonna miss you somethin' awful." Gloria sniffed.

"*Miss* me?" Leona shook her head. "What do ya mean?"

Inhaling deeply, Gloria tried to calm herself. "Daed isn't going to submit to the brethren. . . . I feel sure of it. We're leavin' town."

"But . . ." Tears pooled in Leona's eyes. "I don't understand."

"My father won't repent." Gloria lowered her voice. "He's not gonna budge."

Leona gasped. "Surely things can be worked out in time."

"I'm prayin', but—" Gloria sighed. "Doesn't seem like Daed's waiting around for answers."

Reaching for her, Leona gave her a quick embrace. "I'll ask *Gott* for understanding—wisdom, too. Maybe He can make something *gut* come out of this. We must believe that, *jah*?"

"*Denki*," Gloria whispered. It was just too difficult . . . too painful to say much more. And while it made her feel guilty, in her heart of hearts, she had to question the reason behind Daed's standoff: Did it really have anything to do with the more severe bishop? Or was there more to it?

"Is there anything ya can do?" Leona asked now. "Anything at all?"

Gloria studied Leona's face, memorizing it. "There is something," she admitted. "I could ask my parents if I might stay on here . . . if it does come to that."

Big tears rolled down Leona's cheeks. "Oh, if only you *could* stay."

"Maybe someone will take me in, 'least till I'm wed." With everything in her, she hoped for that, though she didn't want to sound presumptuous. "I mean, think of it—we can't just let our hopes and plans all come to nothing over a spat between Daed and the ministers, can we?"

Leona brightened. "S'pose I *could* talk to my parents 'bout—"

"*Nee*—we best wait an' see." Gloria did not want to complicate things by getting Pete and Millie Speicher caught in the middle, much as she liked the quiet couple. "I really don't know what'll happen," she said, putting on a brave face.

"Well, we ain't sayin' good-bye today. And not ever!"

They clasped each other's hands.

*She doesn't know my father,* Gloria thought sorrowfully.

"If you do end up movin' with your family, you must keep in touch," Leona pleaded, eyelashes wet with tears. "Promise?"

"I'll write every week." Brokenhearted, Gloria turned to go, wondering if there was even the slightest chance her father might permit her to stay behind.

After returning home from work that afternoon, Leona went for a walk, pondering how quickly life could be overturned. She couldn't imagine being without Gloria and her family next door.

Nearing home, she spotted Adam Gingerich heading this way in his courting buggy. *Is he coming to say good-bye, too?*

Adam waved and pulled over. "Ride with me, Leona." His smile belied the tone in his voice.

She hurried across the road and got in. "Your sister stopped by the store," she said, wondering what he might say to that.

Nodding thoughtfully, Adam reached for the driving lines. "I s'pose that means you already know why I want to see ya." He sounded miserable.

Leona nodded. "I'm still hopin' something will change and all will be well." She had trouble getting the words out. Then, not wanting to mention Gloria's hope of staying behind, she fell silent.

"I know it's odd for us to be out together like this, since we're not really dating," Adam said. "Tellin' the truth, I really don't know how things will go with my father. He sure seems bent on packin' up and leaving." Adam turned and gave her a sad smile. "Mighty glad I caught ya." He slowed the horse and turned onto Mount Pleasant Road, toward Jackson's Sawmill Covered Bridge. "Leona, I know we've only been out one time, but I truly care for ya," he said softly. "And I'd hate to lose you."

He reached for her hand as they entered the bridge.

Before she realized what was happening, Adam leaned over and kissed her cheek. Leona's heart pounded in her ears as he leaned near.

A car's horn sounded behind them, and Adam took the reins again. Leona wanted to glance over at him but kept her eyes forward as the horse trotted forward into the sunlight.

They rode northeast to Ninepoints, and Leona wished they might just keep riding till nightfall. She could not bear to think of Adam leaving. *Not now.*

## CHAPTER 5

*P*uh! You mustn't talk that way, daughter." Gloria's father's words smarted. "This family sticks together—you know that. Don't ask again!" She winced as he raised his voice, there in the front room, where he sat warming his stocking feet by the coal stove.

Gloria had expected this response, yet she'd had to ask rather than silently suffer through the ordeal of moving again. Leaving was the last thing she wanted to do.

"Now, go on . . . get your things packed." Daed waved his hand at her and got out of his chair, going over to secure several stacked boxes. "Then help your Mamm with Jonas's and James's things, too."

Biting her lip, Gloria didn't say the words in her head—that this was an impossible thing to ask of them. It was beyond her understanding, and she was ever so sure Mamm felt the same way.

Why *couldn't* Daed see eye to eye with the ministers? What was keeping him from doing whatever was required to be at peace with the brethren?

In the stillness of her room, she rocked silently on the bed, tears threatening. She and Leona had planned their happy futures in this spot, thanking God for their friendship. They'd embroidered here and whispered their secrets, and knelt to pray together, too. Was it all for naught?

Gloria relived her visit to Maggie's Country Store, remembering the shocked look in Leona's eyes at the sad news. And now there might not be time left to tell her the outcome of Gloria's talk with Daed. Or to tell her good-bye . . .

Hands trembling, Gloria did as her father had insisted, opening her dresser drawers and packing her things. She realized this was likely the end of her courtship with Leona's cousin. *I'm not even allowed to say farewell to dear Orchard John. . . .*

Gritting her teeth so she wouldn't cry, she felt too embarrassed to even attempt to go to him and tell him of her father's intent to leave. Oh, she hoped Leona might get word to him. Better he find out from her than someone else.

She hastened to finish the dreadful chore, all the while pushing aside the lovely memories. Each one was precious in its own way, and she promised herself never to forget.

Later, she made her way up the hall to her young brothers' bedroom. Seven-year-old James's lip quivered. Both he and nine-year-old Jonas looked mighty sad as the late-afternoon light poured in through west-facing windows.

"I like it here." James inched over to her. "Why are we leavin'?"

His disappointment made Gloria ache all the more. "The Lord *Gott* will give us peace in this," she said softly. "We know that for sure, *Bruder*."

Rosy-cheeked Jonas squatted down on the other side of the bed and tugged on the old suitcase beneath the box springs, bringing it up onto the bed.

Gloria offered a faint smile. "Now, let's see how fast we can get your clothes organized and ready, *jah*?"

Jonas groaned pitifully but opened the suitcase and began placing his clothing inside. Young James was still fighting back tears, his brown bangs framing his small, solemn face.

Working together with her woeful brothers,

Gloria remembered the sadness she had felt when Daed had hurried her along to help Mamm that other time, too. *The day before we up and left the only home I'd ever known . . . in Salem.* Then Gloria had paid a hasty visit to her schoolteacher, wanting to say good-bye to the kindhearted and patient woman who'd taught her to read. The books at the one-room schoolhouse had been on the shelf near the windows, where she'd sometimes caught herself staring out at the pastureland surrounding the playground, imagining what it might be like to have a sister, praying for one.

*Just like Leona used to,* Gloria thought, returning to packing.

＊＊＊

Oddly enough, Tom's first reaction that morning upon hearing of Arkansas Joe's plan to leave was not to thank God for removing Adam, but to worry for Leona. How would she manage losing Gloria? *Arkansas Joe's answer is to disappear? Why?*

Tom drove the hack toward work with Danny in the front seat, feeling somewhat dazed by all of this.

Unexpectedly, a runaway softball tumbled down the slope near the Amish schoolhouse, and a towheaded boy dashed out into the road, chasing after it.

Shaken, Tom halted the horse and peered down at the chagrined young scholar. Picking up the ball, the child scurried back to the others who were waiting to continue the game.

*Downright dangerous.* What if a car had zoomed past just now instead of his horse and carriage?

Tom decided then and there that whenever he was married and had a family, he would make a point of drilling his children not to run into a road after a ball. "A ball can always be replaced," he whispered, still troubled by the boy's impulsive rush down the hill.

He glanced at Danny, who was shaking his head, his long fingers signing, *A big risk . . . for a ball!*

Together, they rode two miles to the smithy's in Bartville, where Tom pulled into the lot and stopped the horse. He signed to his brother to say he'd return to pick him up after work.

Danny bobbed his head and leaped out of the buggy. Turning, he waved boyishly, then hastened to assist their cousin Michael Petersheim, one of Lancaster County's several experienced blacksmiths.

Clicking his tongue, Tom signaled the mare to move forward and took in the autumn beauty on either side of the road. He had always felt especially fond of Danny and bore a burden of sadness over his deafness. He wondered if it was worse to be born stone-deaf like Danny . . . or to lose one's hearing after an illness or accident. It was, of course, impossible to know.

Danny himself was a great encouragement to the whole Ebersol family, having shown an optimistic determination since his early childhood. He worked hard, too, never shying away from a challenge. *Danny will make his way in life, no doubt about that,* thought Tom, realizing there were other *Youngie* in the community who had fewer strikes against them, yet who demonstrated far less discipline and courage.

⁂

When Tom arrived at Uncle Alan Lapp's office, Alan greeted him and launched into talking about a newly contracted job drywalling a kitchen remodel for an English client. Alan indicated that Tom would be working with another contractor, putting up the walls today. Tomorrow, he would be working alone, installing the ceiling.

"Sounds like an all-day project," Tom said, setting down his cooler. "Mamm sent along her famous chicken salad sandwiches."

"Better keep your eye on 'em," Uncle Alan joked, glancing at the cooler.

His uncle pointed out the location for

the job on the large Lancaster County map thumbtacked to the wall. Red dots indicated past jobs and blue ones upcoming builds and remodels. "See there?"

Tom took a good look, studying the roads. "I'm familiar with that area. Easy enough. I'll let the driver know."

"We'll help ya load the drywall jack into the back of the van when he arrives," his uncle said, then indicated that the other Amish fellow helping today would meet Tom there. "So you'll have help to unload on that end."

"Mighty heavy equipment." Tom recalled the last time he'd used it.

His uncle's eyes turned serious. "How are things at home these days?"

"Not sure what ya mean," Tom said, befuddled by the sudden change of subject.

"It's just . . . well." Uncle Alan seemed a bit uncomfortable. "I s'pose ya know 'bout Arkansas Joe bein' in some hot water."

"Not much," Tom said, purposely remaining mum as he went to pour some black coffee, his first cup today. There'd been no time for coffee earlier as he and Danny had helped his father with barn chores. Anna, their sixteen-year-old sister, had rushed out to help feed the livestock before she left the house to work as a housekeeper for Tessie Mast, Bishop Mast's elderly cousin.

"Is your father in the middle of it?" Uncle Alan pressed.

Tom frowned at the awkward question. "There's been a rift."

"Can't see why no one's talkin' sense to Joe." Alan was shaking his head. "Awful strange, that man."

Tom did not want to discuss it, nor that his father was so sleep deprived he looked ill, with dark shadows under his eyes. The last thing any of the ordained brethren wanted was to lose a church family over a disagreement, yet Arkansas Joe seemed to be giving them no choice.

"Just makes ya wonder . . . Joe comin' from another state like he did, out of the blue." His uncle set an inquiring gaze on Tom. "Guess ya can't tell me what ya know, can ya, son?"

Tom studied his uncle as he took another swallow of coffee. He could trust his mother's older brother, but it wasn't Tom's place to recount the scraps of conversations he'd been unexpectedly privy to in the barn, where his father and the new bishop had talked on more than one occasion while Tom worked nearby. It wasn't in his nature to eavesdrop, but he couldn't help thinking about what he'd heard, and none of it added up. "I'd best not say." He tried to be respectful. "You understand, *jah, Onkel*?"

Alan ran his stubby, callused fingers through his graying beard. "That's what's so *gut* about ya, Tom . . . you're downright dependable. No one can ever doubt it."

Tom finished the coffee, glad his uncle hadn't pushed harder. Then, gathering up his lunch and his gray work apron, he headed out to the parking lot to wait for the company's driver to haul him and the equipment over to the job. Soon, Mamm would be dropping Anna by to take Tom's buggy to a sewing bee. It was odd to think of his sister driving his courting carriage. *A carriage that has yet to carry a single date home from Singing!*

Nevertheless, he knew well enough whom he'd like to escort home . . . and now that Adam was departing with his family, Tom actually stood a chance.

## CHAPTER 6

*L*eona finished up afternoon chores early so she could visit Gloria before sundown. She hoped Arkansas Joe and the brethren had come to some agreement by now.

Drawing her neck scarf closer, Leona was glad she'd taken time to put on the new black sweater she wore under her jacket. A scant few red and orange leaves still clung to branches along the roadside, and Leona already missed the full splendor of fall—*"a brilliant portal leading us to winter,"* Gloria's mother had once described it, inspired by a poetry book she'd gotten from the library.

Leona and Gloria also shared a love of poetry, frequently reading aloud verses for any season or frame of mind. Leona preferred the lighthearted rhyming verses that painted rich descriptions with only a handful of words. Yet for all the girls' love of poetry, neither of them wrote it. Leona preferred to make things using items found in nature—thistles, brushwood, and other bits and pieces from the forest floor—to fashion one-of-a-kind wreaths to sell at Mamma's market stand.

While Gloria seemed to enjoy helping Leona with the wreaths, it wasn't something she chose to do without her friend. In her free time, Gloria made homemade cards and wrote notes and letters, sending them to encourage sick folk and to celebrate birthdays. On occasion, she would even send an anonymous one to other youth in the church who needed a little pick-me-up.

"*Gott* helps you create things with your hands," she would tell Leona, "and I write what He prompts me to share with others."

For sure and for certain, Gloria had a gift for spreading joy around the community, and the People appreciated it. Leona just wished she could do the same for her friend during this difficult time.

The red sun was dropping fast as Leona hurried to Gloria's. To think that same sun had nearly burnt her eyes this morning as she waited for her ride to Maggie's store near Bartville.

Especially this time of year, it seemed remarkable how, in the space of a few hours, the sky could go from blindingly bright to so dim you needed a flashlight before the evening meal was even on the table. Even so, Leona knew the way to Gingeriches' as well as she knew her own family's land, and she could hardly wait to see the frosty-white paths the snow would make in the hollow of the forest come next month. The little red bittersweet berries she enjoyed gathering with Gloria would show up more easily against the wintery landscape. It was right pleasant walking along the perimeter of the trees in that coldest season; better than in early spring, when mud pulled at her boots.

She made her way into the familiar lane and glanced at the house. All seemed quiet. Too quiet, really. Making her way around to the back door, she jiggled the doorknob, which often stuck.

Locked.

*They never bolt the doors,* she thought, dread beginning to pound through her veins.

She saw the family carriage parked where it should be, and the market wagon and pony cart, too. The sight gave her a bit of peace, but it didn't explain the unnatural silence.

Peering in through the back door window, Leona noticed that the row of wall pegs for jackets was bare, as was the area beneath, where the family lined up shoes and boots.

"They've left," she whispered, shocked. *Just like that . . .*

She heard Brownie barking from the stable and saw him coming, tail wagging. Gloria liked to pretend he was their watchdog, but as friendly as the dog was, Leona had a hard time thinking of Brownie attacking anyone.

"Hey, boy," she called as he came to her. She rubbed behind his ears as he leaned his head hard against her, whining. "Are ya glad to see me?" Then her hand brushed against his collar—something was attached. She loosened the white paper next to his dog tag and held up her flashlight to see a scribbled note in Gloria's handwriting.

> *Dearest friend,*
> *Brownie's yours now.*
> *Good-bye till we meet again.*
> *Your sister for always,*
> *Gloria Gingerich*

The note fluttered from her hand. Leona leaned down to reach for the beautiful dog,

wrapping her arms around Brownie and sob-
bing.

There was nothing else to do but head
home with Gloria's dear pet at her side. Such
a sinking, sad feeling Leona had never known.

CHAPTER 7

Winter came and went; then spring arrived in all its radiance. But it was late summer before Leona stopped dashing out to the mailbox every day only to find oodles of circle letters for Mamma, but nothing from Gloria. Month after month, and not a single letter. Why had the friend known for her thoughtful notes suddenly gone so terribly silent?

Leona's parents seemed to know even less than she about what had transpired, merely advising her not to dwell on those days. *"Gott* knows what's best," her father reminded her.

Not even her sister-in-law, Maggie, could offer any leads those first miserable months as Leona's disappointment continued to build. And when Leona had finally asked her brother, Mahlon made it clear this was not the sort of thing Leona should be holding her breath about, wanting news from a shunned family.

"Not all of them were put off church, remember," Leona argued. "Just Arkansas Joe."

"Even so, why would ya want to seek news of 'em?" Mahlon said, shaking his head in dismay. "The Gingeriches never really belonged here."

Whenever Leona walked past the redbrick farmhouse where Gloria and her family had lived, she was reminded to pray. The striking house was rife with childhood memories: baking bread in the sunny kitchen, summer days spent playing with Brownie on the front porch till lightning bugs signaled the girls' curfew, and the rainy Saturdays when they had played in the attic, Brownie ever near.

*Mere memories now . . .*

A year passed, then another. Leona made other friends, but none as dear as Gloria. Leona rarely checked the mailbox anymore, no longer expecting something from Gloria. Evidently their friendship hadn't been as close as Leona had thought, even though Gloria and her family had saved her from her loneliness those six happy years. Leona continued helping at Maggie's Country Store or around the house with the washing, cleaning, and cooking. She missed Gloria and prayed for her daily but tried not to focus on it. She couldn't bear to.

"Life must go on," her mother told her.

The warm scents of springtime—a beautiful bouquet drifting on the breeze—surrounded Leona as she glanced at the large metallic-gray mailbox at the end of the lane. More than three long years had passed since the Gingeriches' sudden departure, and there were fleeting occasions when Leona still wondered about the family, particularly Gloria, most often when retrieving the mail. Indeed, the mailbox had become a painful reminder of what she'd once had and lost.

Adam, too, had failed to keep in touch. *Yet he kissed my cheek,* she thought. She recalled the unexpected stop in Jackson's Sawmill Covered Bridge and imagined he'd found another girl to wed.

Losing Adam hadn't bothered her as much as she might have expected. Attractive as he was, the idea of potentially being courted by him had partly been another way to stay close to her dearest sister-friend and the family that had once seemed to take her in as a bona fide member.

Leona wished she could have written to Gloria. She'd composed numerous epistles in her head, some chatty and caring, others quite direct, even angry. Writing them down would have been pointless, since she had no idea where to send them. Even so, it was one of the ways she'd managed her nagging doubt: *Did I ever really know Gloria?*

With a sigh, Leona turned to the simple chore at hand and began hammering a nail through her homemade sign—*Seasonal Wreaths For Sale*—and into the fence post. She hoped to attract additional customers between Mamma and Aunt Salome's market days to bring in extra money.

*Has Gloria had her baptism, wherever she is?* Leona wondered. After all, her friend would have turned twenty-one this March and would quite probably be married. *Unlike me.*

Of course, it wasn't as if Leona didn't have a serious beau. Tom Ebersol had been seeing her home from Singings these past two and a half years. Much as he had always cared for her, he confessed he had waited for the Lord's timing before asking her to go steady. *"My job for Uncle Alan was so demanding at first that I wanted to get established before seriously courting. And the wait was worth it,*" he'd added, a twinkle in his eyes.

Leona recalled again how pleased she'd been when Tom finally approached her at that fall cornhusking bee, his brother, Danny, grinning nearby as Tom asked Leona if he could walk with her. Oh, how she smiled when he'd asked if she might be his girl! The deacon's handsome, hardworking son could be counted on to keep his word, and Leona was thankful for his thoughtful attentions. *My closest friend since Gloria . . .*

While they rarely spoke of the Gingeriches, Tom had made it clear early in their relationship that he understood what the loss had meant to her. Truth be told, it was more sympathy than she'd gotten from anyone else, and it had endeared him to her all the more. She wondered if he or any other church members gave any thought to Gloria's family anymore. Certainly no one else ever mentioned them.

Presently, Leona glanced down the long, narrow road, hoping Tom might happen by in his father's buckboard wagon on his way to Quarryville. Now that he was his uncle's full-fledged business partner, she assumed Tom would take over the business once Alan Lapp retired in a few years, though Tom had not discussed any specifics with her during their weekend dates.

Pulling a few stray weeds along the bed of irises, Leona was, once again, caught off guard by random memories of Gloria Gingerich. A slew of questions still weighed on her heart.

*I believed she was my sister for always. . . .*

⊷≈≍∗≍≈⊶

Tom glanced toward Pete Speicher's farm, noticing Pete's farmhand out plowing with the six-mule team. The next field over would lie dormant next year, Pete had told him, in keeping with the land sabbath some Plain farmers adhered to every seven years. Not all followed the Old Testament practice, but those who did seemed to reap the benefit of heartier crops.

The morning was warm and humid, and coming closer to Leona's house, Tom spotted a sign for homemade wreaths. *Leona's handiwork . . .*

Impulsively, he turned into the winding lane to see about purchasing one, hoping he might run into Leona. The white clapboard home stood out against a backdrop of fertile green fields and meadows, with the woodlands in the near distance under a wide sweep of sky. Pete Speicher had always made Tom feel welcome, but he also felt a bit nervous around Millie, never sure what she was really thinking, so reticent she seemed. Still, his mother had often spoken of devout and dependable Millie Speicher, an impression that Tom decided meant more than his own brief interactions.

Here lately, Leona herself had been quieter than usual when they were out riding together or playing doubles Ping-Pong. Tom wondered if she might be discouraged at his lack of a marriage proposal thus far.

Or was something else bothering her? He assumed Leona had never quite recovered from the loss of her friend. Then again, he would be the first to say it was challenging to guess what a young woman was thinking, and he'd had plenty of practice growing up with three younger sisters.

He smiled—his sisters would be delighted to welcome sweet-spirited Leona into the family. Tom had wanted to move from courtship to engagement for more than a year, but his bank account had lagged behind his romantic intentions. However, now that he was Uncle Alan's full business partner, Tom was ready to make plans to that end for next year's wedding season. *Lord willing.*

He stopped to pet Brownie before knocking on the back door.

Millie appeared in less than a minute and invited him inside the warm house. "Hullo, Thomas," she said. "Is it one of Leona's Easter wreaths you're after?"

He nodded. "My mother will enjoy havin' one, I'm sure."

Millie eyed him with a twinkle in her eye, her round face moist with perspiration.

*She knows why I'm here. . . .*

He fished for his wallet and smiled at the woman he hoped would be his future mother-in-law. "Why don't you pick out the prettiest wreath."

A quick smile and Millie agreed.

He wondered if Leona was working at Maggie's shop and craned his neck to look when Millie stepped away just inside the mud-room to remove one of several wreaths hanging on the wall. She slipped some plastic over it and carried it back to him.

"Here 'tis," Millie said.

A pressure cooker began to squeal around the corner in the kitchen, and just when Tom was sure there would be no laying eyes on Leona, she came rushing to the gas range from another part of the house, her white *Kapp* strings wafting over her slender shoulders.

"Oh dear," Millie said. "Excuse me a moment." And she rushed to assist Leona, leaving Tom standing there with the wreath and the money still in his hand.

He watched the two women scurry about. Millie seemed to have forgotten him, so he placed the bills on the small table and slipped out the back door. "Wasn't the best timing to plan another date," he murmured, walking back to the buckboard and climbing in, glad at least for the fleeting glimpse of his sweetheart.

Tom set the wrapped wreath behind the seat and reached for the driving lines. *Next time,* he thought.

⚜

"*Ach,* Mamma, I wish you'd *told* me Tom dropped by," Leona said later, all aflutter when she heard.

"Sorry." Mamma looked equal parts remorseful and befuddled. "It just slipped my mind."

"Well, I'll prob'ly see him at Singing in a few days . . . Easter Sunday." Though disappointed, Leona was touched that Tom had come on the very morning she'd been thinking of him—not that he could have had any idea of that, of course.

"Your brother says Tom's a fine young man," Mamma said, carefully removing the lid from the pressure cooker once it was cool. "Your father thinks so, too."

*So I would have their blessing,* thought Leona. "I'm sure the deacon thinks a lot of Tom, too," she said mischievously.

Her mother offered a smile. "Well, Tom *is* his son."

Leona nodded. "Parents tend to think highly of their children, sometimes even when one of them wanders away."

Right quick, Mamma turned her head, the ladle in midair as she stopped removing the stew meat and vegetables from the pot, the broth dripping onto the gas range. "I don't understand, Leona. Your beau ain't thinkin' of—"

"Nothin' to worry about," she said, surprised by her mother's talkativeness this morning. "Honestly, Mamma."

Mamma set aside the contents of the pressure cooker and added a bit of salt after tasting the carrots and meat. "You've been seein' him for a while now, *jah*?"

Leona hadn't expected her mother to inquire. "We're very *gut* friends," she said. Except for reaching for her hand, Tom had been discreet about showing physical affection even when they were alone together. Even so, the thought of his strong hand holding hers made her heart beat faster.

Mamma's blue eyes were serious now. "*Friends*, ya say?"

Leona shrugged. "We're courting, but he hasn't popped the question just yet. Not sure why he's waiting . . . but it's all right, as long as we end up together."

"Well, bein' solid friends is a *gut* place to start." Mamma gave her an encouraging smile.

Leona paused and recalled a similar conversation with Gloria and her mother, Jeannie, about fellows and courtship in general. And after their playful discussion, Jeannie had reached for Leona and hugged her, whispering in her ear, *"Any young man would be delighted to court you, I hope ya know."*

Standing behind Mamma, Leona remembered that long-forgotten moment, and tears sprang to her eyes. "I'll be in my room for a while," she said, wishing very much that the Gingeriches still lived next farm over.

## CHAPTER 8

*E*aster Sunday evening, after Singing, Tom invited Leona to ride in his spanking-clean courting carriage. She thought he seemed especially upbeat as he helped her into the buggy.

"Did your Mamm mention that I stopped in to buy one of your wreaths for my mother?" he asked, grinning as he took his seat next to her.

"She did, *jah.*"

"It's real perty, and Mamm was ever so surprised and pleased."

"Aw, *gut* to know she likes it."

"She also likes your peanut butter spread, so I'll have to get some at your mother's market stand." He reached for the driving lines but not before giving her a wink. "Mamm says it's sweeter than any she's tasted. It sure goes mighty fast at our house," he added with a chuckle.

As the horse stepped onto the road from the drive, he said, "I'd like to take you to a nice restaurant tomorrow night . . . for supper. Okay with you?"

"Sounds just *wunnerbaar*."

"I want it to be an extra-special evening for us." He looked at her, his features clearly visible in the moonlight as he reached for her hand.

She felt her heart flicker and smiled, not daring to let herself assume what he had in mind. Still, she could hope.

Leona spent Easter Monday, a day Amish businesses were closed, visiting with Bishop Mast's teenage granddaughters, Mary Sue and Sarah Ann, after an invigorating game of volleyball with other courting-age girls in the neighborhood. Mahlon had dropped by for Dat and Dawdi Benuel, and they'd all gone fishing, their annual tradition. Mamma, for her part, had been content to visit Maggie and the children for the day.

As each hour passed, Leona found herself

preoccupied with the special supper date that evening. Oh, she could scarcely wait to see her beau again!

The quaint restaurant Tom chose was quiet at this hour, old-fashioned-looking candleholders on each table, the candle on theirs already lit. It was a lovely place, one Tom had not brought Leona to before, but she had always wondered what it was like inside, and here she was, sitting across from her darling beau. His eyes shone as he invited her to order whatever she'd like.

"Are ya sure?" she asked, wanting to follow his lead and not overspend.

"Absolutely. Whatever you wish."

His eyes searched hers, and she reveled in his attention.

Another couple, older and not Amish, came in and took a table in the far corner, and Tom glanced at them, then back at Leona, smiling as if glad their own nook remained private.

The background music was soft and pretty, and the delicate, melodious strains reminded her of something she'd once heard in a driver's van while going to the Lancaster Central Market.

"Do you like it here?" Tom asked, making small talk after the waiter came to take their order.

"Real nice, *jah*. How'd ya hear 'bout it?"

"Well, Orchard John told me."

She wasn't surprised, considering Tom and her cousin had become fast friends during the past few years.

"Orchard John's awful nice." She paused, then forged ahead. "Does he ever mention Gloria?"

Tom shook his head. "Rarely, but I'm pretty sure he still misses her."

"What makes you say that?"

"He hardly ever dates, for one."

"Has he heard from—"

"No letters that I know of." Tom smiled kindly. "You'd think, as fond as Gloria was of writing and all, she might've let one of the two of ya know where her family ended up."

It was still a tender issue, so Leona was rather glad when their orders came—meatloaf and mashed potatoes for her, and a hot turkey sandwich for him. Leona bowed her head as Tom offered a silent prayer of blessing.

"Before we start," he said, leaning forward, "there's something I'd like to ask ya, Leona."

She set down her fork and folded her hands in her lap, not sure what to make of this.

"Ya know I'm in love with you. And not only that but committed to lovin' you for all the rest of my days . . . if you'll have me for your husband."

Oh, she thought her heart might pop right out of her chest. She'd long hoped this day might come, but nothing had prepared her for the rush of emotion she felt now. "*Jah*," she managed to get out, her mouth suddenly as dry as a wad of yarn. "I love you thataway, too, Tom. And I would be happy to be your bride."

A smile encompassed his handsome face, and he clapped his hands once softly as he leaned back in the chair. "I've wanted to ask you for such a long while now."

"Must we keep it a secret from our families, or—"

He shook his head. "I say it's time they know. My father's even been pokin' around the topic here lately, knowing I've been saving up so we could have a *gut* start once we're wed."

"To be honest, the other day, after you dropped by for the wreath—my mother was fishin' around for details 'bout us. I told her we're *gut* friends, but apparently she was hopin' for more."

"If I could have managed to swing it sooner, believe me, we'd be married by now."

She took small bites of mashed potatoes and gravy, but Tom's sandwich soon lay nearly forgotten as he talked about getting married at the start of this year's wedding season.

"Early November, then?" she asked.

"All right with you?"

Leona nodded, so delighted she could hardly think of eating. Tom hadn't said where they would live, but some newlyweds stayed with parents or in empty *Dawdi Hauses* until the spring. Whatever Tom decided would be fine with her. *Wherever we can be together...*

On the ride home, Tom's horse trotted faster, or maybe it just seemed that way to Leona, who felt like she wasn't riding at all but rather floating through the silvery moonlight, her hand in Tom's.

As they passed over a bridge near some marshland, the smell of a newly plowed field mingled with the fragrant night air, and Leona knew she'd never been happier.

⁓⁓⁓

Tom saw Leona home and said good-night, which was mighty difficult since, as usual, he really didn't want to say good-bye. Even though he'd been almost certain of Leona's answer, he was so relieved she'd said yes.

Once home, he made swift work of unhitching his mare, then stabled and watered her. That done, he moved the courting buggy into the carriage shed and outened the lantern.

He felt too keyed up to head for bed, thoughts of making a home with Leona filling his imagination. Instead, he was hungry again and found some of his mother's leftover blueberry muffins wrapped in the bread box on the counter. He poured a glass of cold milk from the fridge and walked out onto the back porch and stood there, reliving Leona's joyful expression when he proposed.

At the time, he'd thought it was a good thing they were in a public place, because the temptation was mighty strong to simply take her into his arms and kiss her again and again, sealing their love.

Tom finally headed upstairs, but it wasn't until he was getting ready for bed that he had to push back the nagging question that sometimes haunted him when he least expected it. *If Arkansas Joe hadn't up and left with his family, would Leona be mine?*

He sighed and closed the laundry hamper. *It doesn't matter,* he reminded himself, pulling back the bed quilt. *Adam is long gone, and the Good Lord has seen fit to answer my deepest prayer.*

## CHAPTER 9

As was typical, the supper table conversation had a slow start that Tuesday evening. Mamma passed the chicken and waffles to Dat first, holding the platter while he dished up his meal.

*Should I tell my parents about Tom's proposal before or after dessert?* Leona mused while sipping her iced tea. She observed how her parents glanced at each other, rarely saying more than a word or two—Dat about the tasty food and Mamma thanking him—the same thing every meal. Leona often wished there might be something worthwhile to talk about, something interesting like other families talked about when they sat down to eat together.

Tonight, of course, she knew just the thing.

"Tom asked me to marry him last night," she announced, immediately getting her parents' attention.

"Oh, my dear girl," Mamma said, looking at Dat, a bright smile on her face as she turned to Leona.

This pleased Leona. "*Jah*, and I'm ever so happy," she assured them.

"Tom sought me out after Preaching Easter mornin', while we were waiting for the shared meal, askin' for my blessing," Dat surprised Leona by saying.

She was deeply touched to know this.

"He's a *gut* young man."

"*Denki* for tellin' me." She rose to hug his neck, then stopped herself and sat back down, not wanting to embarrass him, even though this was a moment like no other for the three of them.

"I'm real glad for ya, Leona." Mamma said it so softly, Leona almost wanted her to repeat it, but she turned to thank her for the cherished words.

"Tom will be like a second son to ya, Mamma."

"A welcome addition to our family," Dat emphasized.

*Thank You, Lord.* Leona couldn't have been more delighted. "We should've invited Dawdi

Benuel over to share the meal and the news," she said, knowing Dawdi would have broken the ice a bit more and asked questions, too. *I would have felt comfortable hugging him . . . if he didn't get to me first.*

"Invite him for breakfast tomorrow," Mamma suggested.

"S'pose I could, but I'll be leavin' for work in the morning, so maybe I'll just go an' tell him myself later."

Mamma nodded, then went back to eating, and that was that.

Later, Leona asked her mother if Leona might accompany her to market next Saturday, trying to find a way to prolong the sense of contentment she felt.

"My sister will be there, of course," Mamma said. "Your *Aendi* Salome. I think I've told ya we've started sharing the market table."

"Well, maybe sometime we can plan ahead so I can join you, too," Leona suggested. "Or Salome might like a break."

"If you wish, dear."

"I really do," Leona said, thrilled with her mother's response.

⁓⁂⁓

Leona deliberately looked to see if the ground was there beneath her feet as she walked into Maggie's shop the next day. Now she understood better why the engaged girls amongst *die Youngie* seemed to exude a radiance that wasn't as evident during their dating days.

Leona went around lowering the shades a bit, the sun beating in hard just now. She caught herself wondering if Gloria had ever thought of working amongst fancy folk and tourists. Would *she* feel comfortable doing so? Leona imagined an invisible wall between them where there had once been complete openness and sharing.

*Does Gloria ever think of me?*

"You certainly look wide-awake today, Leona." Maggie had just rung up a purchase for a customer, then began to tally the morning's sales behind the counter. "Did ya have a *gut* sleep?"

Leona waited for the customer to head out the door before replying. "Actually, I slept great last night, but it wasn't easy falling asleep Monday night." She had to smile. "Oh, Maggie, I'm engaged to marry Tom Ebersol."

"Such *wunnerbaar-gut* news!" Maggie rushed to embrace her, crying for joy. "Does your Mamma know yet?"

"I told her and Dat yesterday."

"I'd be surprised if they weren't holdin' their breath for it."

Another customer came in just then, and Leona turned away, refolding doilies that had been handled and mussed up by shoppers.

The minute Maggie was free, she came over and asked if Leona and Tom had set a date, to which Leona whispered, even though no one else was around to hear, that their wedding would take place the second Thursday in November.

"Too bad yous have to wait more than a half year."

Leona blushed at that.

"Must seem like a long time when you're so in love," Maggie added.

"There are plenty of things to be done yet, so I left the date up to Tom."

"*Ach*, such a patient wife you'll be." Maggie nodded her head and patted Leona's hand. "Patience goes a long way, let me tell ya."

Smiling, Leona didn't mind the interruption when four Mennonite women walked in, the bell on the door jingling at their arrival.

The following Sunday was an off day from Preaching, and Leona rode with her parents to visit Mahlon and Maggie and the children. Sitting in the second bench seat, Leona petted Brownie on her lap; Mahlon's children had been pleading for him to come along. Brownie was as much Leona's now as he had been Gloria's, and every bit as fondly cared for.

She recalled Dawdi Benuel's joyful whoop when she'd gone to tell him her news last Monday evening. *Akin to Maggie's exuberant response,* she thought. Mahlon had always been somewhat reserved, like their parents, but he had married a woman as people-oriented as anyone Leona had ever known, besides Gloria and her mother. Tom, on the other hand, could be serious yet also liked to have fun . . . and enjoyed a good conversation. A nice mix.

The afternoon was warm, and sunlight glimmered on the flat surface of the pond behind Bishop Mast's farmhouse as they approached the ordained minister's large spread of land. Leona looked away. Things had definitely changed for the church members back when Preacher Reuben Mast was chosen by lot to take the deceased bishop's position. Yet the only person unwilling to submit to his strict leadership had been Gloria's father.

Leona stared out at the newly cultivated fields on the opposite side of the buggy. The roadside ditches were thick with grass, and the flowering trees were in their glory, as were the pink peach blossoms in the nearby orchard.

"Mahlon's hired a farmhand just till young Samuel's older," her father was telling Mamma as they neared her brother's place. "Have ya heard?"

Mamma shook her head. "Mahlon works too hard."

"That's the way life is for anyone who's a keeper of the fields, ain't?"

Silence prevailed until Mamma slightly shifted in her seat. "Maggie tells me her shop's doin' well."

"She has quite a few repeat customers," Leona volunteered. "It's *wunnerbaar* to see them come in with their long lists for birthdays, 'specially, and other wants and wishes."

"*Jah*, wishes . . ." Mamma's voice faded away.

"Wishes are like hopes, right?" Leona yearned yet again to talk about something of substance, something that didn't just fill up the space between their house and Mahlon's. But neither her father nor her mother responded. Leona wouldn't let it bother her, though, thankful for the changes she'd seen in her mother, more talkative, at least, in the years since Gloria and her family had left town. *Maybe I've calmed down some, too. . . .*

Leona focused her attention on Brownie, whose eyes were at half-mast as she stroked his graying neck and back, grateful for her near-constant companion.

While Mahlon and the children visited with Dat and Mamma in the front room, Leona stayed with Maggie in her kitchen and quartered apples. She placed them on a round tray with Ritz crackers and cheese spread, a tasty snack for midafternoon.

"Did ya tell Mahlon my news?" Leona asked, itching to know.

"I don't recall ever seein' him grin like that."

"Honestly?"

Maggie nodded. "It was really kind of sweet, his reaction to his little sister getting engaged and all."

"I'm not so little anymore." Leona didn't mention that most of her friends were married; Maggie was as aware of this as she was.

"Well, he's your only brother, so he's very protective of you—prays for you every day. Did ya know that?"

Leona smiled. "I'd never have guessed it."

"Well, it's true. Like your father, Mahlon has a list of folk he prays for . . . keeps it in the front of his *Biewel.*"

"Dat has a prayer list?"

"I'm surprised you didn't know." Maggie lifted the tray of food and motioned for Leona to follow her into the front room. "We have some mouths to feed."

Leona hurried along, trying to imagine her father writing a prayer list like Maggie said. *She must be* ferhoodled *about that.*

In the front room, she spotted her nine-year-old nephew, Samuel, teasing his younger sister, five-year-old Marianna, hiding her rag doll first behind his chair, then behind Dat's, next to him. Young Marianna smiled but didn't make a peep as she scampered back and forth, swift as a mouse, trying to snatch her doll from her mischievous brother.

Samuel and Marianna's middle sibling, seven-and-a-half-year-old Sadie, sat next to Leona's mother, her petite hands folded primly against her long blue apron while the adults chattered away. *She's being so good.* Leona recalled trying to sit still like that as a child, to be only seen and not heard. It had never been easy for her. Or for Mamma, considering how it had fallen on her to rein in Leona's overenthusiastic temperament.

Maggie placed the tray on a low table in the midst of the gathering, and Leona took a chair beside Sadie. "Did ya help the school-teacher again last week?" she asked.

Sadie brightened, her soft blue eyes blinking up at her. "I cleaned the chalkboard during afternoon recess. It didn't take long, 'cause I wanted to go outside an' play before the bell."

"I once filled in for my teacher when she was ill."

Sadie smiled. "How old were ya?"

"Fourteen . . . almost finished with eighth grade." Leona told her how exciting it had been when the school board permitted her to step into the teacher's shoes for those two days. "My friend Gloria had already graduated and was at home helpin' her mother cook and garden, but she would come after school to meet her little brothers, and then we'd walk back home together. She always brought Brownie along, too."

Sadie twisted one of her *Kapp* strings. "Brownie was hers first?"

"You prob'ly don't remember Gloria—you were only four when she moved away." Leona sighed. "She wanted me to take care of Brownie."

"Is she comin' back for him?"

"Well . . ." Leona realized her mother was overhearing all this; Leona had certainly gotten herself into a corner. "*Nee*, Brownie's mine now," she said, making it clear.

"Let's go an' play with him," Sadie suggested, looking to Maggie, who granted permission with a quick nod of the head.

"Sure." Leona was glad for an excuse to exit the stuffy room.

"*Kumme,* Aendi Leona," Sadie said, reaching for her hand.

They found Brownie lying in a blanket of sunlight at the southern end of the front porch, his long nose resting on his paws. Leona craved the sun, too, and loved how it fell over the dark bricks lining the walkway, warming them like toast. There was something about the intensity of the sun's rays that reminded her of their heavenly Father's constant love and grace.

In less than a minute, the back door opened, and here came Samuel and Marianna, too. "Come join us," Leona said, happy to be surrounded by her spunky nephew and his little sisters as they all squatted near Brownie and made over the precious pet.

*Gloria would be tickled,* Leona thought, momentarily wishing she could share these moments of her life journey with her long-lost friend.

## CHAPTER 10

The breeze was soft that Tuesday after-noon, rustling the dogwoods and mov-ing through the willow trees near the neighbors' springhouse. Beneath the new leaves, the sun speckled the roadside with shifting light.

Leona had decided to walk the last half mile home after working at Maggie's shop, asking to be let out of the van. She yearned for the peace of a pleasant walk on the heels of having helped customers all day.

When she neared the house, Leona spot-ted her mother heading toward the end of the lane to check the mail, waving when Mamma noticed her. *How she loves writing and receiv-ing letters,* Leona thought, aware of the hours her mother spent each week corresponding with relatives in other districts, sometimes five pages or more.

Leona caught up with her, and they strolled back toward the house together. "Did you get lots done today?" Leona asked. Her mother nodded, and Leona went on. "If you'd like, you might come in with me to the store sometime . . . see Maggie's new merchandise."

"That'd be nice, if you're sure I wouldn't be in the way."

"Just let me know so I can plan it for a day when I'm working shorter hours, all right?"

They reached the house, where Brownie had wandered out the dog door onto the porch, his tail thumping eagerly against the post. Leona bent to pet him as her mother went inside.

After hanging up her coat in the mudroom, Leona went to the kitchen, where she noticed an envelope with her name on it lying on the counter. Recognizing Tom's printing, she sat to read it at the kitchen table while her mother sifted through her own stack of mail.

*I'm looking forward to seeing you again this Saturday evening, Leona,* he wrote, signing off, *With love, Tom.*

It was so like him to send her a note to reassure her of his care and devotion, but it was the first time he'd ever written *with love* for a closing.

Looking over at her mother, Leona folded Tom's note. "I'll make supper for us, all right?" she offered.

"*Denki* . . . so thoughtful, dear," her mother said, briefly looking up before returning to her letter reading.

"How 'bout an extra big batch of chicken and noodles to take over to Dawdi?"

"*Des gut,*" Mamma replied, her eyes still on her letter.

*Maybe I should invite him to eat with us,* Leona thought. *There'd be no shortage of conversation with him at the table!*

And she did just that.

Later, at the meal, Dawdi smiled, clearly delighted with the company. He talked of Leona's grandmother and how she had enjoyed rolling out noodle dough, taking a whole morning to make a large amount to dry and use for later. "She sure did love her noodles," Dawdi said, digging into his plateful. "For sure and for certain, she would make over these, too."

"*Jah,* she knew how to put a feast together," Leona's father said, then looked at Mamma. "Much like you, Millie dear."

Dawdi Benuel grinned and gave Leona a knowing look.

Mamma laughed softly. "No need to say that."

"Well, I mean it," Dat replied.

And to reinforce her father's remark, Leona said, "I've enjoyed your feasts as much as Mammi's."

"It's not a competition," Dawdi Benuel added.

Leona smiled, glad she came from a long line of wonderful cooks. *Tom will be thankful, too!*

It rained lightly for a few hours Wednesday afternoon, and Tom finished up the drywall for a large master bedroom suite and two spacious walk-in closets, thankful for a shorter than usual workday. He gathered up the drop cloths and other tools, counting the days till the weekend, when he would next see Leona.

He still recalled how utterly happy he'd felt when she agreed to let him court her, two and a half years ago now. From his earliest school days, he'd had his eye on Leona Speicher, admiring her shining spirit and kindness toward everyone. Her patience, too. *It was only right that I be patient, as well, waiting for the right time to finally approach her.*

That windy yet sunny late-October afternoon of the cornhusking bee was still crystal clear in Tom's memory. *Die Youngie* had arrived at Preacher Miller's place and divided into several teams with four teenagers each racing the clock. Turning the chore into a work frolic had been more common decades ago, but the Millers had kept up their family's annual tradition, eager to provide an activity for the youth in their church district.

Leona and Tom found themselves on opposite sides, but that didn't keep Tom from paying close attention to Leona's masterful way with the task. He stole glances at her every now and then as they worked, noticing how gracefully her hands flew as she husked and snapped the ear off the stalk, then tossed the ear into the waiting bin. Most of the youth on both teams wore sharp-ended pegs on their fingers to split open the husk, their swift movements like second nature, they'd shucked so much corn.

Tom recalled now how much fun Leona seemed to be having as part of her team, laughing and smiling as jokes were told over the course of the first hour, and then while their teams took a break to enjoy refreshments when the next two teams of youth took their place.

Leona's team's pile of shucked corn

weighed more than Tom's by only a few pounds, and several of the fellows on Tom's side asked for the corn to be weighed yet again. But when all was said and done, it was Leona's group that triumphed and was rewarded with delicious hard candy.

Later, Tom caught up with Leona out on the road as she headed for home on foot, asking if he might walk with her, just the two of them. He had been looking forward to this moment all day.

"*Ach,* so much fun," she said, massaging her right hand. "Not sure I could go that fast for much more than an hour, though."

He agreed, still mulling over the words he planned to say.

"Were ya surprised at how many youth turned out today?" she asked, giving him one of her candies.

Nodding, Tom decided to forge right ahead. "Would ya like to go for steady, Leona?"

Her sudden smile was all the encouragement he needed. "*Jah* . . . I thought you might ask me today," she replied.

Tom hadn't expected such a response, but he certainly liked it. He liked *her*. "*Denki* for the candy," he said, enjoying the pleasant day more so now than even before, thankful that it was still warm this late in the season.

Leona removed another piece from her

pocket. "Here's one more for ya." She was all smiles as he accepted.

Tom unwrapped it and popped it into his mouth, thinking he'd never been happier.

Presently, Tom hitched up his mare to the open buggy and contemplated his upcoming date with Leona this Saturday. *The day can't come quickly enough,* he thought, imagining walking hand in hand with her amidst the ferns and trees in the woods near her parents' home. The clearing in the woodland there was Leona's favorite spot in all of Lancaster County. *"On earth,"* she liked to say.

It was only fitting that Tom point out to his sweetheart-girl the spot where, in another few weeks or so, he planned to break ground for their house. Not far from the clearing was a knoll where they could overlook the land his father had graciously given them to farm and live as newlyweds. *Where we will grow our family* . . .

Making the turn into his father's lane, Tom's heart swelled with affection at the thought of his beloved Leona becoming his bride come fall. *At long last.*

amma, did ya order something?"
Leona saw the mail carrier coming
up their lane with a large parcel as she and her
mother chopped celery, carrots, and onions
for a pot of beef stew that Friday afternoon.

Mamma smiled. "*Jah*, chust wait and see."

Ever so curious, Leona wiped her hands
on her work apron and dashed outdoors.

The tall postman set the box down on the
back stoop and reached into his gray pouch.
"Here you are, miss . . . and while I'm at it, I've
got your mail." He bobbed his head. "Good
afternoon."

"You too." She put the mail atop the
box and carried it inside, setting the box on

the counter opposite the cut-up vegetables. *Mrs. Peter Speicher* was printed clearly on the address label. "Want me to open it?"

"Go ahead." Her mother nodded.

Leona slid the mail off to one side and used a knife to slice open the top. Peering inside, she saw a set of flat-bottom copper kettles sent from the Lehman's Ohio warehouse. "So perty!"

Mamma made her way over and pulled out one of the kettles. "Mighty nice, ain't so?"

"They're *wunnerbaar,*" Leona agreed.

Mamma's face broke into the brightest smile. "Well, I'm glad ya like them. They're for your hope chest—a pre-wedding gift."

"*Denki,* Mamma. You're full of surprises."

"I'm not lookin' forward to you movin' out, but I couldn't be happier for ya, Leona."

*We've managed to get a bit closer lately,* Leona mused, thinking ahead to her wedding day, her feelings surprisingly bittersweet. There had been a time when Leona would have said she was *dying* to leave home, so she was glad that her mother would voice the opposite sentiment.

Did Mamma really feel that way?

⸺⧓⸺

Near suppertime, Leona heard her father scuffing his boots on the rag rug in the outer room. An array of jackets and a few shawls, work coats, hats, shoes, and boots were arranged along one wall.

Leona had long since put the hearty beef and vegetable stew on to cook, wasting no time in baking a big pan of corn bread, too. While the bread cooled, she brought up a jar of sweet-and-sour chow chow, as well as some pickled red beets. Dawdi would be joining them again for supper, and she wanted things to be extra nice.

Before her father washed up, he made his way into the kitchen and placed something on the table as Leona laid out the paper napkins. "I found this lyin' on the sidewalk," he said, his chin jutting forward. With a nod, he returned to the outer room.

Her mother picked up the envelope and squinted her eyes. "It's from Hill View, Arkansas," Mamma said. "Looks an awful lot like Gloria Gingerich's handwriting."

"Wha-at?" Leona's knees felt weak as she hurried around the table to take the envelope. She stared at the familiar handwriting and the return address, so far away. Tears pricked her eyes, and despite her frustration with her former friend, she couldn't stop them from coming.

Mamma was quiet, appearing to take this in stride.

*Can it really be from Gloria?* Leona thought as anticipation trickled through her. Quickly, she tore open the envelope, ignoring that it was so close to suppertime.

Her father returned stocking-footed to the kitchen, his left arm tucked into Dawdi Benuel's elbow as he slowly and steadily guided his father to the table. "Seems Leona has some excitement," Dat observed as Dawdi set his cane to one side and lowered himself into the sturdy chair they had scooted up to the table.

"Will yous excuse me a minute?" Leona said, suddenly wanting nothing more than to sit somewhere quietly and absorb every word Gloria had written.

But Dat shook his head, instead glancing toward the gas range and Leona's chore at hand. "In its proper time. It can wait, daughter."

Obediently, Leona pushed the envelope into her dress pocket and went over to dish up the stew into a large tureen, which she carried to the table while it was nice and hot.

"Your mind's a hundred miles away," Dawdi Benuel said when she took her seat across from him.

*Farther than that,* she thought, wondering where exactly Hill View, Arkansas, was. She'd have to look at a map somewhere.

"Gloria Gingerich sent me a letter," she told him. "I can scarcely wait to read it."

"Ah," he said, eyes widening as he offered her a wrinkled smile. "'Tis a long time comin', ain't so?"

Mamma looked on silently, her emotions veiled as Dat kept busy eating.

Leona had a difficult time paying attention to the subdued conversation, and she wondered if her parents and grandfather were as curious as she was about what on earth had prompted Gloria to write at last.

*Probably not,* Leona thought. And when she glanced her mother's way, Mamma sighed softly, looking quite sad.

*Other than Gloria, she never cared much for the Gingerich family. . . .*

After a dessert of leftover chocolate cake, Leona's father saw Dawdi safely back to the small addition next door. Lest Gloria's letter burn a hole in her pocket, Leona excused herself to the front room, promising Mamma that she would redd up the kitchen the minute she returned.

So many different thoughts were running through her head.

Heart pounding, Leona began to read.

*Dear Leona,*
*I hardly know how to begin. And I wouldn't blame you for not opening this*

*letter. You have every right to be put out with me, or worse.*

*It feels like forever since we last talked, and I've missed you terribly. We left in such a rush! That first week after we moved, I sat down and wrote a long letter to you, but my father found out and insisted he wanted our family to cut all ties to the People there. Sending it was out of the question.*

*I did my best to honor him, but oh, was it hard! Wasn't long before I wished I'd never listened to him, yet I felt too humiliated at not keeping my promise to write to you. I hope you've made new and better friends. Maybe someday, you might see fit to forgive me.*

*While we returned to Arkansas, we lasted just nine months in the Hill View church district—different than the Plain community where I was born.*

*The story is too long for me to write here, but ultimately Dad decided it was best for us to go fancy, with no more strict church ordinances to follow.*

*I am embarrassed to tell you all of this, dear Leona, but I feel like I've reached the end of my rope, and I need the wisdom of the truest friend I ever had. Is there any chance you might call me? I realize it's asking a*

*lot, and that you have every right to refuse,
but you're the only one I can turn to now.*

*Please call me anytime at this number:
555-649-0230. It's my cell phone, so you
don't have to worry that anyone else will
answer.*

> *Still your sister-friend,*
> *if you'll have me,*
> *Gloria Gingerich*

Shaken that Gloria had gone fancy, Leona read through the letter again. Was there something she'd missed, something that might explain why ever-confident Gloria had admitted to being at the end of her rope? What was happening? And why was she reaching out to Leona *now*?

## CHAPTER 12

While frying bacon the next morning, Leona gingerly shared with her mother some of what Gloria had written, including that the Gingeriches were no longer Amish. She held her breath, then added, "She wants me to give her a call."

A frown appeared as Mamma poured the mixture of eggs, milk, and onions into the hot black skillet. "Is that a *gut* idea?"

The same worrisome thought had nagged Leona late into the night, but she couldn't let her friend down—not when Gloria had finally reached out to her.

"She *needs* to talk to me . . . she said as much." Leona paused. "You don't mind, do ya?"

"Well, I s'pose if you want to call her . . . there's no reason why ya can't."

"*Denki,* Mamma."

Her mother added Swiss cheese to the thickening eggs. "You're clearly concerned for Gloria," Mamma said.

Turning the bacon strips, Leona nodded. *She was practically my sister . . . and I want to be there for her if I can.* She couldn't help wondering what her old friend might have to say.

All that morning at Maggie's shop, Leona tried to imagine what Gloria's life was like now, especially since they hadn't shared any goings-on for this long. Had she changed considerably in looks since she'd become an *Englischer?* Did she wear earrings and short hair, paint her nails . . . her lips? Gloria hadn't mentioned being married, or having a serious beau—a *boyfriend,* as she would surely refer to a fellow now. Was she working somewhere . . . maybe even attending college?

Ach, *such a terrible shock. Gloria has followed her parents out of the Amish church!*

"You all right?" Maggie asked Leona in between sales. "You look simply *bedauerlich.*"

"*Nee,* ain't sad. Just thinkin', is all."

"Well, I sure wouldn't wanna think *that* hard, or my face might crack."

Leona smiled at that. "I received a letter from Gloria."

"Wha-at?"

Nodding, Leona told her everything. "They're no longer Amish, she said. And she sounds desperate . . . wants me to call her."

"Well, what the world! Why now, I wonder?"

"That's what *I* thought," Leona admitted, worry niggling at her.

⁓⁘⁓

By her best calculations, Gloria assumed Leona had received the letter by now. "Either yesterday or today," she murmured to herself on the drive home from the diner where she worked as a waitress. It wasn't the kind of job she wanted long-term, but it would do for now, since she only had her GED—something she knew she should consider remedying.

"Will Leona even give me the time of day?" she whispered, recalling the dozen or more times she'd started the letter, each version ending up crumpled on the floor, until she'd finally written one she dared to send. One she was *permitted* to mail off now that she was twenty-one. Her father had told her he would not stop her, even though she knew it was with much reluctance.

Sighing, she glanced in the rearview mirror, glad for this time alone after juggling orders for the cook, wiping down tables, and making small talk with customers. She needed time to process everything, including what she would tell Leona in the event she called.

Driving the back roads here reminded her of happier days, of taking the horse and buggy to a quilting bee, or to market in Lancaster County. Yet she mustn't let herself brood; she'd come too far to reminisce for long. According to her parents, as Englishers, they were right where they all needed to be.

At the stoplight, Gloria glanced at her phone on the console to check that the ringtone volume was set loud enough. She did not want to miss Leona's call. And surely she would come through for her, despite Gloria's silence. *Not the way I planned it,* she thought, resentment swelling again.

Initially, she hadn't understood why her father had prevented her and her brothers from staying in touch with friends in Colerain. What harm could have come of a simple letter? Still, her father's anger toward the brethren— or had it been uneasiness, even fear?—made her comply with his wishes. Well, that and the tongue-lashing when her father caught her writing to Leona their very first day back in Arkansas.

Eventually, Gloria had made new acquaintances amongst the nearly three hundred Amish in the community of Hill View, but never any as close as Leona. With just a few Amish settlements in Arkansas, naturally her father had chosen the church district most similar to that in their former community of Salem.

Now, seeing Adam's old blue beater parked in the driveway, Gloria grimaced and wondered how he'd gotten home so early from his job at the car repair shop. She gathered up her purse, phone, and jacket, glad she hadn't told him about writing to Leona. However, if she received a call from her friend, she would have to tell him something, especially if Leona agreed to come for a visit.

*Surely our parents won't object to having an Amish houseguest for a few days. After all, it's been three and a half years since we left Pennsylvania. . . . What can it hurt now?*

* * *

Leona ventured out of her room and passed Mamma in the hallway late that afternoon, saying she would be back shortly to set the table. "I want to call Gloria right quick."

Her mother gave a faint smile, and Leona flew down the stairs and headed outdoors, startling a gray cloud of birds in the maples at the far end of the yard. Oh, to speak with her friend again!

She clung to Gloria's phone number on a piece of paper as she hurried through the meadow, feeling a sudden tentativeness now. Her father's mules were still out grazing, enjoying what was left of the daylight, and the sounds of deep springtime chorused up all around her. *Lord, please be ever near as I talk to my friend.*

Leona spotted the little wooden phone shanty, glad when she saw through the window that it was vacant. The door squeaked open and shut, and she stood before the telephone, realizing she was out of breath.

*Gloria can't be happy outside the Amish church,* she thought as she dialed the phone number. *How could she be?*

After only two rings, Gloria answered, "Hello?"

Hearing her voice, Leona was momentarily speechless. Then, "*Ach*, Gloria! This is Leona Speicher, callin' from—"

"I *know* who you are," Gloria said. "Am I ever glad you received my letter!"

Just hearing Gloria express herself so

brought back a flood of memories. "It's so *gut* to talk to you."

"You too, Leona." Then the sound of sniffling came through the line. "I . . . I hardly know what to say."

She heard Gloria blowing her nose. "What's happening?"

"I'm on the brink of making a huge decision . . . and feeling so much pressure from all sides." Gloria paused for a moment, then sighed. "Maybe this wasn't such a good idea, talking by phone."

Leona recalled the letter, its urgent tone. "I'm glad to help, if I can."

"I just don't know. I . . . don't want to inconvenience you."

"Calling doesn't put me out. You know that."

More sniffles.

Leona felt frustrated yet compelled to do something. A crazy notion struck her. "What if I came to visit you?" she suggested. "We could talk things through face-to-face—whatever's troublin' ya."

"You'd *do* that? You'd come all this way?"

"We said we were sisters for always, remember?"

There was another long pause. "Well, if you're serious," Gloria said slowly, as if thinking this through. "I was actually going to ask if you'd come, but now you're offering. I honestly didn't expect that."

"Sounds like we're in agreement, then." Leona laughed softly.

"I insist on helping pay your way."

"Let me see what's available for transportation. It might take me a day or so to make arrangements."

"Oh, Leona, I can't believe this! It means so much to me."

"I'll call you again when I know more, all right?" She spotted Brownie nudging his way inside the phone shack, pushing the door open with his nose. "Here comes your old pet."

"Aw . . . how's Brownie doing?"

"Getting up in years for a dog, of course." Leona told her what a special part of the family he had become. "*En wunnerbaar Hund.*"

"I'm so glad he's with you, Leona. I really am."

They talked for another minute or so before Gloria initiated the end of the call.

"*Jah,* till we meet again," Leona replied, echoing the words Gloria had written in her final note, attached to Brownie's collar.

They said good-bye and hung up.

Leona shook her head. Whatever the reason Gloria had reached out to her, she was pleased she had. Breathing deeply and thanking the Good Lord for the opportunity to help her friend, she leaned down to hug Brownie, whose small tail thumped against her. "I just talked to your first owner," she said light-heartedly. "Do you remember Gloria?"

Brownie tilted his head to look at her, and she laughed.

But as she began to walk back toward the house, Brownie by her side, concerns began to rise in her mind. *Will my parents or Tom object? And will Maggie even give me the time off?*

Leona's happiness quickly dissolved into a long list of uncertainties. *Was I too impulsive just now?*

## CHAPTER 13

That evening, after supper dishes were washed and put away, Leona took time to brush her hair and put it back into a fresh bun, donning her best blue dress and matching apron for her time with Tom Ebersol. She'd scrubbed her face extra well, peering into the small mirror over the bathroom sink to look for blemishes but seeing none. Now, thinking it might rain, she decided to take along her umbrella.

"Where are you headin'?" her mother asked.

"For a walk with Tom."

Mamma nodded, a twinkle in her eye. "Enjoy your time together."

On her way out, Leona walked around the barn, past the stable and the corncrib, full of thoughts of Gloria and all the fun they'd had together here.

She planned to tell Tom about her surprising letter, and of offering to go see Gloria, soliciting his advice on whether she should speak to his father, perhaps—or to one of the preachers—before she left. It wasn't required, but as a baptized church member, she certainly didn't want to cause undue concern.

The heaviness in the atmosphere portended rain, although thankfully there was no lightning or rumbling thunder in the distance. Still, she had been wise to bring the umbrella.

She tried to relax, anticipating seeing her betrothed. As she walked, she was ever so thankful that her and Mamma's relationship had improved some during the years the Gingeriches hadn't been a part of Leona's life. *Things have gotten even better since I announced my engagement, as well.*

Nevertheless, it wasn't as if they were close. Most conversations were initiated by Leona, and her father was just as close-lipped. Truth be told, she still missed Gloria's family and the easy feeling of belonging.

*It'll be so gut to see them again,* she thought. *No matter the changes . . .*

Just ahead, she saw Tom, also holding

an umbrella, standing near a tree so tall it dwarfed him. He was wearing his straw hat with its black band, his face beaming as she approached him at the perimeter of the clearing. She picked up her pace, delighted to see him, too.

––––––––

*Leona gets prettier every day,* Tom thought as she quickened her step toward him.

"Hullo," he greeted her.

She looked up at him, eyes blinking. "*Wie geht's?*"

"*Wunnerbaar-gut,* now that you're here." He offered his left arm, and she took it to begin their familiar walk. "Was Maggie's store busy this week?" he remembered to ask.

"Lots of customers bustling about," Leona said quietly. "Spring fever, I guess."

He measured the flow of their conversation as she shared about her day. When was the best time to reveal his surprise?

Suddenly, Leona stopped and turned to him. "Oh, Tom, I feel like I might burst if I don't get this out right now."

How he loved her zest for life! "What's on your mind?"

"You'll never guess, so I'll just tell you: I talked to Gloria Gingerich earlier today!"

"Gloria?" Shock coursed through him. "But . . . how?"

Leona touched his arm gently. "She wrote to me, apologized for not keeping in touch, then asked me to call her." She went on to say that something seemed terribly amiss. "Something more than the obvious. You see . . . Gloria and her family have left the Amish church out there."

"That's terrible news."

"I was actually hoping you might advise me." She paused. "You see, I offered to go an' visit her."

*Visit Gloria . . . and her family?* He hardly knew what to say as he reached for her hand.

"You must be as surprised as I was," Leona continued before he could respond.

"That's one way to put it." Tom began walking again, slowly setting one foot in front of the other in the hope it would help him think. With a sideways glance, he asked, "Are you really considering going?"

"Now that she's gotten in touch with me, I can't stop thinking about her. I can't believe she's happy with the life she's living, and I'd like to talk with her heart to heart, like we used to." Leona had never sounded so earnest. "Just think, Tom—what if I could persuade her to return to the Amish?"

Simply put, Tom had deep misgivings about his fiancée spending any time with such a family, but at least she was looking to him for guidance. "I'm not too keen on it," he finally admitted, "considering that Arkansas Joe is a shunned man."

Leona shook her head. "This is about Gloria, though. Remember how dear she always was to me?"

He stopped walking again. "If I told ya I'd rather you didn't go, would you at least think about it?"

Leona's face grew solemn. "Gloria's reachin' out to me for a reason," she said, her lower lip quivering. "And if there's any chance of bringin' her back to the fold, then I feel I should go."

"Well, tellin' the truth, I'm not surprised they abandoned the Plain life," he blurted.

"Please don't say that." Her voice wavered as her eyes filled with tears. "Please, Tom."

"Joe Gingerich was the most underhanded church member to ever farm in this area!" The words escaped his mouth before he could stop them. He was never supposed to voice this. *Not to a soul.*

Leona looked stricken, and Tom felt foolish. Furthermore, he questioned his own motives. Was he worried for Leona, or for himself? After all, for a short while, Adam had been a very promising beau.

Tom took a deep breath. *I can trust her,* he

assured himself. *The Gingeriches aren't even Amish anymore.*

"I'm so sorry," Tom said, reaching for her. "I shouldn't have said that. You and Gloria always were like sisters, ain't?"

She sighed. "That's exactly why I need to go, Tom. You know my heart in this, but I want your blessing."

For a long moment, he held her near. "Promise me you'll be careful."

Leona gave him a small smile as she nodded. Then he gently led her out of the beautiful area she so loved just as the rain began to fall.

The news of his father's gift of land would have to wait for a more suitable time.

❧

When Dawdi Benuel joined them for Sunday breakfast, Leona told her family about the call to Gloria and her desire to make a trip to Arkansas, hoping the news might go over better with them than it had last night with Tom.

Mamma gasped, and Dat gave Leona a long look. "Arkansas?" he said. "Have ya thought this through, daughter?"

"I really don't know how everything will fall into place," she confessed, passing strawberry jam to Dawdi for his toast, "but it sure sounds like Gloria's in a pickle. I'd like to help if I can."

"And they ain't Amish any longer, ya said?" Dawdi Benuel frowned.

Mamma, calmer now, said nothing, her attention seemingly on buttering her toast.

"That's what Gloria told me," Leona replied.

Dawdi Benuel raised one thick gray eyebrow and shook his balding head. "*Ach,* such a shame." He sighed. "I often wondered 'bout Joe . . . comin' all that way with his family to join our community like he did. Why would anyone do such a thing?" He raised his coffee cup and took a slow sip. "Never seemed quite right."

"No one questioned it back then—or did they?" Leona asked, glad to have this opportunity to discuss something she'd long pondered. "I was too young to notice."

Dat wiped his mouth on the back of his wrist. "As I recall, some of the ministerial brethren did."

"Is that right?" Leona wondered now about her father's willingness to let her stay with the Gingeriches when she was in fifth grade. He must have done so with serious reservations.

Mamma nodded her head and finally spoke up. "I remember the family dressed different when they arrived. It was clear they were from a more progressive district."

"It didn't take long, though, and Jeannie sewed new clothing like ours here," Leona pointed out.

"And Joe and Jeannie joined church right quick, too . . . never seemed to hesitate," Dawdi noted, then asked for some water from Leona, who got up right away. "They joined nearly as quickly as they left," he said thoughtfully, thanking Leona when she brought back a tumbler full.

Leona agreed. "It does seem peculiar."

"Guess we shouldn't be surprised they went fancy, really," her father said with a glance at Mamma. "Would have been a challenge for them to adapt to a stricter *Ordnung*."

When they were finished eating, Leona rose and cleared the dishes to the sink while her parents and Dawdi talked further around the table. The subject of the Gingeriches had certainly made for a lot of conversation tonight, but she realized her parents hadn't really addressed her hope to visit Gloria.

By the time she rejoined them, Dawdi's eyelids were beginning to droop. What with all he'd eaten of the simple fare, it wasn't surprising. *How will he stay awake through Preaching now?*

"I'm glad we talked 'bout this," Leona said softly.

"You and the Gingerich girl practically grew up together, ain't?" Dawdi said, perking up a bit. "All the hours you spent with her and her family. There for a while, before they moved away, I was beginning to think you'd adopted each other."

Leona blushed and hoped his remark wouldn't upset Mamma.

"Yous were awful close." Dat sighed. "Yet that's never affected your respect for the Old Ways."

Dawdi ran his knobby fingers through his lengthy gray beard and pressed his thin lips together as if considering this. "I 'spect you pray for Gloria, now and again."

"Oh, every day."

A gentle smile spread over his wrinkled face. "Well then, the Lord above knows your heart, Leona. He knows why you want to go all that way out there to see her."

She nodded, grateful. "I want to see things made right between Gloria and her heavenly Father."

"Is Tom okay with this?" Dat asked. "If so, then I s'pose a short visit with Gloria would be all right. The brethren would likely be fine with it, too, knowin' your reasons."

Leona replied that Tom knew. "And I feel

so strongly that this is the right thing for me to do."

Dat gave a nod of acknowledgment as he folded his hands, ready for the silent prayer. But it was Mamma who surprised Leona by patting her hand beneath the table.

## CHAPTER 14

After Preaching service, while waiting for the fellowship meal, Leona found Maggie outdoors with her three children. "Could ya manage if I took a few days off work?" she asked timidly. "How would ya feel 'bout it?"

Maggie turned to her in surprise. "Am I workin' ya too hard, maybe?"

Leona shook her head. "I called Gloria Gingerich yesterday. She sounded all *ferhoodled*—my heart went out to her, so I offered to go and see her, and she agreed."

"That's a big step." Maggie looked momentarily happy for her before becoming somber. "Well, I suppose I can manage for a bit, but not for too long, *jah*?"

"I sure don't wanna be replaced . . . and I understand if you can't spare me." Leona felt self-conscious about asking for favors even from her sister-in-law. "I've already talked with my parents and Tom. I'm also going to try to see the deacon 'bout it later this afternoon."

Maggie nodded thoughtfully. "'Tis prob'ly wise, since Gloria's a Yankee now."

Hearing this spoken aloud made Leona feel unsettled. "It's still hard to believe it even though she admitted it to me herself."

"I'm sorry for your friend." Maggie bowed her head. "What a disgrace."

Leona felt on edge as they waited together on the bishop's side porch while the appointed women readied the meal of cold cuts and homemade bread for the first of several seatings. "I best be makin' some calls from the phone shanty tomorrow. I need to find out what the trip will cost—Gloria's offered to help pay."

"You really think this is a *gut* idea, goin' clear out there, spendin' time with folk who've left the People?"

Leona wondered if she was getting the carriage before the horse. Even so, she was willing to do whatever she could to bring Gloria back home—where she belonged.

*My dearest wish.*

Leona didn't feel at all nervous about talking with Deacon Moses Ebersol, well-known for his kindness and care—"*a gut man,*" her Dat had said of his longtime friend. And trusting that all would go well, Leona knocked on the back door of the deacon's big farmhouse.

No one stirred inside, so she knocked again. Yet all remained quiet.

Leona had moved to one of the windows to peer in when Miriam emerged. Tom's seventeen-year-old sister looked a bit wide-eyed when she saw Leona there. "Hullo, Leona," Miriam said, holding open the door.

"Is your father home?" Leona asked, moving toward her.

"He and Mamma went with Rachel to check on my mother's sister up in Bird-in-Hand."

"Hasn't taken ill, I hope."

"Well, she's had some trouble with her asthma flarin' up." Miriam looked sad, like her aunt was worse than she was letting on.

"Do ya happen to know when they might return?"

"Oh, not till after supper." Miriam gave her a searching look. "Can I help?"

"*Nee* . . . I'm sorry to bother ya."

124

"Tom's round here somewhere." Miriam motioned toward the barn.

"That's all right." Leona smiled. "*Denki*, though."

"Have yourself a nice evening."

"You too." Heading home, Leona wondered what she should do. Since her parents and Tom had given their okay, wouldn't it be all right for her to commit to a quick trip before talking to any of the brethren? *Surely so . . .*

Tom was amused when his sister Anna insisted that her beau, and Miriam's, too, would be counting on both girls being at the evening's Singing. The fact was, he didn't really want to take both of his sisters to Singing tonight unless they were certain of a ride home. He was holding out for an opportunity to spend time with Leona, mighty curious if she was still planning to go to Arkansas. After mulling it over further, he continued to have concern about Leona's spending time with anyone under Joe Gingerich's influence, Gloria included. It had crossed his mind that it seemed strange for Gloria to reach out to Leona now. *Can any good come of it?* he wondered. *I'd hate to see Leona hurt again.*

"Please, Tom?" Anna asked from beside his perch on a stool there in the front room.

"Why don't yous get a ride with Danny—he's taking his buggy tonight," Tom suggested.

"All right, then," Miriam said. "As long as he's goin', too." She pitched a small throw cushion at him, and Tom caught it, tossing it back.

He frowned. "Where *is* Danny, anyway?"

"Still in his room." Anna motioned toward the stairs.

"By the way, I think he *does* have a sweetheart-girl," Miriam whispered, "so don't let him play innocent next time ya ask."

Lately, Tom had seen Danny talking with Preacher Miller's granddaughter at youth activities, and while Linda Miller wasn't deaf like Danny, she had picked up sign language remarkably fast. And Danny could read lips pretty well, too.

Just then, Danny wandered downstairs, his hair all scruffy, something Anna pointed out to him.

Seeing the mischief in his brother's eyes, Tom grinned and decided to stay out of it. If Danny *was* courting Linda, he'd want to look his best for the evening. Who knew but Danny might marry this year, too?

*I'm a blessed man,* Tom thought, remembering again Leona's happiness at his proposal.

Things were falling nicely into place, and he promptly dismissed any further thoughts of the Gingeriches.

⌑

As it turned out, Tom drove Miriam to Singing that evening, and Danny took talkative Anna. Upon arriving, the girls hurried inside, saying it was too chilly to dillydally in the open carriages while Tom and Danny tied up the horses.

Tom didn't mind the chill now that the sky was clear and the breeze had let up some. He was anxious to see Leona when she first arrived, so he waited near his horse, presuming her father would drop her off, as usual.

When he spotted Pete Speicher drive in, Tom hurried over to meet them, offering his hand to help Leona down and greeting her father. Pete dipped his head in return, then headed back out. "How are ya, Leona?" asked Tom.

"A bit cold." She smiled at him. "How are *you*?"

"I was hopin' we might talk before the Singing begins."

Leona nodded, pulling her black coat closer around her. "All right."

She fell into step with him as they made their way around the barn to stand on the west side, where the late-afternoon sun had warmed the wood siding. "Miriam mentioned you stopped by to talk to my father," he said, letting Leona stand closest to the barn.

"Hope I wasn't a nuisance."

He shook his head, assuring her it was fine. "I'm just sorry Dat wasn't home. But I daresay there's nothin' wrong with goin' to visit Gloria, considering what you hope to accomplish. I'll be praying 'bout that, for certain." He paused. "I trust ya not to disappear into the Ozark Mountains, of course. It's Gloria's father I'm worried about."

"Despite the rumors, Joe always treated me fine."

Tom reached to hold her hand.

"I'll make some calls tomorrow and let you know more," she told him.

One of the parent sponsors called to alert the stragglers to come inside and take their seats on the long benches.

"We'd better go in," Leona said, turning to go.

"In a second." He wanted to say something more. "I'm hopin' you'll be traveling with other Amish . . . maybe with one of the van drivers. Have ya thought of going that way?"

"*Jah*, that'd be my first choice."

"The Lord will be with you, Leona."

Though he meant the words, Tom said them as much for his own sake.

She gripped his hand. "Oh, Tom, I know you'll remember to pray for me."

He was impressed by her fervor. Tom looked at her, taken by her beauty—her gleaming dark blond hair, her sweet smile. He stepped closer and bent near, intending to kiss her cheek.

"I hope ya won't worry 'bout me," she said softly, her breath warm on his face.

There was a rustling in the grass, and then the sponsor loudly clapped his hands, startling them apart and shooing them around the barn and inside.

Tom felt mortified, but he refused to let it ruin the rest of the evening. He sang heartily, joining in with the other young men on one side of the long row of tables. He'd taken a place next to Orchard John, who had made a rare appearance.

Leona had found a spot next to his sister Anna, whom Tom suspected was either engaged or close to it. The two young women exchanged quick smiles, Leona's cheeks still red with embarrassment. Tom looked away, knowing he was the cause, getting caught alone by the barn as they had.

*Not such a good send-off to Arkansas.*

CHAPTER 15

*E*arly Monday morning, Leona helped Mamma pin the washing to the cellar clotheslines Dat had strung up for rainy days such as this. While she worked, she made a mental list of the various items she wanted to pack once the clothes were dry and folded. *If I can make arrangements soon.* Gloria's relief at her offer to visit was fixed in her memory, and Leona felt that time was of the essence.

Later, Leona headed to the phone shanty, where first she called the Amtrak listing and then, after discovering how unaffordable it would be to go all that way by train, called the bus station. She jotted down the information in her notepad, disappointed at how costly both modes of travel would be.

Discouraged yet determined, she placed a call to her favorite van driver, Ted Bell, in case he knew of anyone else headed in that direction who might be willing to share the cost.

"As a matter of fact, two older couples are leaving for Hot Springs, Arkansas, this Wednesday morning. I'm sure they'll be glad to divide the cost with yet another passenger." Ted assured her there would be plenty of room for her to ride along. "We'll stop for the night along the way and get an early start Thursday morning. Eighteen hours is too long a drive to safely make in one day."

"Sounds fine."

Ted told her the amount, which was more reasonable than either the bus or the train.

"That's better than I'd hoped." She said for him to count on her going, recalling Gloria's offer to help with the cost.

"All right, then. Be ready by nine o'clock Wednesday morning."

"My friend will likely be able to pick me up in Hot Springs," she said, hoping so.

He agreed.

They hung up, Leona delighted to see how quickly the details were falling into place.

The moment she got off the phone with Ted, Leona called Gloria back with her good news. "It might be inconvenient for you," she said, explaining that the driver was going to Hot Springs, then somewhere south of there to pick up some other passengers. "I have no idea how far your town is from there."

"Don't fret; I'll pick you up." Gloria sounded gleeful. "This is just wonderful."

Leona explained that she could only stay till early Sunday. "Will that suit ya?"

"Sure, but I'll have to work some on Saturday. Maybe you can hang out at the diner where I waitress for a while that afternoon and meet some of my friends."

Leona took it all in. "This is such short notice, I understand if ya can't get off work the whole time." Then she added, "I can scarcely wait to see ya, Gloria."

"It does seem like forever, doesn't it?"

Leona felt like she might start tearing up. "I'll see ya real soon."

The silence that ensued felt so long that Leona thought the line had gone dead. It wouldn't have been the first time such a thing had happened out there in the middle of the neighbor's field.

Just when Leona was going to hang up, Gloria spoke again. "Keep my number handy, and let me know if your plans change, okay?"

"I'll call from the driver's cell phone when we're three hours or so away from Hot Springs, *jah*?"

Gloria laughed into the phone. "It's been a long time since I heard anyone in my family say '*jah*' or anything else in *Deitsch*."

This struck Leona as really surprising. "We can speak *Deitsch* together my entire visit, if you'd like."

"I'm sorry to say my father's forbidden any of us to speak Pennsylvania Dutch around him."

After they said good-bye, Leona walked slowly back to the house, pondering what Gloria had said. Truly, it sounded as though the Gingeriches had left behind every jot and tittle of the Plain life, and considering the forthcoming trip, Leona felt anxious. *Is it a mistake, going away from the People . . . deep into the outside world?*

⁓≈⋙⋘≈⁓

Gloria was dragging her feet about helping Mom clean the house that evening, wishing her mother would put away their collection of springtime decor. Even one papier-mâché rabbit seemed inappropriate with Leona coming to visit. Amish folk didn't have frivolous knickknacks, let alone an Easter egg tree or fake baby chicks. *Dust catchers,* Gloria thought, annoyed by her mother's interest in buying such pointless things.

"This could be jarring to Leona, you

know," she told her mother as she dusted the seasonal collection along the bay windowsill.

"Well," Mom reminded her, "she's not your typical sheltered Amish girl, remember. She was working at her sister-in-law's tourist shop when we moved away."

Gloria knew little about Leona's life now. But she knew one thing: She should not have lost track of her friend, and more and more, Gloria placed the blame on her parents. "You once said the best way to get over the pain of leaving Leona was to put the past behind me," she said.

"Right . . . and I told you to keep it there, too. Do you remember that?" Mom's tone was annoying.

"Honestly, that wasn't the best advice. Not for me."

"Now, honey . . ." Mom reached for her shoulder, but Gloria pushed her mother's hand away. "I really hope you and Dad aren't going to make things uncomfortable while Leona's here," she said and left the room. Let her mother finish fussing with all the decor.

Despite her mother's obsession with trinkets, Gloria was relieved that her parents had ultimately seemed tolerant of, if not okay with, Leona's visit. Her father had objected the most, asking what Gloria was thinking inviting her without first getting their consent. But even he had relented once Gloria made her case. What problem could a solitary visitor like Leona possibly pose? *"After all, she's always been a friend to us,"* Gloria had argued. *"And I'm twenty-one now—old enough to take care of myself."*

Gloria sauntered down the hall to dust and vacuum her room, staring at the wall-to-wall carpet, trying to see it—and everything else in the house—through Leona's eyes. *No hardwood floors here,* she thought, wondering if her parents would blare the TV each night after supper, when they watched their favorite sitcoms instead of having family worship like they used to. And of course Adam's beloved NBA was in the midst of play-offs. No, she would steer clear of the living room if the TV was on. *Leona's in for a shock if she's still devout.* Recalling how curious they both had been about television, back when Gloria herself was Amish in Colerain, Gloria wouldn't think of tempting her.

She finished cleaning her room from top to bottom and then wandered to the kitchen, where her father was sitting at the table in the far corner, balancing his checkbook. Adam was at the kitchen island talking to Mom while she wiped down the microwave. Respecting her brother's privacy, Gloria walked past them and headed toward the downstairs rec room, where the boys' air hockey and Ping-Pong tables were located, and where her father had built in bookshelves on the other end of the room.

Mom called to her. "Come join us, Gloria."

She turned back and pulled out a stool at the end of the island. "What's up?"

"Your brother's landed an apartment." Mom smiled at Adam. "A big step."

"He's moving out?"

"Splitting the rent with one of his mechanic friends," Mom said, still doing all the talking.

"Is your new place far from here?" asked Gloria.

Adam shrugged. "Too far to walk, if that's what you mean." He chuckled. "Close enough to the diner that I won't starve."

"Well, I hope your roommate knows how to cook."

"His sister says he can reheat leftovers." Adam reached for an apple from the fruit bowl on the counter and chomped into it. "But you and Mom can come over anytime." Here, Adam grinned. "Any extra crumbs will be welcome."

"Absolutely." Mom dried her hands on a towel. "Certain dishes are actually tastier reheated."

"It's a good thing Leona's visiting this

week, because I'm moving a week from Wednesday," Adam said.

"I'll be glad to help you pack," Gloria volunteered. "Be sure to take a few of the knick-knacks from the living room, okay?"

Mom's gasp meant she didn't appreciate that suggestion, and Adam grimaced, then joked that he wouldn't be caught dead with anything from Mom's shelves.

"What'll you do with his empty room?" Gloria asked Mom as she helped herself to an apple of her own.

"Oh, I've got plans." Mom's eyes sparkled. "A craft room, maybe . . . or we might move the reading room upstairs."

Adam groaned and pleaded with her not to spoil his former room with floral fabric or her poetry books.

Mom laughed, looking more relaxed than she had in a long time.

"What's this 'bout a craft room?" Their father got up and wandered over. "Hey, I live here, too, don't I? I have in mind a computer room—a real home office. It'd be mighty nice to do my paperwork at home on weekends instead of the welding shop."

Then, looking Gloria's way, he asked, "How long's Leona here for?"

"Just three nights. She heads back early Sunday morning."

He pushed one hand into his jeans pocket. "I guess we can hold things together that long." He clapped Adam's right shoulder with his free hand. "What do ya say, son?"

"We wouldn't want to scare her now that we're fancy folk," Adam said.

Mom looked worried. "Leona always was a very sweet girl."

"And still is," Gloria piped up.

"Good thing she won't be here over a Sunday," Dad murmured as he headed toward the living room.

"I'd be happy to take her to *my* church," Gloria said softly.

"Hope you've told her we ain't—*aren't*— Amish anymore," Adam said.

"I let her know, yes."

Mom blew a stray hair from her eyes. "Well, glad we got that all settled."

*Nothing's settled,* Gloria thought.

## CHAPTER 16

*W*hile at work Tuesday afternoon, Leona shared the specifics of her travel news with Maggie.

Maggie nodded with interest. "Will ya spend the night somewhere, then? It's a long trip, ain't so?"

"*Jah* . . . not sure where, though. Ted said it was too far to go without stopping for rest," Leona said, glad she could talk to Maggie about this.

"At least you'll gain an hour goin' west."

Leona hadn't thought of that. "*Des gut.*"

Maggie glanced around the shop, where only a pair of customers lingered. She lowered her voice. "It wonders me . . . the whole family up and leavin' the faith."

"'Tis troubling." Leona recalled Gloria's remark about not being permitted to speak *Deitsch* in the house. She couldn't imagine it, not as friendly and fun loving as Joe had always seemed.

"Have ya told anyone outside the family 'bout your plans?"

"Just Tom."

"I s'pose he's mentioned something to his father," Maggie said, frowning a bit.

"I'm sure he has by now. At least I have Tom's and Dat's approval."

"Well, don't forget . . . you have mine and Mahlon's, too. You can depend on our prayers."

Leona thanked her, accepting the gentle squeeze of Maggie's hand.

***

Upon returning from the shop, Leona slipped away to her bedroom and dropped to her knees, praying that Gloria might be reconciled to God and the People. "O Lord, please guide me in all I say and do. Make me a tool for Thy mercy."

Then, after supper, once she'd redded things up for her mother, Leona slipped out of the house and hurried across several fields to talk to Tom before her Arkansas trip in the morning.

She found him in the stable, freshening the straw in the horse stalls. "Just came to catch you up on my plans. I leave at nine a.m. tomorrow."

Tom took off his work gloves and reached to hold her hand. "So glad ya came. I was just thinkin' of walking over to see you."

"Well, I don't want to keep ya from your work. Just wanted to say good-bye," she said softly, glad it was just the two of them out there with the milk cows lowing as they settled in for the night. "I've never gone so far away."

"I'll be thinking 'bout ya, Leona . . . and sending up prayers, too."

"*Denki*," she whispered, thankful again for his caring nature. "Will ya keep Gloria and her family in prayer, too?"

"I will now," he said, a smile creeping onto his face.

"Well, I s'pose I should get home and try to close my suitcase."

He chuckled and offered to walk with her, but it was still light enough that she insisted she was fine on her own.

"Good-bye, Leona." He gave her a brief hug. "Have a safe trip, and I'll look forward to seein' ya when you're back."

She smiled. "*Jah*, won't be long."

The sky was a metallic gray the next morning as Leona rode west in the van. The two middle-aged couples talked softly in *Deitsch* in front of her while she did a bit of crocheting to pass the time. Mostly, though, she enjoyed watching the landscape change from rural areas to busy cities, each place new to her.

When she felt tired after stopping for hamburgers, Leona leaned her head back, giving in to the sway of the van, which made her sleepy. In her haze, she recalled a blizzard that hit Colerain when she was twelve years old. Farmers were socked in for several days, and for a full week, there had been no school or Preaching services in many districts around the county. Leona's and Gloria's fathers had taken their driving horses down to the general store to get flashlight batteries, toilet paper, and ground coffee. And Leona had managed to get over to Gloria's by wearing Mahlon's old snowshoes he'd once gotten for Christmas. She, Gloria, and Jeannie had baked dozens of sugar cookies that day, which Jeannie let them decorate at their whim using all sorts of colors and designs. Gloria and her mother carried on about Leona's three-cookie blue-and-red snowman as though it were a work of art.

When Leona awakened, the van was vacant and Ted Bell was standing outside filling the tank with gas. She stretched and yawned, wondering where they were as she got out to use the restroom and buy a small bag of salted peanuts. A few customers did double takes, gawking at her and the other Amish folk, as well. *We certainly aren't in Lancaster County!* Leona thought, relieved that she was traveling by van rather than on her own.

⌊⌋⌈⌉

That afternoon, Gloria drove her mother to the grocery store, where they stocked up on sodas, chips and dip, and other snack items, including ingredients to make Chex mix for the guys watching basketball on TV. At the store, her mother spotted a round loaf of sourdough bread and snatched it up to put it in the cart.

"We used to bake our own bread," Gloria commented.

Her mother stopped walking, turned, and stared at her. "Do you know that was my least favorite thing about being Plain?" She swept her long bangs over her brow. "That and hitching up the horse and buggy. You probably never realized how much I disliked that job, either, especially when I did it alone."

"It *was* a challenge, but I really thought you enjoyed the bread making, Mom, and all the other baking we did together." *With Leona, too . . .*

Gloria pushed the cart forward while her mother turned her attention back to the shelves, deciding what she needed to stock their small pantry. "We could bake a special cake to welcome Leona. What do you say?"

"It would be simpler to purchase a ready-made cake."

"Okay with me." Gloria smiled at her mother's attempt to cut corners, but she was pleased to see her warming up to the idea of Leona's visit.

*So much has changed since my parents welcomed her like one of us!*

⁘

Carefully, Gloria removed her mother's favorite vase from the hutch, having already stacked the supper dishes and utensils in the dishwasher. "Mom, where do you want to display the fresh flowers we picked up?" she asked as she arranged them in the vase. Her mother had already settled onto the sectional with a magazine she'd bought on impulse at the store, her feet up.

"You decide, honey. You have a good eye."

Adam glanced up from a chair on the opposite end of the room, his phone in hand. "Aren't you gonna blow up some balloons and put up some streamers, too? Those ought to make Leona feel right at home."

Gloria almost laughed at his sarcastic tone.

"Come now, Adam," Mom said, flipping the page of her magazine. "Leona can surely live with a few cut flowers. After all, this is *our* home."

Gloria hoped her mother was right, but looking around, she couldn't help but feel embarrassed at how very English their place looked. She glanced at Adam in his ripped jeans. *What have I done, encouraging her to visit?*

"When does she arrive in Hot Springs?" asked Adam, still staring at his phone.

"Tomorrow afternoon."

He groaned. "I can't get off work, or I'd offer to drive you down there."

"Aren't you nice," Mom murmured.

Adam set aside his phone. "I'm actually lookin' forward to seeing her—wondering if she's still as Plain as ever."

Gloria looked at him. "Maybe you'll have a chance to talk. Did ya ever really get to say good-bye?"

Adam shrugged. "I did my best. We weren't really dating—only went out that one time . . . but if our family had stayed, I suppose we would've."

It all came back to her—Leona's excitement over Adam's interest, their hope of maybe being related through marriage one day. . . . "Well, you're with Donnalynn now, and she's wonderful. Bet you're glad I coaxed you into coming to church with me, right?"

Adam gave her a thumbs-up and took up his phone again, returning to texting.

Mom rose and headed toward the kitchen. "I think I hear your father scouting out a second helping of dessert."

Gloria found a spot for the bouquet on the side table, where it wasn't so noticeable.

Leona was surrounded by pleasant chatter as the van rolled across the miles. Manny Stolzfus, one of the Amishmen from a neighboring church district, moved up front to the passenger seat to visit with Ted for a few hours, so his talkative wife, Sarah, sat with Leona and struck up a conversation.

"Have you ever been to Hot Springs?" Leona asked.

"Oh, a couple times . . . we just love to walk at Garvan Woodland Gardens," replied Sarah. "Will this be your first visit, then?"

"I'm heading on to a small town northwest of there—Hill View. An old friend of mine is pickin' me up."

"My goodness, some of our Amish cousins live there." Sarah leaned forward to pull a bit of mending from her sewing bag.

"Seems like the People live almost everywhere now, doesn't it? I read recently that Amish are settled in at least thirty states."

Sarah shook her head. "Well, ain't that somethin'!"

Leona opened her poetry book and started to read, remembering how she and Gloria had enjoyed reading aloud to each other from this very book. She still could scarcely believe that, after three long years, she would see her former friend tomorrow. *At last!*

## CHAPTER 17

Gloria had traded Thursday shifts with another waitress and gone in extra early to serve the large breakfast crowd, knowing she'd need a head start for Hot Springs later.

She'd made up her mind not to wait for Leona's call, deciding she could take it while already en route. She was glad she'd splurged on a car with Bluetooth. Dad would have made a ruckus if he knew she used to drive her old beater while listening to music on her phone with earbuds, unable to hear a siren or another car's honking.

With Leona's visit imminent, Gloria was having more reservations about it, especially considering how infrequently the rest of her family attended church these days. *And Dad never goes at all.* Last year, they'd stopped attending the small fellowship where her parents decided they would go after leaving the Amish church here. Gloria was beginning to think they as a family did not fit in anywhere for worship, though she had found a little church to attend on her own.

Even living surrounded by Amish farmland as they were, Gloria still felt the most adrift from her past on the Lord's Day. At times, she wondered if it was merely a childish yearning for the past, something common in young adults who had rejected the church of their upbringing.

*What beliefs do I want to embrace as my own?*

***

"Would ya mind if I use your phone?" Leona asked Ted Bell that afternoon, glad for the rest at a motel last night.

He reached for it on the console and handed it back to her. "Help yourself."

She thanked him and located Gloria's phone number in the zipped compartment of her purse. Punching in the numbers, she soon heard ringing.

Gloria answered on the fourth ring, but

it sounded like she had a cold or had even been crying. "Are you all right?" Leona asked right away.

"I will be . . . once you're here."

Leona wasn't convinced Gloria was okay. "We've just passed Forrest City, so our driver thinks we'll link up with you in close to two and a half hours. Meet us in the Staybridge Suites parking lot." She gave the address. "He says it's easy to find."

"You must be worn out," Gloria said. "Such a long trip!"

"I was a little tired of riding till I heard your voice just now."

"Well, I'm thrilled you're coming, Leona. I really am." Gloria sounded perkier now. "Safe travels."

Yet when they said good-bye, it wasn't Gloria's words that lingered, but the melancholy tone in her voice.

Unable to shake his nagging qualms about Leona's venture into unfamiliar territory, Tom had talked out his concern about Joe's checkered past with his father as they worked together oiling saddles yesterday evening.

"I'm afraid Leona's setting herself up for disappointment," Tom had said, still questioning whether his own motives were muddled.

After all, in a way he actually *hoped* she'd be let down enough by this visit to get the Gingeriches out of her system for good, although he really didn't want to see Leona suffer the depth of sadness she had after they left.

His father had been as understanding about the trip as Tom expected, focusing on Leona's close friendship with Gloria as a youngster. But the one thing that stuck in Tom's mind gave him both comfort and pause to the point he felt a bit convicted. "We must never turn our backs on the wayward, son," his father had said. "Leona is quite right to make the trip if her intentions are pure."

"I know her heart's in the right place," Tom confirmed. "She's gone for the best of reasons."

"Then your place in all of this is to pray for a *gut* outcome," Dat told him. "Nothing less."

So pray Tom did, every which way he could think of, including for traveling mercies and wisdom once Leona arrived safely.

Leona tried to be patient as the two couples gathered their belongings and disembarked from the van near the hotel entrance in Hot Springs. Eventually, Leona, too, was able to climb out of the van and stretch her legs. She wished Manny and Sarah and the other couple a relaxing vacation. Then, turning, she spotted what she assumed was Gloria's car creeping up behind them while Ted unloaded the luggage.

"I think she's here!" Leona waited to move toward the car. Gloria had rolled down the window to smile and wave at her before jumping out of the vehicle. The sight of her former friend as an *Englischer* was a shock, and for a moment, Leona wasn't altogether sure it *was* Gloria. The young woman wore pencil-thin jeans and a white sweater, her deep auburn hair loose and bouncing around her shoulders, her lips tinted by gloss.

*Look happy!* Leona told herself as Gloria gave her a quick hug.

"Let me see you." Gloria stepped back, smiling. "You haven't changed. I mean it . . . you look exactly the same."

Leona wished she could say the same about her. "Let me get my sewin' bag and purse so my driver can get checked into the hotel, *jah*?"

Gloria reached for the luggage and carried it toward the car, opened the trunk, and stashed it inside, then returned for Leona, who was paying the driver.

"I can pick you up in Hill View early

Sunday morning if that'd suit you better,"
Ted Bell offered.

Leona conferred with Gloria. "Would it
help you out?"

"If that's no trouble, sure."

"All right, then. Let's plan on that."

"Just give me the address," Ted said, pulling out his phone to enter it into his contacts.
"Be ready at six-thirty in the morning, sharp."

"How many passengers will there be on
the way back?" Leona asked.

"Five that I know of," Ted said. "We might
be fairly full with all the luggage."

"*Denki* ever so much."

"Here's my number if anything comes up
and you want to stay longer." He handed her
a business card. "Travel safely, young ladies."

Leona followed Gloria to her car, which
seemed low to the ground compared to the
vans she was accustomed to. Inside, the car
smelled new. "My legs feel like rubber," she
admitted, sliding in and reaching for the seat
belt. She had never ridden in a car before,
and the seat belt felt extra snug against her.
She tugged at it a bit until Gloria mentioned
she should unfasten it and try again if it was
too tight, which she did.

Looking around at the interior, the front
dash and the console with all the gauges and
whatnot made her feel distinctly out of place.

"It's too bad you have to ride two more hours to get to my house," Gloria said as she started the ignition.

"That's all right, really."

"I can never repay you for putting yourself out like this," Gloria said, slowly pulling out of the parking lot, then making the turn onto the main road.

"*Ach,* you would've done the same for me, ain't so?"

Gloria smiled at her before switching on some soothing music. "Maybe you can rest a bit."

"Do ya really think I can doze off now that we're together? *Nix kumm raus*—nothin' doin'—in case ya forgot what that means."

Gloria didn't reply, and Leona wondered if she should have said it quite like that.

"How's your family?" Leona asked, not wanting to start out on the wrong foot.

"Mom's anxious to see you. She bought a cake to celebrate."

"Hope it's no bother."

"Are you kidding?" Gloria reached over and squeezed her arm. "I still can't believe you're here."

Wondering when Gloria might reveal the reason for her pressing letter, Leona decided to wait till her friend opened up on her own. She glanced over, still trying to reconcile her memory of Gloria's familiar Plain attire with the person next to her. She should have mentally prepared herself. After all, what *had* she expected—a former young Amishwoman who still wore an apron and the sacred *Kapp*?

"How's *your* family doing?" Gloria asked. "Are your parents well? And your Dawdi Benuel—is he still living?"

"Everyone's doin' all right just now, *jah*." She mentioned seeing her nephew and nieces recently, how much they loved playing with Brownie. "I doubt you're surprised, 'cause he always liked children. Remember how we played fetch with him for hours on end?"

"Seems like a lifetime ago."

"Well, we're all grown up now. Naturally things are different. . . ."

"Different's good," Gloria replied and began to talk about her waitressing job. "I meet so many fascinating people traveling through town. The regulars are great, too. If I were a storyteller, I could fill a bunch of notebooks with the tales I hear."

"I'm glad you're happy, Gloria."

"Happiness is a choice, right?"

Leona nodded. "Maggie used to tell me that when I was lonely, back before you moved to the farm next to us."

Gloria nodded but fell silent once more. The music on the radio was so tuneful and sweet, Leona could have gone on listening to it for hours. "Do you have a radio like this in your room, too?"

"Not in my room," Gloria said. "And it isn't the radio we're listening to, but the play-list on my phone." She explained how her phone connected wirelessly to the speakers.

Leona sighed—this was all so strange. She felt like Lucy Pevensie must have when opening the door to the old wardrobe and falling into the very different world of Narnia.

## CHAPTER 18

When they finally arrived at Gloria's house, Leona was aware of the two cars parked in the driveway, as well as the gleam of the outside porch light. Gloria insisted on carrying Leona's luggage up the driveway for her, and Leona could hear what turned out to be a TV as they entered by way of the front door. *Not around to the back?*

"Come in, come in," Jeannie Gingerich said, rising from the sectional and motioning for one of Gloria's younger brothers—James, it looked like—to turn down the TV. She came to the front door to greet Leona, reaching to hug her. Leona found herself momentarily comforted by the woman's familiar scent, so at odds with her changed appearance. *Like coming home,* she thought, torn between delight and sadness.

"I hope you stopped for supper somewhere," Jeannie said.

"We ate on the run, anxious to get here," Gloria said and excused herself to take Leona's bag to the guestroom, leaving Leona there with the rest of the family. With the boys' cropped hair and jeans, they couldn't be mistaken for Plain. Joe, however, still wore a bushy beard, which surprised Leona.

"Welcome to Arkansas, Leona." Joe flashed his old smile. He was a blend of Amish and English with his long beard and khakis and checkered blue shirt. "You picked a nice time to visit . . . everything's bloomin'."

Adam stepped forward to shake her hand, and Jonas and James came over and did the same. *Prompted by their parents ahead of time?* Leona wondered.

"We'll visit more once you're settled," Jeannie said, showing her the way down a hallway lined with numerous framed family pictures. They found Gloria in the spare room, folding a handmade afghan at the foot of the bed. "Be sure to show Leona the bathroom, dear," Jeannie told Gloria.

*Thoughtful as ever,* thought Leona.

"*Denki* . . . thanks so much." Despite their

kindness, Leona felt overwhelmed with the Gingeriches in such modern attire and surroundings. The reality of their new life was mind-boggling.

*Are they happy living this way?*

---

Gloria invited Leona to come over when she was unpacked, then slipped off to her room to change into sweats.

"Such a perty place you have here." Leona's eyes grew wide when she entered later.

Gloria relaxed against the headboard, her pillow behind her. "It's just stuff Mom's bought me," she said. "She's a housekeeper for several families, but I wonder sometimes if she just works so she has money to spend on stuff. Thank goodness I'm a penny pincher—I'm savin' up for college classes."

Leona didn't comment on that. "So many bright colors," she said. She seemed curious, laughing softly, pointing out the large white net holding oodles of stuffed animals. "Where'd ya get all of these?"

*She means in the short time we've been Englishers. . . .*

Her friend turned to look at her. "Did it seem strange, at first, having fancy things?"

"Sure, but after a while it became just the usual thing. Normal as white bread."

Although Leona smiled politely, this seemed to bother her.

"Doesn't Maggie sell some of these kinds of trinkets and things? Do you still work there?" Gloria had to ask.

"Well, I do, but we offer mostly homespun goods, remember? Tourists love locally made items."

"Oh, I guess I forgot." Gloria laughed as she climbed off the bed. She couldn't stop staring at Leona. It was remarkable how little she'd changed.

<hr />

The following morning, Gloria awakened to sunshine spilling through her white lace curtains. She squinted over to see Leona standing at one of the windows, staring out, already dressed for the day, her dark blond hair up in the traditional bun. "Morning," she said groggily. "Did you sleep all right?"

"*Jah*, but I think I woke up too early."

"Oh, the time change, maybe," Gloria reminded her. "It's an hour earlier here than back at your house."

Leona came over and sat at the foot of the bed. "Hope ya don't mind me wanderin' in here."

"It's just fine."

Leona smiled. "Like the old days, when you and your family welcomed me in."

"I remember when your mother was so sick."

Leona nodded. "It was a scary time . . . and your family was so nice to me."

Gloria wondered why she was bringing this up. "Maybe if I shower, I'll be able to wake up and join the human race." She yawned.

"I'd like to help make breakfast, all right?"

"Good luck with Mom on that. I think she has coffee brewing . . . sure smells like it. But wait for me, okay?"

Leona smiled. "I'll do that."

Gloria gathered up some clean clothes. "Feel free to stay in here, if you want to look around more," she said, still trying to absorb the fact that she and Leona were together at last.

Leona was surprised at Gloria's hospitality. The room seemed ornate, though, very different from her friend's former bedroom back in Colerain.

Looking at the bookshelves, Leona noticed the book of limericks she'd given Gloria, as well as a few devotional books from those days. *Does she still read these?*

Then on the bureau, Leona spotted something that looked familiar—a small pink net sachet with potpourri like the kind Maggie sold in her store. Leona raised it to smell the scent, which had faded. Then, looking more closely, she saw a tag: *With love, JS.*

She pondered this. Then it came to her. "I *know* those initials," she murmured. "My cousin's." She found it quite touching that Gloria had kept something of her Amish life.

Even so, Leona was deeply aware now of the enormous challenge before her, her hope that Gloria would give up all of this to return to a simpler life in Lancaster County. *More obstacles than I'd expected.*

She headed back to the spare room and located her Bible in the suitcase, then went to sit in the comfortable chair in the corner near a little fake tree, a writing desk nearby. She found her bookmark and began to read chapter thirteen of Hebrews. When she came to verse five, she read it aloud. ". . . Be content with such things as ye have: for he hath said, I will never leave thee, nor forsake thee."

Leona continued reading, and when she'd finished, she rose and looked out the window, then back at the cheerfully decorated guestroom, getting acclimated to the new environment. Silently, she knelt and asked the Lord God for strength to see this visit through for His glory and honor.

When the knock came at her door, Leona was ready to have breakfast with her friend.

"Mom had to rush off to work, but she put a roast in the Crock-Pot and left a note," Gloria said at the kitchen counter. "One of her clients requested an extra cleaning; they must have company coming." She explained that her mother was always glad for any extra hours. "It'll be just us for breakfast, since Adam's also at work and Jonas and James are in school."

Leona felt a spark of nerves at the thought of seeing Adam again. He'd seemed friendly enough last night, but they hadn't really talked.

Gloria pushed her mom's smiley-face-laden note across the counter. "Do you want eggs and toast for breakfast? I can heat some water in the microwave if you'd rather have tea than coffee." She opened the refrigerator and removed a container of eggs. "Or I can rustle up something more hearty and Amish style, if you'd like."

"Don't go to any trouble." Leona eyed the microwave but insisted on cooking up some fried eggs and bacon on the stove, and Gloria seemed fine with that. *Unless she's just being polite*, thought Leona as her friend went to set the table.

Once they'd eaten their fill, Gloria suggested they take a drive. "I want you to see where I work, for one."

"If ya want to, sure." Leona was not thrilled about the idea of getting back into the car, but Gloria seemed awfully restless. *Why?*

## CHAPTER 19

Gloria could hardly wait to show Leona their town nestled amidst mountains, rivers, forests, and lakes. First, she drove around the large, mostly Amish neighborhood, explaining that her father had rented the house when they moved here. She pointed out several Amish ministers' homes, especially the bishop's, slowing as they drove past the oversized black mailbox and two purple martin birdhouses nearby. Two *Dawdi Hauses* had been built onto the tall main house. *Just like back in Colerain . . .*

"Does it seem strange to still live under the noses of all these Amish farmers?" asked Leona.

"Sometimes, to be honest."

"Not to be nosy," Leona said, "but does it cause any tension for your family?"

Gloria wasn't ready for this, so she steered the discussion into safer waters. "By the way, I want to show you the one-room schoolhouse up ahead. I used to walk there to chat with the teacher and to see Jonas and James home afterward."

"Do ya think they miss it?"

Again, Gloria felt tense. "It's been more than two and a half years since we left the Amish. We've moved on—all of us."

"I think I might've enjoyed teaching school," Leona said wistfully.

"Why didn't you?" Gloria glanced her way. "You're so good with kids."

"Well, as you know, most of the other girls my age had higher grades."

"I doubt any of them have a better heart than yours."

Leona ducked her head. "Ain't necessary to say that, ya know."

"Still, it's true. You came all the way out here to visit with the likes of me."

Turning to look at her, Leona paused as if deciding what to say next. "I can't help but wonder if ya miss bein' Plain, Gloria."

Gloria bit her lip. She forced humor into her voice and smiled wryly. "Have you *looked* at this car? What's not to like about getting somewhere fast?"

Leona laughed, but her eyes looked pained.

Gloria instantly felt regretful. "Sorry."

"That's okay. I can imagine how easy the *Englisch* life must be."

"But I was flippant."

"No, you were *honest*," Leona said softly; nevertheless, she seemed much more subdued than when they had set out.

*Not entirely honest.* Gloria *did* miss her Amish years, the warm fellowship of the womenfolk at work frolics and all the home-made food. She also missed grooming the road horses and riding in the enclosed carriages, the peaceful sound of the *clip-clop-clip* keeping time with her heart.

Leona found it curious that Gloria was so eager to drive downtown next. They pulled into a parking space on the square busy with shoppers.

"The antique shops and boutiques are very popular with both the locals and the out-of-towners," Gloria explained as they got out of the car. She pointed out the courthouse and its grounds, where crape myrtle shrubs were coming into bloom. "These are my favorite, since they blossom till fall. Do I sound like a tour guide yet?"

Leona laughed.

They stopped at the old Missouri-Pacific Railroad Depot, which now served as a museum and displayed many interesting historical artifacts.

Later, by the time they drove to the diner where Gloria worked, Leona felt all in, dismayed by the gulf that separated her and Gloria. Their lives had changed in every way imaginable, and their conversation seemed to come to a halt whenever Leona bumped up against their past. A couple of times, Gloria visibly shrank back, her expression troubled.

Leona wasn't sure how long this could continue. Would it only end when one of them broached the subject of why Gloria had broken her silence, contacting Leona after all these years?

Music blared as Leona stepped inside the diner—she'd never been in such a loud place. She looked at Gloria, taken aback.

"It's just the oldies. C'mon, you might enjoy it."

Leona put on a brave face and followed.

The diner was filled with smiling customers, many of them Plain folk sitting in booths along a wall of windows or at the long, narrow counter where black stools trimmed with aluminum swiveled on chrome pedestals.

At least here no one gawked at her

Amish dress and *Kapp* the way some Lancaster County tourists did upon first entering Maggie's shop.

She trailed Gloria past the counter and back into the kitchen.

"Is Hampton around?" Gloria asked one of the cooks dressed in white, including a tall chef's hat.

He motioned toward his right. "Check back in the office, but I think he may have slipped out early to go to the ER. His wife fell and hurt her foot. Might be broken."

After getting more details and expressing concern, Gloria waved Leona on toward a small room, its door ajar. "Nope, he's gone all right." She sighed.

"Is Hampton your boss?" Leona asked as they headed back out to the car.

"He's nearly like a father to me. Such a kindhearted soul." Gloria sat behind the steering wheel, leaning both wrists on it. "He's become my go-to person . . . but nothing like you."

It occurred to Leona that, despite the distance and the passage of time, she had remained alive in Gloria's imagination, just as Gloria had in hers.

*Even with all the changes, we're still friends,* Leona realized.

"Hampton Brockett's actually almost old

enough to be my grandfather," Gloria was quick to clarify. "He's established several successful diners in a few of the surrounding towns. And he and his wife have a son, Darren, born late in their marriage."

Smiling, Gloria went on to say she wanted Leona to meet Darren while she was here. "Would you feel awkward having lunch with him and me tomorrow?"

Leona was taken aback. "Well, if he's a *gut* friend of yours."

Gloria blushed. "We've been dating a short while, but Darren wants to move too quickly to suit me."

*Too quickly?* Leona wondered what exactly Gloria meant by that.

"Darren's nice, but there are issues we don't see eye to eye on—or we could, but . . ." Gloria turned the key in the ignition and backed out of the parking spot. "Listen to me babbling," she murmured. "Let's go home and bake some shoofly pie. Want to?"

Leona agreed, though she felt glum after hearing of Gloria's serious beau. *This is definitely a big setback*—the biggest complication yet. *How on earth am I going to get her to think about going home to Colerain?*

"Do ya remember the ingredients?" Leona teased Gloria as they each tied on one of Jeannie's half aprons.

"How could I forget?" Gloria went to the pantry and brought out the flour, brown sugar, salt, and shortening for the crumbs, then went to the freezer to remove a frozen piecrust, which made Leona gasp. That brought a smile to Gloria's face, though, and she was quick to apologize.

"Remember when you were so determined to make the perfect piecrust?"

"Do I ever!" Gloria laughed again.

They assembled the dry ingredients and cut shortening into the flour mixture with a pastry blender. Then Gloria preheated the electric oven.

"I don't know when Mom or I last made this," Gloria admitted, a sad look in her eyes. "Mom isn't one for baking anymore. In fact, did I tell you that she never liked baking bread?"

Leona stared at her. "*Ach,* but your Mamm's bread was the best. I can't believe it."

Gloria shrugged. "I was as surprised as you are to hear it, but it's true."

Leona turned her attention back to beating the eggs and then the syrup with an electric mixer, no less!

Working together, they soon had the pie

ready to slide into the hot oven. Gloria set the timer on the appliance, saying she wondered what her mother had done with the old wind-up one.

"*Ach*, we still use ours," Leona said. "And Mamma bought a day clock with a second hand."

"Goodness—she's got her recipes down to the second?"

This brought peals of laughter from both of them, and Leona was truly relieved at how much less tense things were now that they were working together in the kitchen. *One as modern as the day is long. But a return to old times nonetheless!*

⌒⌒⌒

Leona was glad to see Jeannie return, coming in through the garage door.

"Something smells fantastic," she said as she hung her car keys on a peg near the bulletin board.

"It's shoofly pie—the wet bottom kind, of course." Leona was curious what she'd say.

Jeannie went over to the cooling rack and leaned down to take a sniff. "You two really are something. You could open a bakery!"

"It was my idea." Gloria grinned. "Of course Leona was happy to help."

Jeannie moved around the island to greet

Leona as she had yesterday. "Do you mind if I give you another hug, my dear?"

Gloria laughed. "Go ahead, Mom—she's our same wonderful Leona."

Leona embraced Jeannie, too, but she was still having to get used to all her makeup and the silver hoop earrings, partially hidden under shoulder-length blond hair. Gloria's mother's appearance was as altered as her daughter's— the trim black leggings and long flowing red top. *Such strange cleaning clothes,* she thought.

"Come into the living room and tell me what you did today," Jeannie said, going to the sectional and patting the cushion next to her. She continued to talk, saying how sorry she was about missing breakfast with them. "I hope you saw my note."

"Mom," Gloria said, patting her chest, "relax. It's just us. Okay?"

Jeannie leaned her head back for a moment, sighed, and then folded her hands on her lap. "All right . . . I'm better now. It was a hectic day. Evelyn Russell wanted all of her light fixtures polished along with the special spring-cleaning. Her sister and hubby are coming for a week's visit."

"She's known to be a perfectionist," Gloria explained to Leona.

Jeannie agreed with a raise of her eyebrows. "The woman keeps me on my toes."

"When will Dad be home?" Gloria asked.

"In time for supper, as always."

"You have a real nice town here," Leona said, noticing how distant Gloria seemed sitting over in the farthest corner of the sectional, hugging a brightly patterned throw pillow.

"I guess we're drawn to small communities," Jeannie said, exchanging glances with Gloria. "Aren't we, honey?"

Gloria merely smiled.

"My parents send their greetings, by the way," Leona said, realizing as soon as she'd said it that she should have waited till the whole family was together, perhaps at the supper table.

Jeannie's smile was as warm and endearing as ever. "Be sure to tell Pete and Millie hello from all of us."

"I will. *Denki.*"

Jeannie rose suddenly. "If you girls just want to relax before supper, feel free. I need to check on my roast in the Crock-Pot." And she headed off toward the kitchen.

Gloria got up, too, and said Leona should make herself at home. "I need to freshen up a bit," she added, exiting the room.

Leona wandered to the fireplace mantel, which displayed a colorful glass egg and a framed picture of Joe and Jeannie posing cheek to cheek. How had this family moved so thoroughly into the fancy world so quickly, and with so little effort?

Then, of all things, she spied a statuette of a horse-drawn buggy on one side of the mantel. *Interesting*, she thought. *Someone has at least one fond memory of Plain life. . . .*

Leona left the room to wash her face. Glancing in the extra large bathroom mirror, she saw that her hair bun was still secured beneath her *Kapp*. Was seeing her prayer covering convicting to either Jeannie or Gloria? Did they miss putting up their hair each morning and wearing the sacred symbol of devotion and modesty?

She returned to the living room just as Adam came in from work, looking altogether grimy. "I picked up the boys from school, Mom," he called.

"Hullo, Leona," Jonas and James said before dashing downstairs with their matching navy blue backpacks.

Adam chuckled. "They're still full of energy, as you can see." He offered a smile. "Was your first full day here lots of fun?"

"It's sure different than Lancaster County."

He sniffed the air. "Did someone do some baking?"

"Gloria and I couldn't resist."

"The house smells like it used to." He

looked away briefly, then shrugged. "Like when we were Amish."

Leona hardly knew what to say as Adam excused himself to take a shower.

---

While Leona waited for Gloria to return to the living room, her mind spun with all the changes in the Gingeriches' life—Gloria's English boyfriend; Adam, who seemed like a stranger now . . . and Jeannie. Even Jonas and James looked like any two Yankee boys she might see at market.

It was beyond her how their former bishop here had permitted them to live in such a modern house, one with electric, too. That aside, how had things gone so wrong that they slipped away from the Amish church?

*To think I once yearned to belong to this family.* It had been a childish, if not naïve fancy. In spite of that, Leona still wished for her sisterly friendship with Gloria to continue. Above all else, she wanted Gloria to open her heart and share her pain, whatever it was. But it was apparent something was holding her back.

## CHAPTER 20

Seeing Leona sitting there alone in the living room, Gloria wondered again how she felt spending time in their modern house. *How much better would this visit be for her if we were still Plain?*

Later, in the kitchen, Leona asked if she could set the table, but Mom refused the help even when Gloria offered. Mom looked cute, if not quaint, in her gray work apron, something she must have unearthed from the back of a drawer.

"You haven't seen Leona in a long time," her mother said. "I'll cook; you visit!"

Gloria also noticed that the Our Daily Bread Promise Box was centered on the table—it had been missing for at least a year. The family Bible was also set to the left of her father's placemat. Seeing it again was sobering. Was Leona's impression of them so important that Mom had resurrected a few remnants of their previously pious life?

*Maybe Leona's visit is good for us. . . .*

A few minutes later, Adam emerged from the basement, and Gloria had to smile. "Well, don't you clean up nice." He'd washed his hair and put on his best blue shirt and khakis. She suggested that he and Leona join her in the living room, where Leona sat in the chair nearest the sectional and Gloria sat where her mother had been sitting before, moving the magazine back to the barnwood coffee table. Adam took a spot on the floor in front of the TV, as though blocking it from Leona's sight.

"I s'pose Gloria gave you the town tour," Adam said.

Leona nodded demurely.

"Is our town smaller than you imagined?" he asked.

"I didn't have any expectations, to be honest."

Adam nodded. "If you'd like to do more sightseeing tomorrow, just say the word. I have a friend who could loan us a Jeep to do some exploring at White Rock Mountain."

He paused. "Or maybe Gloria took you up there already."

"We were too busy to hike," Gloria said.

"Maybe another time, then," he said.

Leona smiled at Gloria. "Really I'm just here to see your sister . . . not to be a tourist."

"We had a great time baking together," Gloria mentioned. In fact, now that she thought of it, she'd enjoyed it far more than driving around.

"What're you two cooking up for tomorrow?" Adam asked. "And I don't mean food."

"We're meeting Darren for lunch at the diner."

Adam told them that he'd promised to take Jonas and James to play basketball with some other kids at a nearby park.

"I'm not sure yet what Leona and I will do the rest of the day," Gloria said, "but I'm sure we'll find something fun."

"You don't have to entertain me," Leona said.

"Well, if I ever want you to visit again, I can't have you sitting around here, right?"

The garage door rumbled open, and Adam got up from the floor. "Sounds like Dad's home," he said. "He likes to eat on time." He glanced at Leona and headed toward the kitchen.

"I'm with Dad—I'm starving!" Gloria

rose quickly, waiting momentarily for Leona to join her. "My father will be thrilled about the pie."

"'Tis *gut* we made it. *Jah?*"

Gloria laughed as she linked her arm in Leona's to make their way to the kitchen.

Leona picked up right away that everyone was going overboard to make her feel included at their first supper together. Jeannie made over Jonas and James, practically reintroducing them. The boys stood near the kitchen table, behind their chairs, Jonas shifting his weight, arms folded, and his younger brother glancing away, not making eye contact. Jonas, still blond as ever, handled the fussing better than James, whose round face turned bright pink.

Had Jeannie always been like this? Leona wondered. Or had she just never observed it before?

Joe looked tired from his day, a crease on his forehead where perhaps he'd worn some sort of protective helmet at the welding shop.

For a moment, as they gathered at the table, Leona recalled the camaraderie she'd experienced at their former cheerful haven. In fact, when they all sat down, she realized they were each seated in the same order as then. Leona was to twelve-year-old Jonas's left, facing Gloria across the table. *Some things are just ingrained*, Leona supposed.

Arkansas Joe asked Adam to offer a verbal blessing before the meal. Evidently, Adam was as surprised at this as Leona, since he sputtered out a short prayer that contained only a few grateful sentences. It was his father who added the amen before asking quickly for the pot roast.

As the food was being passed, Joe again made a point of making Leona feel welcome. "I'm sure you can see how glad Gloria is to see you."

Leona nodded at Gloria. "And I really appreciate your hospitality."

"Any time." Arkansas Joe smiled more broadly now.

"*Denki,*" Leona replied, embarrassed when she realized every eye was trained on her.

She was relieved when the eating commenced and the attention turned to Joe, who told about his day at work. From what Leona gathered, it sounded as if he and another man had become partners not many months ago. Adam and Jeannie interjected various questions while Jonas and James dug into their large helpings of food.

"Hill View is in the midst of a growth spurt, so there may be an opening for you at some point, son," Joe told Adam.

"I prefer fixin' cars," Adam said politely, sitting straighter.

"Why're you all dressed up, Adam?" James asked, glancing at Leona.

"We have a guest," Adam replied before taking another bite of mashed potatoes and gravy.

"Um, you never look that good," James added, grinning.

"Hush now, son," his father said, reaching for more coffee. "Your brother's got a girlfriend, and I'm sure Leona's spoken for, pretty as she is." He winked at Leona, who felt herself blush.

Gloria offered Leona a smile. "My guess is she's well on her way to engagement."

"I am," Leona said, happy to share her news. "To Thomas, our neighbor's son."

Adam nodded. "If it's the Tom I remember, he's a good guy."

"Tell us more," Gloria said, smiling mischievously.

*She forgot who Tom was,* Leona realized.

"Well, Tom's in partnership with his uncle at a construction firm," Leona explained. "You might also remember that he's our deacon's eldest son."

Joe's expression dimmed. "You can leave Leona be with the questions. We should remember that Amish courtship is a private matter." Abruptly, he turned back to Adam and asked a question about the car he was refurbishing.

Gloria looked terribly uneasy.

Listening to Adam talk animatedly about engines, Leona observed Gloria's father, puzzled at his awkward response. Was it the mention of Deacon Ebersol?

---

When they'd eaten, Gloria suggested they read the Bible by passing it around the table, asking her father to go first.

Joe looked startled, then grudgingly went along with it, starting with verse one of Psalm 136. "'O give thanks unto the Lord; for he is good: for his mercy endureth for ever.'" But after a single verse, he passed the Bible to Adam, who read the next verse, and so on around the table.

Joe's hesitancy to participate didn't escape Leona's notice. *Yet how can a life without faith be satisfying to a formerly Amish family?*

Jeannie, however, read the seventh verse with expression, even lifting her eyes to look at Leona as she read, "'To him that made great lights: for his mercy endureth for ever.'"

All of them continued the shared reading through verse twenty, and when it was Jeannie's turn again, she read verse twenty-one. "'And gave their land for an heritage: for his mercy endureth for ever.'" Her voice broke at the final word, and she coughed quietly.

Leona tried to keep her attention on the reading, but when the Bible was closed and there was no time set aside for silent prayer, she felt sad. She could see a twitch in Joe's jaw and wondered if he, too, had felt convicted by the Scripture.

Leona was pleased when Gloria asked the boys if they wanted to play Dutch Blitz with her and Leona following supper cleanup. Jonas bowed out, saying he was meeting a friend for a sleepover, but Adam and James remained. Gloria's parents left for the living room, where the drone from the TV drifted into the kitchen. Leona had only seen Joe and Jeannie together for a short time since her arrival, but from what she had observed, things seemed very different between them. Gone, it seemed, was the affection she remembered, the couple they appeared to be in the framed photograph.

The familiar game was enjoyable, yet Leona kept recalling the former days, how they'd all sat around the table for hours—Joe and Jeannie, too—playing games and laughing about one thing or another, reveling in the fellowship. Was the draw of TV the only reason why Gloria's parents hadn't played the game tonight?

One by one, her best and fondest memories of this family weren't adding up with what she was witnessing now.

*When did all of this change?*

A thought crossed her mind: Maybe the Gingeriches had never quite fit in with the People. After all, they'd changed church districts more than once. Had it been a struggle for more than just Joe to submit to the various church ordinances? Or was he too stubborn to come under the unwritten rules of the *Ordnung*? *And if so, why didn't I notice this before?* she wondered.

Once Gloria had dressed for bed and slipped on her warmest bathrobe, she went over to the guestroom, and seeing the door open slightly, she looked in. There, in the soft illumination from the hallway, Leona was kneeling beside the bed, hands folded and her long blond hair, free of its bun, cascading down her back.

Gloria stared at the white cotton nightgown, similar to the ones she'd often worn, and the length of Leona's hair, which, like all Old Order Amishwomen's, had never been cut, only trimmed. A rush of recollections from a world away poured into her mind.

*Is Leona praying for me?*

She stayed a moment longer, touched by the tender sight, then tiptoed off.

Leona's visit had stirred up memories of the best part of Gloria's life, the years she'd tried to forget but hadn't. Not like her family, who'd so easily adopted the fancy life.

*Yet what can I do about it?*

The thought filled her mind long after she, too, said her prayers before falling asleep.

## CHAPTER 21

Tom Ebersol headed to Mahlon and Maggie Speicher's house early that Saturday morning, taking some jam from his mother. Danny rode with him, asking along the way if Tom planned to inquire about Leona. *Has anyone heard if she has arrived in Arkansas?* Danny signed.

Tom shook his head. He'd hoped she might think to call and leave a message for him at Uncle Alan's business, but so far, no word.

The sun's rays bounced off the neighbors' twin silos, and the fields absolutely glistened. The dew point was high, and as he drove, it crossed Tom's mind to pray that Leona would have nice weather for her trip home tomorrow.

Danny poked his elbow. *Are you worried about Leona?* he signed.

Tom nodded and smiled, turning to him as he drove so Danny could read his lips. "Not too much."

*She will be back soon,* Danny signed.

*And hopefully her fascination with the Gingerich family will be a thing of the past,* Tom thought.

When they arrived at Mahlon's farm, Danny wanted to wait in the open buggy. Tom quickly carried the small box of blueberry jam, Mahlon's favorite, to the back porch.

Maggie flung open the door and ushered him inside. "You're out and about early for a Saturday," she said. Her children were sitting around the table putting a puzzle together. "I'm glad ya caught me before I head to the shop."

He placed the box on the table. "Mamm sent these over for ya."

"Isn't that thoughtful!" Maggie said, lifting one of the pint jars out of the box to show the children, who applauded. "Please thank her for us, won't ya?"

"Dat will want some for snack," Samuel said as he looked up from the puzzle. "Ain't so, Mamma?"

"For certain."

"Well, have yourself a nice day," Tom said, turning toward the door.

"Oh, Tom, in case you wondered, we haven't heard from Leona," Maggie said. "Still, I'm sure all's well. She wasn't going to check in unless she had a chance."

He smiled. "The Lord's watchin' over her."

"Remember, the Gingeriches' story isn't finished."

Tom agreed.

"The Lord might just honor Leona's prayers—and her visit—and use her to remind them of His long-suffering nature," Maggie added.

Hearing this encouraged Tom, and he thanked her. "Danny's prob'ly wondering what's become of me." He waved and headed out the back door. "*Denki!*"

⁓⊱✦⊰⁓

Though it was the weekend, Gloria's parents left the house early for work, and Adam took Jonas and James to the park before Gloria had even budged from under her covers. She'd heard their voices coming from the kitchen, and then the sound of the garage door opening and closing.

Sitting on the bed, she wished she wasn't scheduled to work that afternoon and evening, as well. But this was the busiest day of the week, and her boss was temporarily shorthanded. Hopefully Leona would feel all right about hanging out with the family until Gloria arrived home that evening.

At least she and Leona had the morning to themselves before they met Darren Brockett at noon. Leona intended to sit in one of the booths doing needlework or reading, whatever suited her, until Mom picked Leona up before supper.

Plumping her pillow, Gloria reveled in the stillness before dressing for the day, having showered last night. Once ready, she went out to the kitchen to mix up some batter for chocolate chip waffles. Mom never made them anymore, but she hadn't forgotten their old recipe. *Dad always piled whipped cream on his when we were Amish. . . .*

Thinking of that, Gloria realized again how strange it must be to Leona to be in a houseful of newly minted Englishers. *Leona's as devout and certain of her path in life as ever.* And Gloria couldn't help but be envious.

⁓⁓⁕⁓

Leona was on the lookout for a parking spot on South Third Street, leaning forward in her seat and scanning for available options as Gloria's car crept along.

"Let's talk more about *you*," Gloria said, tapping on the brake when it looked like there was an opening, but they were mistaken. "Other than that you're engaged, I don't know much about what's going on in your life."

Leona noticed how gentle Gloria's voice was, as if she didn't want to sound nosy. "Well, I still enjoy workin' for Maggie several days a week—I like to talk with the customers. Most of them are curious 'bout the Amish life, as you can imagine."

"Do you still attend the Singings and other youth gatherings?"

"Most of the time."

"Is your fiancé baptized yet?"

Leona nodded and smiled. "Tom joined church right after his twentieth birthday. He's always known he wanted to be Amish."

"Always knew . . . that's something."

"He wasn't boastin' about that, though. Tom's not like that."

Gloria spotted an opening and pulled into a parking spot. She turned off the ignition. "What about you—have you joined yet?"

"I did, the year after you moved away." Leona said it softly. "You must've joined out here, then?"

Gloria shook her head as she slipped the keys into her purse. "I took a few baptismal classes here, but my father pulled the family out of the church district before I could finish." A sad little laugh escaped her lips.

Leona didn't bring up the fact that they'd always planned to take the lifelong kneeling vow together. "It was ever so special . . . *nee*, a most sacred experience for me."

"I'm real happy for you," Gloria said, sounding as if she meant it. "If only my own situation had been within my control."

They got out and put money in the parking meter and walked around downtown, window-shopping and enjoying the warm breeze. All the while, Leona wondered why Gloria hadn't stayed with the Amish community here when her father broke away.

"Did you find another church home, then, for yourself?" Leona asked.

Gloria sighed. "At first, my father felt strongly about us staying together as a family, so we had church at home, so to speak, taking turns reading verses from the Bible and singing some of the old hymns from the *Ausbund*. But after a few weeks of that, he decided we could visit a nondenominational church not far from our house. At the time, I felt like I might just wither up and die without going to worship somewhere, so I went along with it." Gloria suddenly motioned toward a tearoom and antique shop. "Hey, let's stop in there and rest our feet awhile."

Leona agreed, thinking perhaps Gloria wasn't comfortable talking where people could overhear them. *Or maybe this is an excuse to change the subject.*

The tearoom was charming, decorated with touches of soft pink and with abundant cream-colored lace at the windows, on chair backs, and on the paper doilies that graced the small tables.

"Isn't this the sweetest place?" Gloria pointed out the large glass display case featuring pastries. "This is my treat, by the way, so choose whatever you'd like."

Unplanned, they both ordered hot orange zinger tea and pastries at the counter. "Maybe we aren't so different now after all," Gloria remarked with a smile. She picked out a cozy table toward the back of the room, near a soothing water feature. A pink rose in a round glass vase was centered on the table beside the heart-shaped salt and pepper shakers. Only a few other customers were in the room.

"Perfect," Gloria said, putting her napkin on her lap. "Now we can talk more privately, *jah?*"

Leona pricked up her ears at the *jah* she'd slipped.

"Oh dear." Gloria laughed a little. "Bits and pieces of Amish life must still be lurking inside me."

"I'd be surprised if they weren't."

Shortly, a server brought a tray with

individual teapots, cups, and saucers, as well as a petite pitcher of cream and a small glass dish of sugar cubes with a tiny silver spoon.

When the delightful woman returned with their midmorning pastries, she mentioned the royal raspberry cake, saying she highly recommended the daily special, but both Gloria and Leona politely declined.

"This pastry is plenty for me," Leona added, thanking her.

When the server left, Gloria turned to Leona. "Now, where were we?" She stirred a sugar cube into the tea in her floral teacup. "Oh yes . . . we were talking about church."

Leona held back, letting her make the return path to the delicate conversation.

"We were all bored to death with the church Dad randomly chose. Eventually, my family stopped attending, and I pleaded to be able to visit other churches on my own. I settled into one where I attend now every Lord's Day," Gloria said, taking her first sip of tea. "I hoped my parents and my brothers might follow, but only Mom and my brothers have ever gone with me, and none of them regularly. It's where Adam met his girlfriend, Donnalynn. But Dad . . . he never goes anymore."

She glanced out the window and wrapped a lock of hair around her pointer finger. "I'm not like my father," she said, returning her gaze to Leona. "I doubt you ever saw this side of him, but he really seems to chafe under New Testament teaching. It was the same with the expectations of the brethren. No wonder the Amish church was such a challenge for him."

"Is that what happened in Lancaster County, too?" Leona felt sad for Gloria, caught in the mire of her father's choices.

Gloria seemed to steel herself. "This is hard for me. . . ."

"Please, don't feel that ya must—"

"I *need* to tell you," Gloria insisted. "You're the only one who will understand." She glanced around nervously, then leaned forward, her words coming out in a hushed tone. "I learned most of this from Mom long after we left Colerain . . . but Dad had some underhanded business dealings that eventually caught up with him. It was a terrible time—the worst trial for our family. I still don't know what to think of it. My father supposedly still owes quite a lot of money to one of the Amish farmers in your church district, and there are other farmers who never went after him for payment on certain items, forgiving him of debts or just overlooking them."

*So this is what Tom was referring to!*

She drew a deep breath, determined to reach out to her friend. "You're not at fault for what he did."

"He's my father, though, and it *feels* like I'm partially to blame."

"But you're not," Leona objected.

Gloria wiped a tear and looked away.

A moment of silence passed. "Do ya ever miss the Amish way of life?" Leona asked.

Gloria grimaced. "I'm not sure how to answer that. I thought I was fine . . . but yesterday, when we were baking together, I thought I might cry. It was just odd." She sighed. "Your visit has stirred up all sorts of emotions."

Leona studied her. "You must've been terribly distressed when you wrote to me."

"I was a train wreck that day. It was all I could do to even write what I did." Tears sprang to Gloria's eyes. "I needed to see you again, Leona. I had to know if you were still willing to be my friend . . . and if you were still Amish."

This tugged on Leona's heartstrings. "It matters that much?"

Nodding, Gloria asked, "Have you ever found yourself at a crossroads, not sure which way to go? It keeps me awake at night—every single night." She looked down at her shiny bracelet and touched it. "Let's just put it this way: If I decide to go one direction, I will have sealed my future . . . there'll be no turning back."

Leona listened but was confused—Gloria was being too vague. "Wouldn't that be true no matter which road you take?"

Gloria folded her hands on the table. "You're right, of course. But sometimes, I don't even know my own heart."

Sipping her tea, Leona pondered the misery in her friend's expression. "The Lord does, though."

"I'm not sure of anything. . . ."

"Well, here's something else to consider. You know that I care about you, *jah*?"

Gloria nodded thoughtfully.

"Can ya imagine how much more *He* cares—the One who created you and knows your pain, your hurts, your disappointments?"

"People hide their truest selves . . . keep the secret pieces of their heart under wraps," Gloria said, faltering. "My father does it, obviously, or he wouldn't jump from one church to another, running away from his wrongdoing when confronted. Running is his escape, I guess you could say. My mother said your bishop told him that he runs out of fear, because he's afraid to self-examine."

*Trying to hide from God . . .*

Leona wanted to remind Gloria of what she'd said earlier: She wasn't her father.

Instead, she sadly observed how torn Gloria seemed to be.

"Oh, goodness, look at the time!" Gloria pushed her small plate aside and took one last sip of tea. "I say we have more walking to do before lunch, especially if we want to eat again so soon." She laughed, but it didn't sound very natural. "Why don't you just take the rest of your pastry in your napkin? Time's a-wastin', as the Amish say."

Leona drank the rest of her tea, seeing through Gloria's sudden bluster. And just when she thought they were getting somewhere . . . perhaps even to the root of Gloria's frantic letter.

## CHAPTER 22

*G*loria gave the impression of wanting to show Leona every nook and cranny of her remaining favorite downtown haunts. So when Gloria wanted to poke her head into yet another gift shop, Leona asked to borrow her phone to call Maggie. "There's a telephone at her store, and she'll relay a message to my parents." *And to Tom.*

Gloria opened her shoulder bag. "You should've said so sooner!"

The truth was, Leona hadn't wanted to ask and was surprised when Gloria gave her the car keys. Feeling strange about having both the mobile phone and the car keys in her control, Leona opened the car door and stepped inside, where for a moment, she sat and stared at the phone. She leaned against the headrest and thought about Gloria's shocking statements about her father. *Something's dreadfully wrong.*

With only today left to visit, Leona prayed that what she'd shared with Gloria over tea might prove helpful.

*Dear Lord, let my words be acceptable to Thee. Help Gloria understand and grasp Thy great love for her.*

Leona punched in Maggie's number and heard the ringing on the line. She hoped her sister-in-law wasn't swamped with customers at this hour. Another ring, and there was Maggie's voice, as clear as if she were sitting here in the car.

"Hullo, Maggie. It's Leona. I wanted to let you know I arrived all right and I'm doing fine."

"Tom was over here earlier askin' in a roundabout way."

Leona perked up, hearing of Tom.

"He brought over a batch of blueberry jam for all of us, and I took the opportunity to assure him you were all right, or we would've heard somethin'."

"*Denki*, Maggie. Kind of ya."

"Your young man's definitely smitten."

Leona smiled into the phone. "Well, please

be sure to tell Dat and Mamma I called—and Tom, too, if you see him. Maybe I'll be home before ya have a chance."

There was a pause. "So how are the Gingeriches?"

"Honestly, since you asked, I think they're a bit *ferhoodled*."

"*Ach*, aren't we all sometimes?"

Leona nodded. "That's not the response I expected."

Now Maggie was laughing. "Let's just say people are really enjoyin' the store. It's been one *fleissich* day."

"Busy is *gut*, though, ain't so?"

"I'll be mighty glad when you're back," Maggie replied.

"I miss you, too. *Da Herr sei mit du*."

"*Gott* be with ya, too, Leona."

She wished Maggie a good day and ended the call.

*Tom went out of his way to ask about me*, she thought, and in that moment, Lancaster County seemed much too far away.

⸱⸱⸱✦⸱⸱⸱

Gloria did her best to dismiss her discussion with Leona at the tearoom, and while browsing in yet another shop, a display of stationery caught her eye. She picked up the pretty set, turning it over and thinking she ought to buy it—Leona would enjoy getting letters from her on this paper. At the thought, she dreaded her friend's visit coming to a close. *And I still haven't come clean with her!*

Glancing out the shop window, she noticed Leona still sitting in the car, apparently finished with her phone call. Quickly, she made her purchase.

"Not many young women come in for stationery anymore," the clerk said.

"Email and texting are so convenient." Gloria smiled at her. "But there's nothing like a card or letter." She thought of the journals she'd kept after first moving here. *Like a long letter to Leona that never got sent.*

"Thanks for dropping by," the cheerful woman said as she counted out Gloria's change. "And come again."

"Have a wonderful afternoon." Gloria exited the shop and walked toward the car. Momentarily, she considered showing Leona the journal stashed away in the back of her closet—a chronicling of those painful months.

*Too depressing,* she decided.

⚜

A light drizzle began falling just before noon, and Leona wondered aloud if there was more rain in the forecast.

"Let's find out," Gloria said, pulling her

phone out of her purse at the red light. "Here, check my weather app. It's at the top of the screen."

Leona clicked on the app's radar, which depicted a small weather system moving across the screen. "Looks minor. *Ach*, this is really something. Like a moving version of what's in the newspaper."

"Better not get too attached to it," Gloria teased as she made the turn onto the street where the diner was located.

Leona smiled. "No chance of that."

"Oh, you really can't say that. The modern world can be like sin—at first we're repulsed by it. Then, after a while, we open our arms to it, welcoming it. It's as simple as that."

"Do ya think havin' a phone is sinful, then? You used to think that . . . remember?"

For a moment, Gloria was silent. When she spoke again, she seemed a bit choked up. "Like I said at the tearoom—there are still many lingering Amish bits and pieces in my heart."

Leona wondered what it had been like for her friend to say good-bye to a life she'd seemed to love—a life she was forced to leave because of her father's crooked business dealings. *No wonder Joe wouldn't permit his family to contact any of us back home.*

Gloria seemed determined to find a quieter spot at the homey diner, eventually selecting a booth near a window, away from the long counter where a few customers were drinking sodas and eating hot dogs and burgers. "How's this?" she asked, sliding in opposite Leona and pushing her hair back from her face.

*Does she want to continue our talk?* With Gloria's boyfriend joining them, Leona really doubted it.

"You hungry for lunch yet?" Gloria asked.

"That delicious little pastry took the edge off my appetite." Leona placed her canvas sewing bag on the seat beside her and reached for the menu. "What's *gut* to eat here?"

"Everything—and I mean it." Gloria rummaged in her purse. "I can use my employee discount, so lunch is on me."

"Let me treat *you*," Leona argued, determined.

"You're my guest, silly. Besides, you've come a long way."

"Still, I'd like to."

Gloria caught Leona's eye. "You have no idea how much it's meant to me, having you here, sharing like this."

Hearing this warmed Leona's heart, and she thanked God that she and Gloria were together again, even if only for a while.

The tinkle of utensils on plates and the low hum of people talking were somehow comforting to Leona as she looked over the menu.

"Darren texted me to go ahead and order his usual," Gloria said. "He'll be here by the time the food comes." She laughed. "Although you and I might want to opt for something lighter after those pastries. And . . . Mom's planning a big meal tonight. I'm really sorry that I couldn't get off work. I hope you understand."

"My visit came up so quickly, it can't be helped," Leona said, then decided on a half tuna sandwich and a cup of tomato soup.

The friendly waitress took their order, and Leona mentioned to Gloria that hardly anyone seemed to look twice at her Amish attire.

"I noticed that, too, back when we first moved here. But this is a small town, and everyone's likely aware of the Plain community here."

"Well, they sure seem more courteous than in some places." Leona thought of the gawks she'd received while buying peanuts at one of the gas station convenience stores on the trip out.

"Maybe so . . . but everyone also knows everyone else's business," Gloria said. Then her attention seemed to focus elsewhere, and she waved to a tall, dark-haired young man who was coming toward them. "Darren's here. Perfect timing." She slid over, welcoming her boyfriend with a dazzling smile.

Leona suddenly felt peculiar, yet she tried to be polite. "It's nice to meet you, Darren," she said, accepting his firm handshake across the table.

"You too," he said, smiling. "Gloria's often talked of you."

Darren had remarkably intense blue eyes, and he engaged Leona by asking about her trip here and then inquiring about their visit so far.

Leona and Gloria took turns responding until their meals arrived, and then Gloria asked what he had been up to this morning. "Did you get everything accomplished in Coal Hill?"

"I checked on one of our diners southeast of here," he explained to Leona, adjusting his shirt collar. "We recently hired a new cook."

While she spooned up her hot tomato soup, Leona tried to gauge things between Gloria and her boyfriend, considering what little romantic experience she'd had herself. Was Darren a good match for Gloria?

After a time, Gloria's boss, Hampton, walked over to their table and asked if everything was to their liking, patting his son on the back. Gloria introduced Leona, and Hampton also shook her hand more gently than Darren had. "You two girls are in good company," he said with a grin. "He's my right arm."

Gloria inquired about how Hampton's wife was doing after her fall, and he assured her that it was merely a sprain, not a break.

When Hampton left, the three of them exchanged small talk for a while, and Darren turned to Gloria and adjusted her gold bracelet, sliding it around so that her initials were showing.

"Have you told Leona about us?" he asked Gloria, glancing at Leona and winking.

"Um . . . that's girl talk," Gloria replied, looking at Leona as if to say, *"Just keep it mum."*

He smiled and reached for his burger and took a bite.

"I stopped by the jewelry store again," Darren said, wiping his mouth with the paper napkin.

Gloria looked startled. "But . . . I thought we—"

"Just wait—you'll love what I'm looking at," Darren interrupted. "I promise."

"Darren, this bracelet is more than enough." Gloria sounded almost childlike as she looked down at her wrist. "It's beautiful."

Leona agreed but didn't feel comfortable hopping into the conversation.

Darren slipped his arm around Gloria. "You wear it all the time, right?"

"Most of the time." Gloria looked at Leona.

"I just want you to be happy with it," Darren said.

Gloria shrugged. "Of course I am."

Leona felt uneasy. Gloria was clearly annoyed by Darren's somewhat dogged attention, although it seemed to her that Gloria was overreacting. Darren certainly seemed pleasant enough.

*There must be more to it,* Leona thought.

## CHAPTER 23

O h, Leona, I hope you weren't twiddling your thumbs while Gloria worked," Jeannie said when she picked her up late that afternoon.

"Not at all. In fact, there were several unexpected blessings," Leona told her. "A little girl eating with her family watched me crochet for the longest time. Finally, she wandered over with her mother to whisper that she was four years old and named Alana, and she wondered if I'd show her how to make loops. *Ach*, was she ever sweet. The cutest little thing!"

"I'll bet she was." Jeannie nodded, one hand on the steering wheel. "And it was kind of you to take time for her."

"Then I went for a walk and met a nice couple who stopped me to visit—said it was my Amish clothes that attracted them, since they hoped to join a Mennonite church soon. Right now, they're in a proving time with the bishop and minister, but the wife said they had Anabaptist roots."

"Is that right?" Jeannie seemed a bit sheepish now.

"They were so friendly and chatty," Leona went on. "After that, I returned to the diner, where Gloria introduced me to three of her church friends who'd dropped by to get something to eat."

"My goodness, you've had a busy afternoon."

"I also met Gloria's boss, Hampton, and his son, Darren."

"Ah yes . . . her soon-to-be fiancé. What a terrific catch." Jeannie tittered. "He's from a great family and has such a sensible head for business, Joe says. Honestly, Joe thinks Darren's the best thing since Amish fried chicken."

Leona listened, wondering whether Gloria really was as serious about Darren as her parents seemed to think.

"I'm glad you met him—was it planned?"

"Gloria set it up."

"No doubt you noticed how crazy Darren is about Gloria."

"Do ya really think they'll get married?" Leona asked.

"Well, it's up to them to set a date, of course, but I expect they'll become engaged any day now. An autumn wedding would be wonderful—it's unbearably hot and muggy here in the summer, and I'd like to have Gloria's wedding outdoors, near one of the lakes." Jeannie paused a moment, glancing her way. "I thought Gloria might've asked you to be her maid of honor."

"They're not officially engaged, right?"

"Well, no, not formally."

Leona recalled that awkward exchange between Gloria and Darren—she assumed he'd been pressing her about an engagement ring, yet Gloria hadn't exactly seemed enthusiastic. "Has your family spent much time with Darren?"

"Joe took him small game hunting last fall . . . they spent two full days together. Adam decided to go along, too, at the last minute. The three of them had a grand time."

"Do Jonas and James enjoy hunting, too?" Leona asked, deciding to try to shift the talk to a subject other than Darren. She didn't feel altogether at ease, discussing him with Jeannie.

"They prefer water sports, but once Darren's in the family, I have a feeling all five will go off in the woods together hunting, at least once the boys are teens. It's kind of what the men out here do. Male bonding, you know."

"My father goes deer hunting with Mahlon every year," Leona said, trying again.

"How *is* your family, by the way?"

"Oh, pretty much the same. Dawdi Benuel's still as talkative as ever, but he's slowing down some."

Jeannie nodded. "And how's your mother?"

Leona wondered if she was thinking about Mamma's hard bout with pneumonia back when. "Mamma's just fine and works circles round most young women." Leona went on to mention how big Mahlon and Maggie's children were getting. "I s'pose just seein' them every so often, I notice the growth spurts more than their parents do."

They discussed Leona's work at Maggie's store for a while, and Jeannie asked about several of the area womenfolk. At last, she said, "Are all the same ministers still there?"

"Well, no one's passed away." Leona wondered why she would ask. "As you know, they're ordained for life."

A horse and buggy was coming toward them when Jeannie turned onto their road. All around, Amish farmers were plowing and planting.

"I don't mean to sound meddlesome," Jeannie explained. "I'm just curious."

"Do you ever think of goin' back?" Leona asked.

Jeannie chuckled. "For a visit, maybe. That would be the right thing to do . . . but it's not my place to decide any of that," she said with a regretful look. "I need to stand by my husband's choices, and I'm sure your mother would do the same."

Leona was surprised at the defensive tone that had crept into Jeannie's voice. Gone were the closeness and understanding Leona had once shared with Gloria's mother.

*This isn't the Jeannie I knew.*

They got out of the car and headed for the house, Leona anxious to get to the privacy of her room. The day had been fraught with awkward moments, yet this had been the most uncomfortable.

*What'll I say if Gloria asks my opinion of Darren?* Leona wondered. It wasn't so much that Darren was bad, if a little pushy . . . more that Gloria seemed to be resisting him. *In truth, she almost seems annoyed by him.*

After Jeannie encouraged her to relax before supper, Leona organized her travel bag, readying it for the return trip and thinking ahead to tomorrow's early morning departure. Leona wished she could stay another day, if only to get to the bottom of things with Gloria, who seemed so conflicted. Yet with Gloria at work until after the supper rush, there was precious little time left.

Going to lie on top of the bedspread, Leona's heart went out to the Gingeriches, Gloria in particular, but she felt at a loss to help, as enmeshed in the world as they had become. She could only guess at the state of her friend's heart, but she was thankful she could pray to her all-knowing heavenly Father, who could heal any hurt. *I trust Thee to give Gloria a tenderness toward the things that matter most in this life.*

Later, Leona wandered out to the kitchen and volunteered to help.

"Everything's under control, dear," Jeannie said, "but you're welcome to stroll out to the gazebo . . . see the yard if you'd like."

"All right." Leona opened the back door and walked along the pebbled path, noticing the wooden rose arbor Joe must have built. A cement birdbath stood near Jeannie's herb garden, and in the distance was a vacant horse barn. *A few things still remain. . . .*

The white gazebo shimmered in the early evening light, and she made her way up the steps and leaned on the banister. She stared at the fertile farmland beyond and counted four barns and silos, plus a windmill. On the road to the south, a farmer was bringing his horse and market wagon home for the day.

She faced hayfields and cornfields. Really, Joe and Jeannie had chosen an ideal spot here.

Then, hearing footsteps behind her, she turned to see Adam. "Mind if I join ya, Leona?"

She smiled. "I was just thinkin' how this view reminds me of Colerain."

"Well, this is all the memory of Lancaster County I need," he said. "I enjoy being English."

She listened, not too surprised.

"But sometimes, I'm not so sure about Gloria."

"She seems fairly happy to me." *Except maybe about Darren.*

Adam shook his head. "It's just a front." He paused, glancing away for a moment. "I often wish my father had allowed her to stay put in Colerain with the People—with *you.*"

Leona was amazed. "I wish that, too—believe me."

"The move here was hard on her. Gloria was blue for days when we were told we couldn't write to you or anyone else back there."

"I appreciate you tellin' me this, Adam."

"Well, she hasn't been the same since—lost some of that plucky spirit she used to have. If you ask me, she just seems a bit unfocused, like she's not sure where she fits in."

Leona pondered this. He'd given insight she wouldn't otherwise have had, and it was encouraging to know she'd done the right thing by coming to visit. "You say you're glad to be English, though."

"Definitely. I wouldn't have had the chance to become a car mechanic otherwise. And I've met a really terrific girl here, too . . . Donnalynn. I hope to marry her someday."

"Gloria said you met her at church."

"Right. She's got a great heart. The whole family really seems to like her, Mom especially." He laughed. "Almost as much as they like Darren."

Soon, Jeannie called for supper, and Adam didn't waste any time hurrying to the house. He held the screen door for Leona, and she thanked him for taking time to chat with her.

At the table, it was Adam who suggested they bow their heads in a silent blessing before Joe reached for the platter of fried chicken. Jeannie passed it to Leona next, not putting anything on her own plate just yet. *Ever the polite hostess,* thought Leona, hoping Gloria might have time to grab a bite to eat during her busy shift.

"Your visit with us is nearly over," Jeannie said after the younger boys had served themselves and passed the platter back to their mother.

"We're glad you could make the trip," Arkansas Joe said, looking Leona's way.

"Well, I'm glad I could get caught up with Gloria . . . and all of you."

Joe nodded, peering at her over the chicken leg he held to his lips.

"And I really enjoyed your view from the gazebo," she added.

Joe groaned. "Seeing all these farms makes me thankful I don't have to get up and feed the livestock before dawn, or groom the horses every day after breakfast. Not to mention hitch up a horse each time I need to run to town."

Leona said not a word.

"Some of us *miss* the farm back in Lancaster County," James piped up. "Don't we, Jonas?"

"Speak for yourself," Jonas said, rolling his eyes. "I'd much rather shoot hoops than pitch hay."

Joe chuckled. "That's my boy."

Jeannie glanced at Leona and gave an apologetic shrug.

*What about once Amish, always Amish?* Leona mused. She could see the appeal of English life, but she could never imagine abandoning the Old Ways and people she'd grown up with to seek it out. *If only the Gingeriches felt the same way . . .*

## CHAPTER 24

*L*eona was all packed when there was a knock at the guest room door. "Comin'," she said, hurrying to open it.

There was Gloria, still in her waitressing outfit—trim black skirt and white apron. "Hampton let me off work early so I could spend a little more time with you."

"Such a *gut* surprise . . . come in." Leona closed the door behind them.

"I don't feel bad leavin' since the supper crowd has thinned out."

Leona sat on the bed, and Gloria pulled a chair over, removing her shoes and socks and resting her bare feet on the bed quilt.

Suddenly, Gloria's eyes were bright with

tears. "I really don't know what to do about Darren."

Leona held her breath. *Please don't ask me.*

"I think I need some space . . . time to think about where my life is heading," Gloria said, wiping her eyes. "I came close to confiding in you earlier today, but I couldn't follow through. Then when Darren showed up for our lunch date, I felt strange, because even though I'd really wanted you to meet him, I was actually sorry when you did."

Leona went to get Gloria a tissue from the box on the dresser and handed it to her.

"Thanks," her friend said through her tears. "You always seem to know just what I need . . . which is why I wrote to you in the first place. I trust you, Leona, and I need you to help me think this through, because if I say yes to marrying Darren, I'll be stuck being English for the rest of my life." Gloria sighed heavily. "On the other hand, if I walk away from him, I'll never know what I could have had *with* him. He's a pretty great guy . . . so generous, and he has such a great future ahead. . . ."

Leona had no words to counsel her, because Gloria was missing the most important ingredient: What did God want for her?

"What should I do?" Gloria pleaded, her makeup all smudged.

"Well, surely ya have a *gut* idea what *I* will say, ain't so?"

"Yes, even after all this time apart, you're still my closest friend."

Leona drew a breath and considered Gloria . . . and everything Leona had observed since arriving in Arkansas. "All right. S'pose to start with, you could ask yourself how you feel now, livin' as an *Englischer*."

Gloria looked miserable. "When I think ahead to having a family and . . ." She couldn't seem to finish.

"And what?"

"Well, to raising my children outside the faith of my Amish heritage." The words seemed to tumble out, and Gloria herself looked surprised.

"You sometimes wonder 'bout your wee ones and the kind of life they might have as *Englischers*?"

Nodding slowly, Gloria's tears welled up again. "It keeps me awake at night, Leona. I'm worried sick I might do the wrong thing for my own future, as well as that of my children." She dabbed her eyes with the tissue, then added, "I know Darren would be a good provider. Well, I can't know that for sure, but his family's done well for themselves."

"Are ya seeking wealth, then?"

"More security than wealth," Gloria admitted.

"Dare I ask where Darren stands on attending worship, and following God's ways?"

Gloria sighed. "He's not too keen on church . . . not yet, anyway. I was hoping I might change his mind."

Leona pondered that. "I'm sorry this is so hard for ya, Gloria. But in the end, it's a choice you alone can make . . . and live with." Leona reached for her hand. "You've been blessed to experience the Amish life, and I know God means for ya to marry a man who respects Him."

Nodding, Gloria said, "I've experienced both sides of the fence now. I just wish it wasn't such a knotty problem. A husband and wife are supposed to be willing to meet each other halfway, right? Isn't that real love?"

Leona hadn't heard it stated quite that way, but she agreed. "And remember, it ain't just the two of you in a marriage. The Lord is ever present to guide you when you ask." She smiled at her friend. "He often speaks in a still, small voice, ya know."

"But how can I get quiet enough to hear it?" Gloria sat there like a helpless child.

"Funny you say that, 'cause I've wondered that, too, sometimes."

"So what do you do?"

"Remember that clearing in the woods not far from our barnyard? I walk there, breathing in the fresh smell of pine and the forest, and remind myself to trust, wait, and hope. Waiting for God's timing is hopeful trust."

"Hopeful trust," Gloria whispered. "I like that."

"When we recognize that Jesus is the Savior of the world, then things fall into place."

"I believe that, too, but it's good to be reminded. Lately, I've been so confused. And I wonder how to tell if what I have with Darren is built for the long haul."

"Love that's true and honest cherishes the *other* person more." Leona was thinking of First Corinthians, chapter thirteen. Surely, Gloria had read it or heard a minister preach about it.

A light seemed to come into Gloria's eyes. "What if . . ." She shook her head. "No, that's just crazy."

"What's crazy?"

"It just popped into my head: What if I could get off work for a while. . . ." Her voice trailed away.

Leona's heart leaped as she sensed what Gloria might be trying to say. "Maybe you'd like to come home with me—have some time away. Is that what you're thinkin'?"

"I don't see how I can swing that. I've

been working hard to save up for some college courses next fall."

"You might just benefit from seeing good old Brownie again. And you could roam the countryside you used to love so. Take time to pray a little?"

"Or a lot." A sad little smile broke across Gloria's face. "Sure, I'll go. Might bring me some peace."

Spurred on toward her goal, Leona quickly suggested, "I could call and leave a message with Maggie. She checks her messages more frequently than my parents do. She'll get the voicemail tomorrow and can tell my parents to get the spare room ready."

Gloria's eyes were puffy. "Are you sure about this?"

"Are *you*?" Leona asked.

"My job's the biggest obstacle. But I'll call Hampton to ask, see what he says."

Leona reached into her purse for Ted Bell's business card. "And I'll check to see if there's room in the van tomorrow, in case you can go, too."

"Forget that—I'll drive us. A road trip together might be fun." Gloria was grinning now.

Leona had never seen such a swift transformation. "All right, then—I'll help ya pack, okay?"

Gloria leaped up and hugged her. "You were always the dearest friend ever."

"Might your father object?"

"Oh, he definitely will."

*Won't my parents be shocked?* she thought, hoping Gloria could get the time off. *And how will Tom react?*

Gloria motioned for Leona to go with her to her room, where she phoned her boss, thanking him at first for letting her take off early tonight. Then she somewhat reticently told him she really needed some time away. "Can you manage at the diner without me for a while?"

Leona felt odd sitting there and listening in, but very soon Gloria's glum facial expression lifted.

When she hung up, she pumped her fist into the air. "We're all set," she said, beaming. "That went more smoothly than I thought. It must be God's will for me to drive you back."

"But you're not doin' this just for me, are ya?"

"Oh no. It'll give us more time together, for one thing. And strange as it may sound, I am looking forward to walking around my old stomping grounds."

"Not strange at all." Leona felt ecstatic.

Gloria handed the phone to her. "Now you

can make your call to the driver, okay?" And she left the room.

When Ted answered, Leona quickly explained her situation and apologized for the last-minute notice. Ted said he was fine with it and mentioned that another couple wanted to ride back to the Lancaster area. "This will be an answer to prayer for them."

"I'm glad to hear it," Leona said, hanging up to call and leave a voice message for Maggie at the phone shed not far from their house, praying that Maggie would relay the news to Dat and Mamma in time.

In the room above Gloria's, Leona heard muffled voices growing louder by the second. Then a loud thump—was it the stomp of a foot as Joe literally put his foot down on Gloria's hopes?

"This is not a good idea, Gloria!" Joe was yelling so loudly now, Leona no longer had to imagine his reaction. She began to fret—what if Gloria caved in and didn't go through with it, and Leona had canceled her spot on the van prematurely? *I'd be stuck here for who knows how long!*

She paced the floor, frustrated. Telling herself to calm down, she decided to put into practice what she'd told Gloria was her best way of handling life struggles. She left the house to go to the gazebo and talk with her heavenly Father. It was a good way to block out the commotion taking place upstairs. She pictured Gloria standing in her parents' bedroom, trying to talk over their objections while Leona prayed for understanding on the part of Joe and Jeannie . . . and for their daughter's freedom to return to Colerain for a reprieve.

Sitting down in the gazebo, Leona was conscious of the soft night chorus of crickets, and the glimmers of fireflies over neighboring meadows. She heard the rumble of a passing carriage in the distance.

*Joe Gingerich gave up that tranquil life,* she thought, befuddled at how he and his family could be so thoroughly encircled by the Amish with whom they'd once rubbed shoulders, yet somehow manage to ignore them daily.

## CHAPTER 25

Gloria's family was still sleeping when she pressed the garage door opener and slipped out of the house with Leona a couple hours before dawn the next morning. It made perfect sense to get on the road before other travelers.

"My father's not pleased that I'm going back with you," Gloria said as they headed out of town.

"Well, I'm so relieved it worked out," Leona said, her hair up in a bun tucked beneath a blue scarf instead of her formal white head covering.

"It's pretty remarkable, to tell you the truth." Gloria didn't know how much she wanted to say about her father's heated indignation. Even her mother had seemed displeased, as though Gloria were somehow judging them by going.

Leona glanced at her, hands folded in her lap. "Miracles do happen."

"Dad was helpful enough, though, to warn me there won't be many places along this highway to stop and eat for quite a distance. And he says there's constant road construction around Memphis."

"That's *gut* to know."

"And Mom, bless her heart, took time last night to help me prepare sandwiches, fruit, and drinks. They're in the cooler in the back seat," Gloria said, mentally forgiving her parents for making such a fuss.

Feeling like a horse escaped out of the barn gate, Gloria pushed the accelerator. She remembered Hampton's exceptional kindness toward her on the phone last evening. *Maybe he senses something's up between Darren and me,* she thought with a glance at Leona, who, from her bowed head, appeared to be praying again. The realization brought a great sense of consolation.

If Gloria were the least bit hard-hearted, she might have clung to the angry words her father had shouted last night, words she believed he would feel sorry about later. *Words that caused me pain.* Instead, she was set on releasing them, along with his belligerent attitude, flinging both to the wind as she followed the directional prompts from her phone on the console.

Before departing, she had also contacted Darren via text. *I'm driving Leona back to Lancaster County . . . hanging out there for a while. I'll be in touch.*

Despite the early hour, he had replied within seconds, naturally surprised but wishing her a safe trip. She decided to text him occasional updates as to their travel progress. *I don't want him to worry.*

Truly, Gloria was relieved to have this short reprieve from so much pressure on the relationship front. "Can you reach the cooler?" she asked Leona.

"Sure, what do you want?"

"Some Coke. I'm still groggy. How about you?"

Leona yawned. "Wish I could share some of the driving." She opened the fizzy Coke and handed it to Gloria.

"That's okay. We'll just stop and run around the car every now and then to keep me going."

Leona laughed softly. "There were a number of gas stations with convenience stores on the way out here. We can stock up on snacks and sweets if we run out, *jah*?"

Gloria adored hearing her quaint Amish accent. *Do I still sound anything like that?*

⁓⁓≫✦≪⁓⁓

It was Gloria's idea to make up limericks to pass the time—some laugh-out-loud funny and others simply ridiculous. Just like old times, Leona loved it. They also read billboards and any humorous road signs spotted along the way, and they played Twenty Questions and I Spy. Leona was finally reconnecting with Gloria in a manner that felt more carefree, and she hoped it would continue when they arrived. She also hoped neither Dat nor Mamma would mind hosting the daughter of a shunned man.

She recalled her conversation with Gloria last evening and how she'd revealed her secret to managing stress and circumstances out of her control: *trust, wait, hope.*

Even now, as she rode along in Gloria's car, she prayed those words might make a difference, with the dear Lord's help.

⁓⁓≫✦≪⁓⁓

When Maggie called back from the phone shanty, Gloria handed her phone to Leona with a serious expression. "It's your sister-in-law," she whispered.

"Hullo, Maggie," Leona said. "Blessed Lord's Day to ya."

"I got your voicemail, Leona. And just as I was walkin' back toward the house, your uncle and aunt pulled into the lane for a visit. When they were ready to leave, I asked if they would drop by your parents' and let them know 'bout Gloria's coming."

"*Denki* for that."

"You sound kinda funny. Are ya nervous 'bout what they'll say?" Maggie asked.

"*En bissel.*"

"Well, rest assured they won't turn Gloria away."

"I'm not worried 'bout that."

"What, then?"

Leona sighed. *That they'll be less than welcoming.* "Nothin'," she said.

"There's always room over here," Maggie offered. "If need be."

"Mahlon wouldn't mind?"

"You're stewin' for nothing; trust me on this."

"All right, then." Leona glimpsed Gloria and hoped she wasn't reading between the lines.

"You still there?" Maggie asked.

"*Jah*, but I'll say so long for now."

"Safe journey, Leona. Good-bye."

Leona sighed after she ended the call. What must Gloria think of her side of the conversation? Surely she'd picked up on Leona's concern.

"Thanks for letting me use your phone, Gloria."

"It's all yours for as long as you need it."

Leona smiled. "That's nice of you, but I better not let myself get used to it."

Gloria turned on the car radio. "You can click the scan button and see what you'd like to listen to. Or if you'd rather, you can look through the music on my phone."

"*Denki*, but that's all right." Leona turned off the radio. "Truth be told, I could get hooked on your music . . . wouldn't be wise."

"I understand, believe me."

They talked about what kinds of things Gloria had been curious to try after abandoning the Plain life: hot rollers, jeans, and of course, driving. "Have you ever tried any of those things?" Gloria asked.

"*Nee* . . . I'll have to take your word for all of that." Leona felt as if she were walking a tightrope, not wanting to judge Gloria, nor to be tempted.

"Honestly, though, not all of it has turned out to be as wonderful as advertised," Gloria admitted at last. "For one thing, it's hard to feel like you're good enough when you're constantly trying to keep up on trends. Modern life can be exhausting."

They rode for quite a while without speaking, and Leona tried to imagine again how Tom would react to Gloria's arrival. Kind as he was, she assumed it wouldn't be a problem. After all, Gloria just needed a few days to get things straight with herself.

*I'll explain if he asks,* she thought, looking forward to seeing him again.

Around midmorning, after Leona had eaten half of her ham-and-cheese sandwich, they took the turnoff to a rest area. They got out to walk along a paved path through a park, trees waving gently, birds flitting about. "I'll race ya to that fence," Leona said to Gloria, who took her up on it.

Leona wished she'd taken time to kick off her shoes, though, because Gloria ended up winning in her tennis shoes, laughing and teasing Leona.

"Let's run barefoot this time, *then* see who wins!" Leona said.

"No fair. My feet are soft as a baby's bottom now, thanks to shoes year round." Gloria grimaced as she caught her breath.

"I don't see how ya went from goin' barefoot to wearin' shoes . . . your feet cramped up all the time."

Gloria shrugged as they walked around the park. "You're poking fun at me, aren't you?"

Leona laughed. "It's just hard to imagine giving up that kind of freedom, that's all."

Gloria suggested they briskly walk two more laps around the walkway before heading back to the car. "My sitter's already getting numb."

"Most folk would prob'ly spend the night somewhere on such a long trip, like we did comin' out in the van."

"We're spring chickens . . . we'll be fine."

"I say we keep drivin' as long as your eyes stay open. You can always get coffee," Leona said, noticing a family with small children getting out of their minivan and rushing toward the restrooms. The youngest child blinked at Leona, undoubtedly seeing her first Amish-person.

"Coffee's the perfect idea," Gloria said, checking her phone to see where the nearest coffee shop was located. "Hope you don't mind stopping right away again."

Leona shook her head. "You're the one drivin'."

"Yep, keep the driver happy."

"And wide awake," added Leona.

Gloria fell quiet for a time. Then she said, "Your parents will be shocked by my fancy clothes and hair."

"They'll certainly have a memory of how Plain you used to be," Leona said gently. "It makes it harder."

"I brought along some long, flowing skirts. I don't want to cause trouble for your parents or amongst the People."

"*Unzucht,* remember?"

Gloria nodded. "Oh, I remember, all right. But I'm a bit rusty. So, would you like to talk in *Deitsch* for a while?"

"Are ya sure?" *Now that she's out of her father's control . . .*

Laughing, Gloria said she had to prove to Leona that she was up for it. So for the next two hours, each time she spoke, it was in *Deitsch.*

Hearing Gloria speaking her very first language gave Leona assurance they were on the right path.

*O dear Lord, I wait in hopeful trust. . . .*

CHAPTER 26

Gloria wasn't quite sure how it came about, but before long, she and Leona got on the subject of Colerain and their favorite people and places there. Leona talked about the climbing wisteria that grew on the redbrick farmhouse where Gloria and her family had once lived, then mentioned which of the farmers had started dividing up land amongst married sons.

"Just wait'll ya see it again," Leona said as they passed through the outskirts of yet another large city. "I can hardly wait to show you around."

Clutching the steering wheel and sighing,

Gloria was surprised how hearing these things stirred up a yearning to see her former home again, especially since she'd given it little thought. "I'm curious how things have changed in the community," she remarked. *And how I've changed in relationship to what I remember. . . .*

Leona nibbled on a cheese stick. "Let me see . . . well, the old one-room school has been replaced by a new one."

"Did you ever wish you could attend high school?" Gloria asked, then wondered if she should have held her tongue.

"Never gave it a thought." Leona shrugged. "Eight grades are all that's necessary, according to the *Ordnung*."

Naturally, her friend would say that. She was her parents' child, and a baptized church member, too.

Gloria recalled her father's insistence that she use the money she'd saved to better herself—*preferably for college*. He maintained that once she and Darren were married, she could easily go to classes during the day while he was at work.

Her father could be so thoughtful sometimes, like when he'd given her Brownie. Yet when it came to the big decisions of life, such as where to live, her father had never seemed to consider anyone but himself. *If only he took my wishes into account,* she thought. Had he always been this overbearing?

*He can be so pleasant and fun . . . when things go his way,* Gloria thought.

Leona offered her a cheese stick, and Gloria accepted. "It'll be fun to see if Brownie remembers you," Leona said.

Gloria tried to picture her former pet. "Has he changed much?"

"He's getting a little gray now and slower than when you had him. It's so cute to see him sniffin' the ground, trying to pick up the scent of a critter."

"That's the beagle in him. He loves to hunt."

"And the cocker spaniel makes him playful and sweet natured."

Gloria nodded. "The day we left, I prayed that God would look after Brownie till you found him. It all happened so fast."

"Oh, he was fine—ran right up to me when I stopped by. I was so puzzled to see your father's buggy and the market wagon parked in the barn. It made me think yous were still there."

"I can just imagine," Gloria said, reliving the traumatic day. "My father put Preacher Miller in charge of selling them to a farmer in Bird-in-Hand. He didn't mail the instructions till we were out of Lancaster County.

Guess he wanted to make sure no one could track us down." She shook her head. "I hate the way we left. I'd wanted to stay so bad, but there wasn't anything I could say to change his mind . . . not after the mess he'd made."

Leona nodded. "I still have the note you left me."

"That was the only good-bye I was allowed." Gloria glanced at Leona. "It was a hard day for me . . . for all of us."

"This might be a silly question, but I often wondered what happened to your chickens and the other livestock. I mean, other than the vehicles, everything was gone."

"Mom told me later that Dad struck a lightning-fast deal with a farmer in Eden Valley, south of Strasburg."

"Everything must've come together right quick." Leona was shaking her head. "It's nearly a blur for me now."

Gloria remembered scurrying about, trying to help Mom carry the smaller boxes to the large moving truck her father had rented, along with a two-man crew to help with the furniture. "At the time, I wasn't paying much attention to anything except my own disappointment. It wasn't till months after we were settled in Hill View that Mom filled me in on a few details."

Leona looked at her. "I still can't believe your father was ousted from the membership. I felt sick about it."

"Well, if you really want to know, the situation in Colerain wasn't the first trouble Dad got into."

"*Ach*, you don't need to—"

"Honestly, I *need* to talk about it."

Expression solemn, Leona nodded. "I'll keep it mum."

Gloria began to tell how, over a period of time, her eyes had been opened to her father's discontent with Amish life. "It seems to have started back when we lived in Salem, Arkansas, where I was born."

"I remember how fond you were of it," Leona said.

"When we moved to Pennsylvania, I missed Salem something awful."

"Remember our walk home from school that first day? You chattered a lot about it . . . made it sound pretty amazing, actually."

Gloria smiled. "Did I?"

"You even tried to show me the size of the rainbow trout in the river your family used to fish."

"I do remember that!" Gloria laughed, glad it was just the two of them in the car. During the years she'd lived in beautiful Salem, Gloria had never realized that her father wasn't in good standing with the Amish church there. "Dad got into trouble with the Salem bishop for playing on a local civic baseball league. It was strange, really, how single guys were allowed to be on the team, but once they were married, that was it. My father was so used to playing, he just kept it up for years after he married Mom, till it finally caught up with him."

Gloria shifted into the left lane to pass a slow-moving truck, then shifted right again.

"Dad must've had other struggles with the Salem bishop and the church ordinance, too," she continued, "but he kept quiet about his growing dissatisfaction. I didn't even know about it till he ran into more conflict in Pennsylvania."

"I never observed any struggle. He was always so friendly to me."

"Oh, Dad's friendly enough as long as he isn't frustrated," Gloria said. "But at his core, I think he's terribly restless."

"I do remember some awkward moments right before you left."

Gloria nodded. "He seemed really disgruntled then." She reached for her coffee to take a sip.

"Has anything changed? I mean . . . now that your father's *English*?" Leona sounded unusually tentative, as if she feared she might be crossing a line.

Gloria had never pondered this. "My father's been known to cut some corners ethically, and he never talks about the Lord anymore. As far as I know, your visit was the first time in over a year that he's opened a Bible." She paused. "Mom tries to keep the peace by going along with what he wants."

"Your parents' decisions aren't your responsibility."

"Well, they're still my family."

"Even so, you didn't make your father's choices. It's not your fault that he took you away from the Amish church."

Gloria considered Leona's words. "I probably made a mistake by not staying when my family left for Arkansas."

"You would've disregarded your father's wishes?" Leona asked.

"It wasn't easy living with him. . . . And there were painful consequences for me." *Like saying farewell to you . . . and my relationship with Orchard John,* Gloria thought, remembering the old heartache.

"Gloria, I—"

"Listen, it's already been a long day . . . maybe I'm too tired to talk about this."

"I'm sorry." Leona sounded sad.

Shaken by the direction their conversation

had taken, Gloria was glad when the gas gauge signaled the tank was a quarter full.

⁓⁓⁂⁓⁓

Tom had been anticipating this off-Sunday from Preaching, an opportune time to go with his parents and sisters to visit some shut-in relatives. His sister Anna had asked to ride with him because the family carriage was nearly filled to capacity with their parents, particularly since their unmarried uncle Dave, who lived in the *Dawdi Haus* next door, had chosen to come along.

"I ran into Maggie Speicher and her little girls when I was out walkin' earlier," Anna said as they pulled onto the lane. "Maggie said that Leona had left her a message on their shanty phone."

Tom snapped to attention. "Leona, ya say?"

"Evidently, she's on her way home." Anna caught Tom's eye. "With Gloria Gingerich."

Tom hardly knew what to think.

"Maggie said Leona called on Gloria's cell phone, and that Gloria's coming to stay for a bit." Anna looked tired from her date last night, but talking about Gloria Gingerich seemed to perk her up. "What do ya make of it, Tom?"

"Not sure," he admitted. "I do know that

Leona's not one to dabble in the world. She's been praying God would help her win Gloria back to the People."

Anna's eyes widened. "You think that's what's happening? Gloria's coming back?"

*Hard to imagine it happening this quick,* Tom thought, then immediately chided himself for his pessimism.

"Time will tell. Why not join Leona in praying for Gloria?" *Instead of talking around about her,* he thought, hoping his sister might catch the hint.

"I used to pray in earnest for that family, but over the years, I plumb lost patience."

"God isn't limited by our time frame or expectations, remember."

"'Tis true," Anna said, looking prim in her royal blue dress and matching apron. She pushed her white *Kapp* strings over her plump shoulders. "I don't remember much about the details. Was it only Gloria's father who was put off church?"

He nodded. "Just Joe."

"All the same, it'll be interesting to see Gloria again. There's no telling what she's like now."

Tom directed the horse to a trot, keeping up with his father's carriage ahead.

Anna lapsed into silence for the remainder of the ride, which was fine with Tom, who had his own concerns . . . ones he wasn't about to voice to Anna or to anyone else. For certain, hearing that Gloria was coming back to Colerain was a surprise!

"With the stops we've been making, losing an hour means we won't get to your house till around two in the morning, unfortunately," Gloria told Leona as they stretched their legs outside a rural gas station that evening. "Will such a late arrival disturb your parents? I don't want to wake them."

"Are ya tired of driving?" asked Leona. "We could stay overnight somewhere. I brought some cash if we need to," Leona offered. "Seriously."

"So did I." Gloria smiled. "It might give your parents more time to prepare for having a houseguest, too."

"On second thought, they might fret in the morning, thinking something happened to us," said Leona.

"We'd better keep going, then," Gloria said, weary of driving though she was. She wondered how she was going to make the long trip back to Arkansas on her own. *I'll definitely need to get a motel halfway.*

Gloria's phone chimed, and she glanced at it quickly before answering. "Hi, Mom. We're near Blacksburg, Virginia, making decent time."

"I've been thinking about you girls. Everything going smoothly?"

"Just fine. I'm glad you're not freaking out."

"Well, this *is* your first big road trip."

Gloria glanced at Leona. "Leona's keeping me company."

"Yes, well . . . I'm glad she's such a good friend to you, but I hope you're not thinking of doing anything rash. Her coming . . . this trip—it's all so spur-of-the-moment that it's got us worried. We love you, Gloria. And Darren thinks the world of you."

She felt trapped, unsure how to answer.

"In fact, Darren just called to talk to your father . . . seems nearly as concerned as we are. This is out of character for you, after all."

*So Dad and Darren are talking behind my back?* Gloria thought. *That's just what I need.*

Mom continued. "Leaving town so abruptly . . . it's a risk you're taking." She sighed loudly into the phone. "Darren thinks you might be breaking things off with him."

"Darren and I have to find our own way, Mom."

"Sure, Gloria. But I don't see how you can do that when you're headed to Pennsylvania." Mom chuckled nervously.

"I really don't want you to worry about me, okay?"

"Well, drive safely, dear. Text me when you arrive, no matter how late."

They said good-bye, and Gloria clicked off the phone.

"Everything okay?" Leona asked.

Gloria mentioned that Darren had called her father. "It's not like him to solicit advice from my parents. I feel even more pressure, hearing this." She drew a breath. "Well, maybe I'm just frustrated. He's nervous because I need some time apart."

"We all do from time to time. *Jah*?"

"But Darren knows I'm struggling with a serious commitment to him." Gloria squinted into the oncoming traffic, promising herself she would never sit down again, once this trip was over. Then, laughing at herself, she told Leona what she'd just thought.

"Funny, 'cause I was just thinkin' the same thing." They both laughed now, and Gloria was thankful once more for such an understanding friend.

It was after two o'clock in the morning when Gloria made the turn into the Speichers' long driveway and parked behind the three-story house in the pitch black. The only light to be seen was the gas light in Millie's kitchen, a yellow glow in a sea of darkness.

Gloria popped the trunk and got out of the car, grateful for the spray of cheerful light. *Like home . . .*

Gloria and Leona kept their voices low as they first hauled their bags out of the trunk, and then the now-empty cooler from the back seat. "I'll come back for it," Gloria told Leona as she followed her up the familiar walkway toward the house.

She breathed in the smell of freshly mown hay, so like the scent of the Hill View Amish farming community. Pausing on the top step, Gloria turned to look at the stars—identical to the sky she sometimes admired back home. Yet there seemed to be something different here, a very different *feel*. Was it because she'd discovered Leona here in sixth grade? Truly, Gloria's years here had been special ones. *Blessed, even!*

"More likely I'm just worn out," she murmured. She heard Brownie yip softly as he came to her from the screened-in porch. "Hey, you sweet, furry thing," she whispered. "Could you possibly remember me?"

Tired as she was, Gloria sat on the step and nuzzled the dog as he licked her chin. Oh, how she'd missed his warm greetings!

Next thing, Leona was beside her, too,

whispering that her mother had gotten up briefly to say they should help themselves to whatever they might be hungry for. "And the spare room's all ready for ya," Leona added quietly. "Mamma's thankful we made it safely."

"Awful nice of her to get up." Gloria smiled in the darkness, relieved the nearly endless drive was over. "I feel bad we woke her."

"Not to worry—Mamma's a light sleeper."

Gloria yawned as Brownie licked her hand.

"Betcha never want to get back in that car again," Leona said.

Gloria stifled a laugh. "Yeah, and I shouldn't have sat on these hard cement steps, either." Giving Brownie another hug, she got up. "Your dog's quite the welcoming committee."

"He was yours first."

"So we'll share him while I'm here. How's that?"

Leona grinned. "I just knew he'd be happy to see ya."

*I wonder if anyone else will be*, thought Gloria as Brownie followed them inside to the kitchen.

## CHAPTER 27

Once in the spare room, Gloria texted her mom by lantern light to let her know they'd arrived. *She'll see this when she wakes.*

Knowing she would sleep better if she showered, Gloria hurried downstairs in her robe to what she recalled was the only bathroom in the house.

*Why am I so wound up?* Then, remembering all the coffees and Cokes she'd sipped throughout the trip, she knew why.

Gloria removed a towel from the beadboard cupboard in the bathroom, recalling that when Pete Speicher built the addition, her father had come over to help. Millie made sandwiches thick with meat, lettuce, and sliced American cheese, and Gloria managed to be polite and ate it, although she'd never cared much for beef tongue. *"You'll learn to like it,"* Gloria's mother had said, chiding her when she'd complained afterward.

*"I doubt it,"* Gloria had whispered to Leona as they helped carry odds and ends of construction debris out to the trash behind the barn.

Presently, Gloria set the small lantern in the corner of the bathroom. She started a bit at her reflection in the old medicine cabinet mirror, small though it was, and turned to get the water running in the tub, noticing the same rust stains where the faucet dripped. For a split second, she was eleven years old again and visiting Leona after school, though Leona had always preferred going to Gloria's house.

*I must be really tired,* she thought as she turned on the shower and stepped in.

Suddenly, she realized that she wouldn't be able to charge her phone tonight, not in a house without electricity. *I guess I failed to take some things into consideration,* she thought, surprised at herself.

Snug in bed, and before she let herself fall asleep, Leona thanked the Lord God and heavenly Father for traveling mercies . . . and for giving her and Gloria ample opportunity to talk heart-to-heart. Stretching out across the mattress, she could smell the appealing scent of fresh air and sunshine on the sheets.

*I'm home. . . .*

When Leona fell into a deep sleep, she dreamed that Gloria Gingerich was the new neighbor girl just over the creek and up the hill. . . .

---

After a quick shower, Gloria dried off and slipped into her bold cheetah-print pajamas—a far cry from what she'd always worn as a Plain girl.

Spotting her phone, she decided the best way to recharge it was to do so in the car, which could wait until tomorrow. If she needed Wi-Fi, there was always the option of going into town to the nearby coffee shop where she and Orchard John had sometimes gone to talk for hours at a time.

As Gloria tiptoed back upstairs, a promising idea came to her. Why couldn't she simply go unplugged? *Can I do it?* she wondered, toying with the notion, and slipped under the sheets, then checked her phone once again. Darren had left several texts, but she was too tired to read them. She did take a moment to let him know she was safe and sound in Amish country, however, momentarily thinking that he might say she was anything but.

⁓ᷓᨔᨔᨳᨷ⁓

Gloria awakened just before five-thirty, feeling surprisingly renewed despite sleeping only a few hours. She got out of bed, put on her navy blue sweats and tennis shoes, quickly brushed her hair, and then made her way downstairs. The house was still at rest as she headed out to the porch, where she saw Brownie's leash hanging from a wall peg.

"*Guder Mariye*, Brownie," she said as the dog came toward her, tail wagging. "Let's go for a walk, okay?"

At his hopeful expression, she leaned down to attach the leash to his collar and led him out the back door, then down toward the familiar road. The morning was fresh and brand-new in the gray light before sunrise, and Gloria's cares began to slide off her shoulders.

"The perfect weather for *Weschdaag*," she murmured, deciding she would return after a morning jog to help Leona and her mother with the Monday washing. "Maybe I'll cook breakfast, too, if they'll let me." She remembered how Leona had tried repeatedly to help in the kitchen during her short visit.

It might not have been the wisest idea to go for a jog on so little sleep, yet she followed the road, moving slowly at first to stretch her muscles, still stiff from yesterday, Brownie at her side. The road turned north and crossed the rippling stream, and then the hill where, as a girl, she'd ridden her scooter or pulled her younger brothers in the wagon. Soon, the stately redbrick house came into dim view.

Slowing but not stopping altogether, lest she be seen as a stalker in sweats, Gloria glanced at the front yard as she neared, taking in the pretty white porch and the long lane to the north. Things looked nearly the same. Even the rope swing still hung from the giant oak in the side yard over near the potting shed.

*Where you could swing so high you might fly . . .*

How she yearned to stroll down the driveway lined with pink-and-white flowering dogwoods to the back of the house, knock on the door, and tell the residents she had absolutely loved living there. Did the new family have any idea what a wonderful house it was? Sometimes in the wee hours, the wind in the eaves had sounded like angels whispering. In the winter, the crackling of the front room's fireplace had given her the feeling of safety, as well.

*Do Amish live here?*

She picked up her pace again but craned

her neck to look back at the barn and outbuildings. There was no sign of a carriage.

The sky was growing lighter, so she could see that the washing was not yet out on the pulley clothesline. "Still early," she whispered.

Leona would surely know who lived there, Gloria assumed, slowing again for Brownie, whose nose was propelling him into the grassy roadside as he followed the trail of some scent. She laughed at the sight of him on such an adventure.

She noticed the old stone wall that edged the pasture, the same grazing land that had offered nourishment to her father's mules and other livestock, and felt a certain longing. Unable to resist, she sat on the wall and found that it was still cool to the touch. Fortunately, the sun's rays began to warm her back as Brownie sat in the grass at her feet, panting hard, not having captured his earlier prey.

What was it about childhood memories? Were they sweeter because they were distant, hazy images? Ones without the stain of disappointment?

Gloria wanted to just sit there in this lovely spot where she used to wait for Orchard John to pick her up in his courting buggy. *If I'd stayed against my father's will, I could be married to Leona's cousin by now. . . .*

Recalling leisurely long walks with her

Amish beau, and the work frolics they'd happily attended, she also recalled going with Orchard John when he went to help build a pig barn for his older brother. Only a few other girls were present that day, mostly there to bring food hampers to share with the young fellows.

*Why did my father choose to take our whole family away from the life we'd built here?* she mused.

Other questions flitted through her mind, but Gloria would not let herself get bogged down during what was supposed to be a time to get her thoughts straight. She needed this respite from the busy world she was now a part of.

Two Amish teenagers—the bishop's granddaughters, Mary Sue and Sarah Ann Mast—came walking, carrying large wicker baskets, looking toward her at first, then glancing away quickly, talking in *Deitsch*.

Mary Sue said, "Would be nice to dress so relaxed like that sometimes, ain't?"

*Thank goodness she doesn't recognize me,* thought Gloria.

"I'd choose something brighter than dark blue, though," Sarah Ann said, tittering at her sister's remark.

Gloria squelched a laugh, knowing they

didn't realize she understood what was being said.

Then, looking down at herself, she knew she must get back to Leona's house before her friend's parents saw her dressed so casually. *I'll do my best to fit in . . . wear the long skirts I packed.*

Three teams of horses and carriages were coming up the road, the second buggy a buck-board with two young men riding atop. She turned away so as not to be recognized.

---

The morning was dewy yet bright, and Tom and Danny had set out with Tom's mare and their father's spring wagon right after sunrise, wanting to get a head start on a few errands before either of them went to work. Tom hoped Leona had gotten home all right, though he guessed her and Gloria's arrival was quite late, probably well after midnight.

How did Pete and Millie feel about host-ing Gloria Gingerich now that she was no longer Amish?

Not far ahead, he spotted a young En-glish woman in dark running pants and tennis shoes sitting on the stone wall with Leona's dog, Brownie. He did a double take.

He turned to Danny. "Say, did ya see that young woman?" he asked, and Danny quickly signed that he, too, thought she looked familiar.

"It might've been Gloria Gingerich," Tom said.

*Red hair*, Danny replied.

*Danny has a good eye*, thought Tom with a smile.

*Whoever it is looks out of place here*, Danny added.

They talked further, wondering who else would have Brownie out on a leash if it wasn't Gloria. But why on earth would she be out so early if she and Leona had arrived in the wee hours?

It was a puzzle to Tom, but he'd already made up his mind to keep out of Leona's way during Gloria's surprise visit.

*How long will she stay?*

CHAPTER 28

Gloria continued to jog in the direction away from Leona's house, now thinking it was still early enough to extend her run before she returned. She passed three more large farms, then spotted a lone windmill amidst a vast pasture—Deacon Ebersol's. Brownie had slowed his pace significantly—it was probably more of a trip than he was used to. She winced and stopped in her tracks in front of the beautifully kept lawn. A wave of emotion overtook her, and she thought she might cry.

*I wish my father would do something about his outstanding debt. . . . If I could go back and change the past, I would.*

But she couldn't fix it. And thinking about it now made her feel vulnerable. *How can anyone here be glad to see me?* It was almost as if Gloria owed the money herself.

*It was my father,* she thought. *My family.* She remembered what a kindly man the deacon had always been.

*College classes could wait,* Gloria thought. *What if I—*

Gloria abruptly shelved the idea and forced herself to think instead of the special breakfast she would make for Leona and her parents, and Leona's Dawdi Benuel, too, if he joined them. She hoped to visit with the older man, dear soul. Being around him as a teenager had often made her wish her own grandfathers were alive. Her only living grandmother resided in a senior residence for Englishers in upstate New York—not her first choice, from what Gloria understood. Grandmother had moved to be closer to Gloria's mother's oldest brother, who'd relocated to the Finger Lakes area to acquire a larger spread of farmland.

Sighing now, Gloria felt bad that she'd never gotten to know her mother's mother. It dawned on her that she might write her grandmother a letter while she was here visiting.

A buggy rumbled in the near distance.

Coming this way were two young men, and a shiver ran down her back. *Can it be?*

Her heart beat a little faster, and she pulled her shoulder-length hair across one side of her face to shield it. She wished for the first time since she'd arrived that she still owned her large black outer bonnet, long since discarded. *Anything to conceal my face.*

But thinking the better of it, she looked up and smiled back as the young men waved in unison. For goodness' sake, she was staring into the face of the most wonderful fellow she'd ever known: *Orchard John.*

Recalling their year of courtship brought back a rush of feelings, and she was thankful he and his cousin kept going, scarcely giving her a glance.

*No beard? But surely he's married . . .*

Feeling off-kilter now, Gloria tried to pull herself together. It would never do to become so emotional about someone who'd probably forgotten her three years ago. Besides, Darren awaited her back in Hill View.

~~~~~

Tired but grateful to be home, Leona dragged herself out of bed, showered, and dressed. On her way back through the kitchen, she spotted Gloria's note—*Out for a quick jog!*

The thought of Gloria having a chance to

clear her mind and gain some perspective on her situation with Darren made Leona smile. *She might miss out on Bible reading and prayer this morning, though,* she thought, going back up the stairs to her room. Her mother was stirring, and Leona wanted to gather up the laundry and take it down cellar to start the first load.

Once the clothes were soaking in the wringer washer, she stepped out to the screened-in porch and saw that Brownie *and* his leash were gone. She laughed, guessing Gloria had taken him along.

She walked out to the end of the lane to pick up the morning paper for Dat to read, once he came in from the barn. The scent of lilacs caught her attention, and she raised her face to the breeze. Redbud trees and azaleas were also in bloom, and she was so glad that Gloria had come home with her and would be able to enjoy the season's spectacular beauty. *Let springtime and renewal be birthed in her heart, O Lord, as Thy grace beckons her back to where she belongs,* she prayed.

Picking up the newspaper, she heard yipping and looked up to see Gloria and Brownie walking along the roadside, Brownie poking along. She hurried to meet them. "Goodness, you must've gotten up at daybreak."

"I did. And while I was over near my

former house, I saw two of the bishop's grand-daughters out walking."

*Naturally, Gloria headed over that way.* "Did they stop and talk to you?"

"I'm sure they had no idea who I was." Gloria smiled and wiped her forehead with the back of her hand.

"Aw... ya don't look that much different."

"Well, I'm certainly not Plain." Gloria chuckled.

"Did ya notice any changes to your old house?" Leona was curious what Gloria thought of the place now.

Gloria fell into step with her. "Things looked quite similar, but it was clear enough it's someone else's home. Time doesn't stand still for anyone or anything, does it?" Gloria pulled her hair back and removed a hair band from her wrist to secure it into a ponytail. "Which reminds me, who's living there now?"

"Jacob and Ada Miller. They've been there for a year and a half. The landlord your father rented from passed away, and nearly the min-ute it went on the market, several farmers were vying for it."

"Not surprising. It's a fine house." Gloria walked with Leona down the drive. "I wonder if they'd let me have a peek inside."

"I don't see why not. I can go with ya to ask."

"Oh, would you?"

"Sure. And you must remember Ada Miller, sweet as a jar of honey. Her oldest daughter, Rebekah, was our schoolteacher when you and your family first arrived here."

"Is that right?" Gloria seemed ever so pleased. "She got engaged the year I was in eighth grade."

"*Jah*, and has look-alike twin boys now."

"Jacob Miller is a cousin to Preacher Miller, if I recall correctly."

"Jacob and the preacher are as close as brothers." Leona laughed as she glanced down at Brownie, who was panting loudly. "*Our* dog isn't used to bein' walked too far, as you prob'ly found out. He romps about the fields on his own, but mostly he likes to lie around."

"He's getting old. Time to spoil him rotten."

They headed around to the back of the house, where rows of red and white tulips grew on either side of the sidewalk. "Let's go an' see your old house tomorrow, once I have the ironing done and before I head to Maggie's shop to work. All right? Unless you have other plans."

Gloria followed her inside and washed her hands at the deep sink in the utility room. "Not for tomorrow, but I do have plans for this morning, as soon as I wash up and change into a skirt," she said. "I'd like to make omelets

for you and your parents . . . and your grandfather, too, if that's okay."

"Oh, I doubt Mamma wants you cookin'
for us when you're on vacation."

"Well, doesn't *that* sound familiar?" Gloria
rolled her eyes.

They had a laugh about that, then Gloria
scurried upstairs to change.

Leona was secretly relieved that Gloria
wouldn't be parading around in sweats. *No
need getting things off to a rough start.*

---

A few minutes after Gloria returned in
her floral skirt in delicate muted tones and
a modest white top, Mamma came into the
kitchen. "*Willkumm,* Gloria. But what're you
doin' in one of my work aprons?"

"Cooking's the least I can do to thank you
and Pete for letting me stay," Gloria replied
with a smile. "Won't you let me make breakfast for all of us? It's my own recipe."

Leona stood back, wondering what
Mamma might say about Gloria's taking over
her kitchen.

"*Your* recipe?" Mamma blinked rapidly.

Gloria pleaded further, and Mamma
reluctantly gave in. "Just this once, then," she
said.

"Not sure I can promise that," Gloria

teased. "What if I end up staying longer than a few days?"

Leona's heart leaped up. "You mean ya might?"

"Wanted to see if you're wide-awake." Gloria winked.

Leona groaned. "Oh, you!"

Grinning, Gloria listed off the ingredients she needed, and Leona was surprised that Mamma went immediately to the refrigerator.

While Gloria oiled the black skillet, Leona wiped off the table and then set it. "Do you need help with bacon or toast or anything else?" she asked.

"Toast, sure."

"No bacon or sausage?"

"Why not let Dawdi Benuel choose?" Gloria suggested. "I'd love to see him here for breakfast, too."

"You'll see him, but he's really not one to come over so early. He prefers his bowl of cold cereal and toast and coffee, which he makes for himself."

Mamma spoke up. "S'pose if he knows Gloria's here, he'll make the effort."

Leona was pleased at how hospitable Mamma was this morning; she hadn't expected Gloria would find such a genuine welcome.

"By the way, I sold all but two of your

wreaths while you were gone, Leona," Mamma said. "You'll need to make more soon."

"Maybe Gloria will help me," Leona suggested.

"Sure," Gloria said. "What else can I do while I'm here?"

"Well, the fence needs to be painted." Leona laughed.

"Oh now!" Mamma said. "We wouldn't think of putting our guest to work."

"I don't mind. Whatever needs to be done." Gloria began preparing the ingredients, telling Mamma about the big cities she and Leona had traveled through, including Memphis and Nashville. "And goodness, we did our share of literally running around at rest stops to get some exercise. All the coffee we drank meant we had more pit stops than we planned."

Mamma tilted her head. "Pit stops?"

Gloria had a time explaining where the expression came from, but eventually Mamma seemed to understand.

"Sounds like quite a trip. But we're glad you're here," Mamma said, nodding. "Thank the Good Lord."

When Dat came in from the barn, he brought Dawdi Benuel with him. "Someone was itchin' to say hullo to Gloria," he said after he, too, had greeted Gloria, who stood next to the gas stove. "How do ya like our springtime weather?"

"It's nearly as warm as it was back home last week," Gloria replied. "It's a beautiful day to be outside."

"That's the honest truth," Dat said. "*Willkumm* to our home." He removed his straw hat and headed to wash up.

Dawdi Benuel took up the conversation. "My, my, if it isn't little Gloria, all grown up," he said, hobbling over to extend his wrinkled hand.

"I was hoping you'd join us for breakfast," Gloria said, accepting Dawdi's handshake. "I think you'll like the loaded omelets I'm making. That's what my mom calls them."

Dawdi chuckled. "Sounds like a rare treat."

"I'm glad you came over." Gloria turned back to the stove and flipped over the first one after filling it with mushrooms, salsa, black olives, and onions. "Now, if you don't care much for my concoction, I'll make you some scrambled or fried eggs instead, okay?"

Dawdi firmly shook his head. "Wouldn't dream of deprivin' myself. Smells delicious!"

Leona helped him to his seat at the table while Gloria beamed as she used the spatula to lift the first omelet out of the skillet and into a warming pan.

"Be sure an' go out and have a look at our day-old calf while you're here," Dat told Gloria when he returned to sit at the head of the table.

"We will go once we get the first washing out on the line," Leona promised, glad her parents were bending over backward for Gloria.

*Like Joe and Jeannie always did for me. . . .*

## CHAPTER 29

*L*eona was tickled to have Gloria help pin the clothes on the line while Mamma took her time redding up the kitchen indoors. "My family really enjoyed your omelets," she told her friend. "You're spoilin' us."

"I loved cooking on your mother's gas range," Gloria replied. "And your Dawdi was so cute, going on and on about how *appeditlich* the omelets were."

"Well, they *were* tasty."

Gloria removed a clothespin from between her lips and used it to pin the shoulder of one of Dat's shirts. "He was always more talkative than your parents."

Leona grimaced. "And a *gut* listener, too."

"Not so easy to find," Gloria said, leaning down for the next item in the laundry basket.

"You were always the best listener," Leona added. "Honestly."

Gloria made a face. "Before I, well . . . disappeared."

"We're past that, ain't?"

"*Jah* . . . and at least you had someone to talk to."

Leona smiled at Gloria's use of *jah*. "Maggie's probably been the person I turn to the most, but there have been a few times when Dawdi pestered me till I opened up. Guess he could tell something was up from my long face."

Gloria laughed.

"Sure ain't the same as sharin' with you, though." Leona wanted her to know that no one had replaced her friendship, not even Tom. "But then, no two friendships are alike. Tom's somebody else I can share with . . . it's a blessing to have a fiancé who cares so much." She gave Gloria a sideways glance. "Do you feel that way about Darren, too?"

Gloria was solemn as she answered. "Darren's a good guy, but I wouldn't say we've built that kind of friendship yet. And he's awfully perplexed now." She explained that she intended to check her phone one last time today, then try to go unplugged for the duration of her stay.

This startled Leona. "Really?"

"I just want to be here and not so *there,* and if I'm on my phone, that won't be the case. It's just for a little while."

"Well, maybe you should tell Darren and your parents first, so they don't worry."

"You're right." Gloria reached down for another shirt from the laundry basket. "You think of others first, Leona. I love that about you."

Leona felt her face turn red as she kept working, hanging up her and Mamma's clothes while Gloria pinned Dat's shirts and britches on the line. The next batch of washing—Dawdi Benuel's things—would be ready to hang out soon.

"Thanks for helpin' with the laundry," Leona said, changing the subject. "You really didn't have to."

"I need to keep busy." Gloria's voice wavered.

"You all right?"

She nodded without speaking.

"This chore must seem time-consuming to you now," Leona observed.

"An automatic washer does make every-thing easier. Put the detergent in, pile in the clothes, leave the room, and it still gets done. Real convenient."

"Sounds like you've been ruined," she joked.

"It's hard to turn up your nose at modern conveniences. There are so many advantages. Surely you noticed that when you visited." Gloria finished hanging up her basketful and came to help Leona with the rest of hers.

"Enough advantages, as ya say, to turn away from Plain living for good?"

"Of course," Gloria said, her tone enthusiastic. Yet Leona noticed that not a speck of that confidence registered on her freckled face.

While sitting at a table outside a fast-food place, about to wolf down a cheeseburger, Tom spotted Orchard John.

*Does he know Gloria's visiting?* Tom squeezed a plastic pouch of ketchup onto his burger, then did the same with two packets of mustard.

John reappeared in a few minutes, carrying a sack and a large fountain drink.

Tom waved him over. "Busy mornin'?"

"Typical Monday." Orchard John took a seat across from him and bowed his head before he dug into his grilled-chicken sandwich and fries.

"Looks like you didn't have time to pack *your* lunch, either." Tom grinned. "*Gut* excuse to grab a burger."

"Mamm offered to send some food along, but she's got enough to do on *Weschdaag.*"

Tom nodded. "Not sure what people did before fast food."

Orchard John agreed as he picked up several thick fries. "Did you take the usual way to work this mornin'?"

"I did, why?"

John shrugged and set his burger down to wipe his mouth with a paper napkin.

Tom studied him. "Did ya maybe think you saw Gloria Gingerich sittin' on the old stone wall?"

"You saw her, too?" Orchard John asked, eyes popping.

"She drove Leona back all the way from Arkansas."

"Why on earth?"

Tom took a drink of his iced tea. "Don't know much 'bout it, but Leona was out visitin' *her* for a few days," he told his friend, "and now all of a sudden, Gloria's decided to come here."

John's face lit up, and he looked like he

might just take off flying. "Well, ain't that the pig's tail!"

"Just a warning, John. She's not Amish anymore."

John nodded. "Her hair was down when I spotted her, and it looked like she had on a running outfit."

"I'll be interested to see if she comes to Preaching service with Leona . . . if she's staying that long."

John seemed to be taking it all in. "'Tween you and me, I'd like to see her again, but . . ." His voice trailed off. "Not sure I oughta."

*Because you're baptized,* Tom thought, certain they were thinking along the same lines. He didn't know what else to say; it was obvious Orchard John had not forgotten the pretty auburn-haired girl.

"Wouldn't it be *wunnerbaar* if she's comin' back to the People?" Orchard John said, his voice lower.

"I wouldn't get my hopes up."

"*Jah,*" Orchard John said. "But stranger things have happened."

"Maybe you and Leona can help the Lord along." Tom instantly wished he could take back the words—he didn't want to encourage his friend to spend much time with an attractive former Amishwoman. *Like walking on thin ice . . .*

"Never told a soul, but I almost proposed to her before she left."

"*Almost?*"

"Went to her house and everything . . . even tossed pebbles at her window."

"And she didn't come to see?"

Orchard John shook his head. "Her room was lit up behind the shade, too. Was so sure she was there."

"Are ya certain you got the right window?" Tom asked. "Plenty of fellas have gotten the wrong one."

"Oh, I'm sure it was Gloria's."

Tom could see the frustration on John's face. "There's always a chance she might not have been in her room," he reassured him. "How many stones did ya throw?"

"I heard two hit the pane."

Tom considered that. "Maybe it's for the best. After all, Arkansas Joe would be a challenging father-in-law. Mighty friendly, but in other ways . . ."

"Like a stubborn child, *jah?*" John finished the sentence. "Digging in his heels."

Tom stifled the urge to say more. *No one really knows what goes on in a household,* he thought. Besides, Orchard John didn't need to know everything about Gloria's errant father.

A moment of silence fell between them, and Orchard John looked to be lost in thought. *Best to change the subject.*

～～～

After breakfast the next morning, Leona ironed pillowcases and her father's for-good trousers while Gloria sat out in her car to charge up her phone yet again, even though she had sounded so sure yesterday about going unplugged.

"She's entangled in the fancy world," Mamma said as she wiped down the kitchen appliances. "Once the fancy grabs ya, it seldom lets go."

"Sometimes it does," Leona said, unwilling to give up hope so easily.

"*Jah*, sometimes," her mother said. "She seems awful *ferhoodled*, poor girl. Kinda doubt she knows her own mind." Mamma reached for a towel to dry the front of the refrigerator.

Mamma was right about that, but Leona didn't want to reveal what Gloria had shared back in Arkansas. Nor did she want to talk about Darren Brockett. "S'pose Maggie's ready to have me back at work this afternoon."

"I'm sure."

"When I'm done with ironing here and Gloria's ready, we're goin' over to see the Millers."

Mamma's eyes blinked.

"Gloria wants to ask if they'll let her look around inside her old home. Seems really bent on it."

"Well . . . how 'bout that." Mamma went to the sink and rinsed her cleaning rag, then wrung it out tight.

"I'll wash the kitchen floor tomorrow mornin'," Leona volunteered.

"It'll need it by then."

"By the way, did Deacon Ebersol ever say anything to you about my trip to Arkansas? I never got a chance to speak to him before I went. Tom planned to tell him 'bout it . . . I hope he did."

"Might be wise to seek out the deacon yourself," Mamma advised. "'Specially now that Gloria's stayin' with us for a bit."

"I thought of that, too."

"Don't wait too long," Mamma added, "or the grapevine will have it to him first."

"I won't." Leona looked forward to asking for her future father-in-law's wisdom regarding Gloria. *Perhaps he knows a way to cut right to the heart of the matter. . . .*

## CHAPTER 30

*L*eona was puzzled when she had to prod Gloria into going over to the Millers' farmhouse later. "You were ever so curious before."

"I'm having second thoughts," Gloria said, still sitting behind the steering wheel of her car, phone in hand. "I'd rather not raise eyebrows."

Leona had been worried because Gloria hadn't returned indoors after some time. Gloria claimed she'd been listening to music and texting, but her eyes were red and swollen. *Did she receive a troubling message?*

"It's all right if you don't want to go," Leona said. "But if you're thinkin' of sitting here awhile longer, I might run a quick errand to the neighbors' before my driver comes to take me to work."

This seemed to be the push Gloria needed, because she immediately turned off the ignition and said she didn't want to seem like she was changeable. "After all, it's not really so peculiar, is it?"

"*Ach* no, lots of folk visit their childhood home."

This brought a smile to Gloria's face, and she slipped her phone into her skirt pocket. "Are you ready to go now?"

Gloria could be quite decisive when she wanted to be, Leona knew, and she matched her stride to her friend's as they walked down the narrow lane toward the road.

Gloria leaned her head back and squinted into the sunshine. She seemed so much more carefree away from her car. *And that pesky phone!*

"I'm glad you talked me into this," Gloria said. "Well, you didn't really . . . but thanks for getting me out of my mood." She laughed. "I feel like a kid today. Maybe it's just being back here again, ya know?"

"We're all children inside, ain't?"

Gloria was quiet suddenly. Then she said softly, "I have to confess I'm not doing very well with twenty-one."

Looking at her, Leona knew from the

ripple in Gloria's jaw and the downturn of her mouth that she was admitting something difficult. "Is that part of why ya came home with me?"

Gloria nodded and slowed her pace. "I'm here to figure that out."

Leona picked up a walking stick she found on the roadside, one Dawdi Benuel may have left there for his occasional afternoon jaunts. "What would you change, if ya could?"

"Some days just about everything . . . and other days, nothing at all." Gloria smiled, reaching for Leona's hand. "Remember when we walked together everywhere, holding hands like sisters?"

Leona had never forgotten. She had been her best self when with Gloria. "It was a *wunnerbaar-gut* time of my life."

"But you have Tom now to take my place."

"No one takes anyone's place, silly."

Gloria's eyes were serious. "You're looking forward to marrying him, aren't you?"

"He's my one and only love." It felt so good to declare it.

Gloria paused, then shook her head. "I can't say that about Darren."

"Maybe sometimes we have to experience more than one dating relationship to know what's best for us," Leona suggested.

"That only makes things more complicated." Gloria frowned. "If I could have experienced the kind of love you and Tom have, I doubt I would have gone out with anyone else."

"Makes sense." Leona was pleased to hear Gloria express herself so openly, yet her frankness seemed to come in waves.

The redbrick house loomed in the near distance, and Leona pointed to the little white potting shed on its south side. "Isn't that new?"

Gloria released Leona's hand. "Oh, I can hardly wait to see my old room again! I sure hope we can."

When they arrived, Ada Miller called to Leona from the backyard, where she was mulching her flower bed. "Hullo there. Are yous out for a nice walk?"

Right away, Leona introduced Gloria, and Ada said she remembered her. "Never forgot those deep auburn locks."

Gloria blushed and glanced at Leona, who knew it was up to her to make their request.

"Gloria's curious if ya would mind letting her see the house."

"Ah—you lived here once, didn't ya?" Ada brushed off her hands on her black work apron.

"For six years," Gloria spoke up. "If it suits you, I'd be grateful."

"*Kumm mit.*" Ada led the way up the back steps and inside.

Leona took it all in. In the kitchen, someone had put down shiny new linoleum similar to what Mahlon chose last year for Maggie's kitchen. She marveled at the beautifully crafted oak cupboards all along one wall, and the new window trim and mopboards. Not fancy, really, just up-to-date.

Gloria remarked on the remodel. "I think my mom would really love to see it the way it is now."

"It was quite a lot of work for Jacob . . . did every inch of it himself. I'm mighty grateful." Ada removed a child's plastic apron from the wooden bench pushed up next to the long trestle table. "The children won't be at school much longer. School's out soon for the summer, so I'll have more help round the house again."

"Everything's neat as a pin," Gloria said. "Just the way Leona's mother keeps house— polished and nearly perfect."

Leona agreed and, at Ada's urging, followed Gloria to the stairs. "Just make yourselves at home, girls."

"*Denki,*" Gloria said. "Real nice of you."

Upstairs, the hardwood floor gleamed in the sunlight from the tall window at the end of the hallway. Leona remembered sliding along the floor on pillows when she'd stayed there during her mother's illness.

Gloria must have remembered, too. "Goodness, we were in so much trouble that night we used our feather pillows for sleds down this hallway."

"Your father wasn't very happy with us," Leona said.

"But Mom didn't seem to mind—she just hung back and looked on while my father raised his voice. I often wondered if perhaps she wouldn't have joined in the fun, had she been younger."

"Your Dat was always the strict one, *jah*?"

"Oh, no question." Gloria motioned to Leona, and they stepped into her former bedroom, where light poured in from two large windows, the green shades rolled up to the tip-top of their frames.

Gloria looked around, a dazed smile on her face. "I've never had another room as nice as this one," she said almost reverently. "One that looked out to tree branches thick with leaves for months on end."

"It almost seems like a tree house. We're so high up off the ground."

Gloria pointed out the dark hues of the bed quilt and the solitary tall chest of drawers without a mirror. "Looks like one of Ada's sons occupies this room now." She went to stand near the north wall, where an oak writing desk was positioned. On a desk blotter, a dozen or more ballpoint pens stood in a black mug. "My bed was here on this wall," she said quietly.

"And your dresser was over there." Leona pointed in the opposite direction.

Gloria sighed, her hand on her chest. "In a way, it's like I never left." She moved across to the nearest window, her shoulders moving up and down.

Leona dared not disturb the moment, whatever was happening. Gloria was clearly struggling.

When she spoke, her voice was hushed. "I used to dream of being married to your cousin." Gloria crept closer to the window, her face inches from the glass, as if looking for something in the fields beyond.

Then Leona realized she was staring at the windowpane.

"There it is." Gloria pointed to the upper right edge.

Going to Gloria's side, Leona saw two tiny nicks in the glass, impossible to detect from across the room.

"Orchard John came to see me a week before we left." Gloria stepped back, still staring at the window. "I always thought he'd intended to propose."

"I'm not surprised," Leona replied. "What did you say?"

"He didn't get the chance . . . I never went to the window. Never went downstairs to greet him." Gloria sighed. "I'm sure he waited for the longest time, hoping."

"But ya loved him—you told me so."

Gloria nodded. "My father thought I should get to know more than one fellow before I settled down. Then we moved away, and it was too late to let John know why I never answered."

Leona's heart was pained for her. "Aw, Gloria . . . I didn't know he meant that much to ya."

Gloria whispered, "I wanted to see this window again to believe it actually happened."

They stood there, side by side, and talked for a while longer about other memories shared in Gloria's room. Then Leona told her, "Orchard John is still single. Not even a steady girlfriend."

Gloria turned to stare at her. "I never thought to ask—I was sure he'd have found someone by now."

Leona shook her head, and Gloria's spirits seemed to lift, if only for a moment. Then she pursed her lips, and her mood slipped again. "Not that it matters anymore."

Quietly, they made their way back downstairs.

Ada Miller was still on her hands and knees, working in her flower bed just outside the back door. "Well, that was quick, girls. Did ya see everything you wanted to?"

"*Denki,*" Gloria was quick to say. "I hope we weren't too bold, just showing up."

"*Kumme* again, if ya want to." Ada wiped her brow.

Leona nodded. "Tell Rebekah we said hullo."

"*Ach,* you should go an' see her and her little ones. Cutest little fellas—mirror images of each other."

Leona knew Gloria was ready to head back to the house. "If there's time, we might." She mentioned she needed to meet her driver soon to head for work.

"Your sister-in-law must have her hands full with a shop and a family." Ada smiled.

"She manages with her parents living nearby. They help with Marianna during the school year and the rest of the children in the summer."

Gloria and Leona thanked her again and waved good-bye.

All during the walk home, the image of Gloria trying not to cry beside the nicked window lingered in Leona's mind. How very different things would be this day if Arkansas Joe hadn't stood in the way of Orchard John's proposal.

## CHAPTER 31

While Leona was busy working at Maggie's store, Gloria offered to help Millie hitch up the road horse to the family carriage. Millie had invited her to ride along to Good's Store in Quarryville for some fabric and sewing notions for a dress Millie needed to make.

Gloria held the shafts as Millie led the horse in, surprised at how much fun this was. She loved being around the farm again, especially the horses. Even hitching up wasn't a bother today.

"I must be a farm girl at heart," she told Millie. "Would you mind if I drove us to the store?"

Millie gave a small smile. "Not so much."

"It has been a couple years, but I still remember what to do." *At least, I hope so!*

"Well, we're not goin' far," Millie replied as they worked as a team to hook the back hold straps. "So why not?"

"Thanks so much. *Denki*, I mean."

Millie looked her way curiously. "Do you miss doin' this?"

"I guess I do," Gloria confessed. "A car sure doesn't have the personality of a horse!"

This brought a rare chuckle from Millie, and Gloria laughed along.

⚜

The cashier at Good's Store was Orchard John's younger sister, Naomi Speicher, who blinked her pretty blue eyes, obviously startled when she recognized Gloria with Naomi's aunt Millie. "*Ach*, goodness! John said he thought you were here visitin'." Naomi seemed flustered and uncertain what to say, not at all like the girl Gloria remembered.

"How long will ya be around?" Naomi asked, her blond hair perfectly twisted along the sides and back into a thick low bun.

"Just a couple more days. I need to get back to work."

"Well, hope ya stay for Preaching."

Gloria smiled at Millie. "If Pete and Millie can put up with me for that long."

Millie replied, "Stay as long as you like."

"That's sweet of you," Gloria said, touched that Millie wouldn't mind a longer visit.

"Is it okay to tell Orchard John I saw ya?" asked Naomi.

Gloria hesitated. *What would it matter to John?*

"If you want to." Gloria waited for Millie to pay for her spools of thread and packet of sewing needles, then said good-day.

Back outdoors, Millie went to the driver's side of the buggy after untying the horse from the hitching post. *Millie must feel more at ease in the driver's seat,* she thought. *Guess I need practice.*

Her phone vibrated in her pocket, and she wished she hadn't brought it. She certainly wasn't doing too well with her plan to go unplugged!

She pulled it out to look.

*I hope you're having a good time,* Darren had texted.

She decided to reply quickly while Millie backed the horse out of the parking spot: *There's no electricity where I'm staying, so I'll be unplugged again today.*

She was about to return the phone to her

pocket when another text announced itself. *Maybe I'll just give you a quick call.*

*So sorry, but now isn't a good time.* She closed the message app and turned off her phone, this time pushing it deep into her purse. *Darren will survive the rest of the day without hearing from me.*

Millie took the back roads, mentioning it was "a real perty way home." Feeling more relaxed, Gloria enjoyed the familiar scenery, thinking how odd it had been to run into Orchard John's sister.

*What if I did stay around for church Sunday?*

⁓⁓⁘⁓⁓

Millie looked altogether pleased when Gloria asked if she could lay out Millie's dress fabric for her on the kitchen table. "I'd really like to help," Gloria said. "I'll be sure to redd up." Gloria knew how spotless Millie preferred to keep things.

"Well, if you're sure, Gloria, I could do another chore."

Her pulse quickened—sewing had always been one of her favorite pastimes. She remembered doing it while her mother baked pastries and loaves of bread. *At least one of us was doing something we loved then,* she thought, glad Millie would be just around the corner mending in the sitting room.

"If you need assistance, don't be shy," Millie said with a glance over her shoulder.

"Thanks . . . er, *denki*." Millie had always impressed her as being a kind and helpful woman, never flashy or insincere. Like Pete, she was also devout. Gloria had sometimes wished her own father was more like Leona's in the way he treasured the old *Biewel*, reverently reading with the family each morning and evening.

*The grass is always greener, I guess. . . .*

When she'd pinned the pattern to the dress material, she asked Millie to double-check everything before beginning to carefully cut along the dark lines, then trimming away the excess fabric.

When she was finished, Millie asked if she'd like to sew the long seams for her, and Gloria readily agreed. "Be sure to open the windows in the sewing room," Millie suggested. "It tends to get stuffy up there."

After a few false starts on the treadle, Gloria's feet got into the familiar old rhythm. It was all coming back. And while she guided the fast-moving needle along the seams, she was reminded of how she used to make little britches for her younger brothers or hand stitch the facing for their small black church vests. She had also sewn a shirt or two for her father, though not to his satisfaction—Mom had taken over to rework some of the details. *"That would be fine for the boys,"* her father had said, *"but I want mine to look store-bought."*

When Gloria had completed the seams, she returned to the kitchen, where Millie set up the ironing board so she could press them nice and flat.

"Do you think your father-in-law would be napping just now?" Gloria asked, wanting to pay him a visit.

Millie laughed. "He perty much naps all the time on days after he helps Pete in the barn. Even if ya have to wake him, he'll be glad to see ya."

Gloria thanked her and folded up the ironing board, stowing it away before heading over to visit with Benuel.

⌘

"I can't be sure, really," Leona was telling Maggie at the shop. She was walking a thin line, trying not to divulge any confidences. "But it seems like Gloria is tryin' to work through some things."

"That would explain why she came back with you." Maggie sharpened her pencil, then pushed it behind her ear.

"Honestly, I thought she just needed to

get away from her boyfriend for a few days. But now I think there's more to it."

They worked together on the inventory of all the handmade linens and whatnot prior to the big summer tourist season, just around the corner.

"Gloria could have been our cousin-in-law by now," Leona said softly, "had she stayed."

"Who knows if you might not have married Adam Gingerich, too," Maggie said, a glint of humor in her eyes.

"*Ach*, Adam and I were never serious." Leona had to laugh. "I know for sure Tom's the man for me!"

Maggie smiled as she jotted down the number of doilies with tatting around the edges.

Leona continued counting the embroidered pillowcases, making sure each was a matched set. She couldn't help but wonder what Gloria was doing at home. *Dear* ferhoodled *friend.*

She thought again of Tom, wondering how soon she might see him. *He trusted me completely, letting me go to Arkansas.*

⁓※⁓

Gloria followed the garden path around to the *Dawdi Haus*, where Millie's tea roses would bloom in June on a white trellis Pete had made years ago. Brilliant lilies would appear, as well, scenting the air close to Benuel's private back porch.

She made her way up the steps and hesitated a moment before lightly rapping on the screen door, lest she startle Leona's grandfather. When no one came, she knocked again, this time more firmly, and Benuel Speicher's frail voice called for her to come in.

"Hope I'm not barging in," she said as she closed the screen door behind her.

"Well, just had myself a long after-dinner nap, so this is a *gut* time." He motioned her into the area where he had been resting. "Sit over there," Benuel said, pointing to the settee. "It's the most comfortable spot—well, aside from this here chair." He patted the upholstered arms.

"I won't stay long."

"*Puh!* Don't worry 'bout that," he replied, leaning forward and making the chair creak. "I enjoy a conversation with a perty girl."

She smiled, enjoying how very Amish he looked with his gray beard and bowl-shaped haircut. "To be honest, I'd like to pick your brain about something."

He chuckled. "Such as it is."

"Seriously, I've been thinking about talking to Deacon Ebersol. Something's weighing on my mind."

"No one's ever regretted seeking out that minister. He has a right agreeable way 'bout him."

Gloria had heard it before. *But my father never seemed to think so.*

"Pete and the deacon are lifelong friends." Benuel tugged on his thinning beard. "Don't s'pose your father wears a beard anymore."

"Actually, he does."

"Well now." Benuel looked serious. "Wonder why he kept it."

"Maybe it's too bothersome to shave every day."

"I s'pose that would be rather vexing. And a beard becomes part of a man's chin and face over the years."

"I've never seen my father without one." She tried to imagine what he'd look like. "But my mother got her hair cut—it was down past her sitter. She donated it to Locks of Love."

"Read 'bout that organization somewheres," he said.

"I'm sure Leona told you that all of us are fancy now—sticking together as a family, as my father likes to say."

"But the Lord *Gott* calls us one by one, Gloria." Benuel sighed heavily. "And 'tis more important to honor God than family."

Gloria pondered that. She didn't recall hearing anything like that before.

Benuel continued, "And to recite a verse I heard often as a lad, 'Wherefore come out from among them, and be ye separate, saith the Lord.'"

"I tried to do that as long as possible," Gloria said, but she knew she had not succeeded. Still, there was something very sincere about Benuel's concern for her. "Leona's real lucky to have such a caring family."

"No luck about it."

"Well, you know what I mean."

Benuel dipped his head. "The Lord alone showers blessings on those who honor His name."

Gloria agreed, then thanked him for the visit and rose to go.

"Gloria, don't forget: When life is hardest, the Lord *Gott* is still to be praised. 'Tis our only lifeline, our best hope, to keep fear from festerin'."

"I believe that, but I can't help worrying sometimes. And I'm not sure what to do in my present case . . . at least now that my life has gone in a different direction," she admitted. "Honestly, I don't know what I think."

"Well, to be blunt, what you or I think doesn't change the truth one iota." Benuel nodded as if to punctuate his remark. "You'll consider that, won't ya?"

She said she would.

"And this time, please don't leave town without saying farewell, all right?"

At the look on his face, Gloria promised to drop by again. Truly, Benuel Speicher was someone she didn't wish to disappoint.

⟜⟝

Gloria took Leona's wicker basket and hurried out toward the clearing Leona so loved and began to gather up twigs and vines and berries for some new wreaths. She missed being out in the woods like this, and she was certain Leona would want to fashion more wreaths before the next market day. *It's only fair I help out.*

She thought of Leona's Dawdi Benuel and what he'd said about God calling His children *"one by one."* It had been so reassuring to talk with him . . . until he'd mentioned how the Lord showered blessings on those who honored His name. That wasn't new to her, of course, but she'd felt uncomfortable all the same. *And convicted,* she thought.

"I can't let this get to me." Gloria shook her head, knowing her father would object to what Benuel had said.

## CHAPTER 32

Gloria placed the basket filled with wreath-worthy material on the worktable in the screened porch and went in to help Millie chop vegetables for a salad. "I had a real nice chat with your father-in-law," she said, going to wash her hands.

"He prob'ly enjoyed that." Millie pulled out an apron from the side drawer and offered it to her.

"When will Leona be home?"

"She's finished at five o'clock, so if you'd like to drive over and pick her up in twenty minutes or so, you could say hullo to Maggie at the same time."

"Okay, I'll do that once I finish up here." She moved to the wooden block to dice the already scraped carrots and peeled cucumbers. Then she washed the lettuce leaves and tore them gently before scooping all of it into a large Tupperware bowl and placing it in the fridge.

"You enjoy workin' in the kitchen, ain't so?" Millie said.

Gloria smiled, guessing what she was thinking. "*Jah*, I'd make a good Amishwoman, if that's what you mean."

"I do indeed." Millie smiled.

Thinking now might be the right time, Gloria asked, "Would Pete mind possibly accompanying me to see the deacon sometime?"

Brightening, Millie nodded. "Don't see why not. Peter would be glad to take you, if ya ask."

"*Denki*," she said, thinking she wanted to talk with Leona about possibly staying till Sunday.

On the way out to the car, Gloria noticed Benuel sitting on his back porch. He waved to her as she climbed into the car, resisting the inclination to check her phone messages.

About a mile down the road, she slowed when a horse cart came rumbling toward her. A closer look told her that Orchard John was holding the reins, and he was motioning for her to pull over.

Nerves clenched her stomach. *This was bound to happen,* she thought, not that she'd been trying to avoid him.

Quite surprised, she slowed to a stop and rolled down her window, shyness overtaking her at first, embarrassed for him to see her driving a car. *What will I say?*

"*Willkumm* back, Gloria," he called from his perch, his straw hat squared on his head, the way he always wore it, and his black suspenders pronounced against his light gray shirt. *He hasn't changed,* she realized, though she couldn't help but note his tentative expression.

"How are you, John?"

"I thought I might run into ya, considering how often I travel this road."

"What've you been up to?" she asked, feeling awkward as she filled in the space. *Leona would say I'm all* ferhoodled!

"Well, ya know . . . workin' long hours." He paused, removing his hat. "Not too busy to meet you for coffee, though, if you'd care to."

For a moment, if she let her mind wander back, it was almost like she still lived around here.

"Okay," she replied without thinking.

"We could meet at our old favorite, say around seven tonight?"

She nodded, hoping this wasn't a mistake. "I'll see you there."

He bobbed his head, put his hat straw hat back on, and signaled the horse to move forward.

"What did I just agree to?" she murmured as she stepped on the gas. *And what if we're seen together?* she thought, concerned for his sake.

Pulling up to Maggie's Country Store, she parked, wondering if she ought to tell Leona about the chance meeting and Orchard John's invitation. *I'll have to eventually,* she thought, considering the plan was for tonight. *Otherwise, Leona will be curious why I'm leaving the house.*

Gloria noticed the pink tulips growing profusely in planters in front of the shop and along the walkway leading to the steps. They reminded her of Ada Miller's flower beds earlier. *What a lovely, welcoming woman,* she thought, still surprised she'd been able to peek in her former bedroom, the very spot where she'd once dreamed of marrying Orchard John. To think he'd stopped his horse to talk to her just now! *And I agreed to meet him for coffee tonight. . . .*

Inside Maggie's adorable shop, she spotted Leona and waved. "I'm your taxi driver today."

"How nice." Leona hurried to gather up her things and called for Maggie to come say hullo. Maggie appeared from the alcove and put on a big smile when she saw Gloria there.

"It's so *gut* to see you again," Maggie said, coming right over. "Leona says you're having yourself a little vacation." Maggie's eyes sparkled.

Gloria glanced at Leona. "Sometimes a person just needs to get away."

"Well, ya picked a mighty perty time to be here, that's for sure." Maggie waved her hand at the front door. "Did ya see the tulips when ya came in?"

"Everywhere I look, there are flowers. It's like one big florist's shop," Gloria said. "I also got a chance to gather some of nature's bounty for Leona's wreaths today."

Leona pulled a mock grimace. "You went to the clearing without me?"

"I certainly did," Gloria teased, to which Leona laughed.

"Well, if you run out of things to do, come back and do a bit of shopping," Maggie suggested as they walked toward the door.

"I'll keep that in mind," Gloria called over her shoulder. "*Denki!*"

They were pulling into Leona's driveway when Gloria finally told her friend about the encounter with Orchard John.

Leona's eyebrows rose. "That didn't take long."

"We're meeting for coffee tonight."

"Tonight?" Leona's face lit up.

"Early evening," Gloria said, trying to put a damper on her own feelings. "Just a friendly visit, is all."

"Oh, I'm sure it will be that," Leona said mischievously.

*He's baptized Amish, after all, and I'm the daughter of a shunned church member,* Gloria thought as she parked the car around back of the Speichers' farmhouse, concealed from the road.

"Might be a good idea not to say anything to your family," Gloria said.

"What's to hide? They'll find out sooner or later."

Gloria nodded. "I suppose."

"Just mention it casually, maybe, at supper or during dessert."

Gloria reached for her purse. "We're making too much of this."

Leona looked at her and frowned good-naturedly. "You're the one stewin', ain't?"

"Yet there's nothing to stew over," Gloria said as she got out of the car. *Nothing at all.*

## CHAPTER 33

At suppertime, Gloria decided to share that she would be leaving the house after evening Bible reading and prayers. Not that she needed Pete and Millie's permission, of course, but she was polite and wanted to follow Leona's recommendation. "I'm meeting an old friend for coffee," she said while passing the mashed potatoes across to Leona.

"An old friend?" Millie asked innocently.

Gloria caught Leona's eye.

"He's not *that* old," Leona said.

"Well now." Millie passed the gravy boat to her and looked Pete's way, though he seemed preoccupied with his food.

"Just a friendly chat," Gloria said. "Nothing more."

Leona's Dawdi Benuel cracked a smile and continued eating.

*There,* thought Gloria. *That wasn't so hard.*

---

Following devotions, Leona spent a few minutes with Gloria in Leona's room. "How was your visit with Dawdi Benuel?" she asked. "What did ya talk about, if I may ask?" She removed her *Kapp* and hung it on the bedpost.

"Oh . . ." Gloria sighed. "I told him I've thought of talking to Deacon Ebersol sometime while I'm here. He's all for it."

Leona stared at her. "Really, you want to?"

Gloria nodded her head but didn't divulge what she had in mind.

"Well, you can be sure Dawdi's advice is trustworthy . . . the deacon's, too."

"Still sorting it all out."

"As long as ya pray 'bout it, too."

Gloria's cheeks turned pink. "If I prayed over every little thing, that's all I'd ever be doing."

"Ain't such a bad thing, is it? The Lord teaches us to pray without ceasing."

"But how is that possible?"

Leona smiled and adjusted the pillows behind her. "Dat once said that it means always being in an attitude of prayer. You know—having your heart tuned to the Holy Spirit."

"Your father is wise . . . and a truly devoted husband and father," Gloria observed.

"I used to think that about *your* father."

Gloria patted the tops of Leona's feet. "Nice of you to say, but—"

"*Nee*, I'm serious. I envied your relationship with your parents."

Gloria grimaced. "Funny . . . I haven't really felt like I can rely on my parents. Not even Mom. She's always in Dad's corner now, whether she wants to be or not."

"I'm awful sorry." She felt sick hearing this, though she'd noticed the flaws in Gloria's relationship with her parents while visiting in Arkansas. Jeannie had talked so sweetly to Gloria whenever Leona was around, but there were definitely some cracks. *Like the pressure over Darren . . .*

Gloria glanced at the day clock on the dresser. "Yikes! Guess I'd better get going." She scooted off the bed. "Remember, it's just coffee."

"Exactly." Leona winked.

"Besides, I'd be a terrible choice for Orchard John, and you know it." With that, Gloria left to freshen up in the spare room.

Leona watched Gloria back out of the driveway and head down the road to meet Orchard John. "She loved him once, and he loved her," she mused as she prepared to write in her daily journal, chronicling the day, particularly Gloria's and her visit to Ada Miller's. *How strange it was to see her standing in her old room,* she wrote. *And pointing out the little nicks in the window—reminders that must cause Gloria a certain amount of sadness now.*

When she finished, Leona closed her journal and redid her hair bun, preparing to go out herself, over to Deacon Ebersol's to get his opinion on Gloria.

She heard Mamma's footsteps in the hallway, and then Mamma appeared in the doorway. "I hope things go well for Gloria."

"She's maybe callin' this a friendly meeting, but I wouldn't be surprised if Orchard John wishes otherwise."

"Poor fella . . . still single after all this time."

"He's gotta be going through a lot, seeing her back."

Mamma stepped into the room and sat on the bed, something she rarely did. "Gloria helped me cut out my new dress pattern this afternoon. She sewed up the seams and pressed them, too."

"She didn't tell me."

Mamma linked her hands in front of her. "I daresay there's a tug-of-war taking place in her heart."

"I sometimes think she's ashamed because of her shunned father."

"The dear girl . . . I pray *Gott* shines peace into her troubled soul."

"*Denki*, Mamma." Leona went to sit next to her mother, just being quiet there with her. A treasured moment, for certain.

"Gloria's blessed by your loyal friendship, 'specially now. Not too many folk in our district would welcome her back when she hasn't made any declarations 'bout returning to the church."

Leona placed her hand over her mother's callused and wrinkled hand. "You've been so kind to my friend, Mamma. It means ever so much to me."

The coffee shop seemed quiet even for a weeknight. As Gloria entered, she immediately spotted Orchard John sitting in the corner at the table they'd always frequented. He waved to her, straw hat removed and his blond hair looking fresh from a recent shower.

He stood up to greet her, sitting down again only when she did.

Gloria noticed a latte awaited her, and smelling it, she realized it was her favorite kind. "You remembered?"

"Of course," he said softly, eyes shining. "How could I forget?"

"Well, thank you." She took a sip, and the familiar taste and surroundings reminded her of the many wonderful times she'd spent with the smiling young man across the table.

"Are you enjoyin' your visit with Leona?" he asked.

"I guess the grapevine's caught up with me."

John smiled. "Sometimes a person just has to come home again, *jah*?"

"Well, I'm only here for a short break." *An escape from my life . . .*

"I was curious 'bout why."

To keep things from becoming too personal, she quickly said, "Leona and I had an interesting morning over at Jacob Miller's house."

Orchard John took a sip of his coffee before speaking. "It was providential that Jacob got all that land when he did."

"Well, he's a terrific carpenter. I saw his handiwork in the kitchen." She described the handsome cupboards and built-ins. "I'm not sure my father could have gotten my mother to leave if it looked like it does now."

John nodded, chuckling. "A woman and her kitchen."

Gloria thanked him for inviting her.

"When I saw ya sitting there on the stone wall yesterday mornin', I knew I needed to see you again."

She found herself nearly holding her breath and wondered what more he would say.

"It might seem like a long while since you lived here, but for me it was just a matter of time before you'd miss all of us and return, if just for a visit." He paused, clutching his coffee cup with his right hand.

"And now, seeing me in these fancy clothes, you must wonder how I could've left it all behind—right, John?"

He held her gaze. "You always were a devoted daughter. Naturally, you'd want to follow your father . . . stay with your family. 'Specially if you were just goin' along to get along, ya know. Not really buying into their beliefs."

"I hadn't thought of it that way." She reached for her cup, glad for the comfort of something to hold.

"I'd rather not embarrass ya, Gloria, but I'd like to ask ya something."

"You were never shy." She smiled.

"One night before you and your family

moved away, I tossed some stones at your window. . . . Were you in your room?"

She looked at him, stunned that he was bringing this up. "Yes . . . I heard them." Drawing a long breath, she continued, "But my father wanted me to date other fellows before settling down with a serious beau. It had only been a year since I'd started going to Singing and other youth gatherings, remember?"

He nodded thoughtfully. "I only asked because I wanted to know if it was your choice . . . or someone else's."

It wasn't necessary to go a step further and say how distressed she'd felt. *Pointless now.* "I simply could not disobey my father . . . you understand."

"And he was right: You hadn't had much chance to get to know other young men." Orchard John kept his attention on her as she sipped more of her latte. "What about now, Gloria . . . are ya seein' someone?"

She'd hoped he wouldn't ask. "Actually, I'm here to sort things out with my boyfriend. Well, not *with* him, but about him. And there are some other things to mull over, too."

"I see." His eyes squinted in confusion. "Do yous have much in common, then? Has he always been an *Englischer*?"

Her thoughts right now were beyond her

ability to verbalize. Besides, John's questions were tying her stomach in knots.

"I'm sorry, but what if we talked about you instead—your work, your family and friends?" she suggested.

John didn't seem to mind switching topics and told her about his day tending to hundreds of apple and peach trees with his father and other workers. He also mentioned that his sister Naomi had left a message on their father's barn phone to say that Gloria had stopped by the fabric and notions shop where she worked. "Daed heard the voicemail first and wanted me to listen. Guess he doubted I'd believe him if I didn't hear it myself."

Gloria was embarrassed they had made such a big deal of it. "It was real nice seein' your sister again, even so briefly." Then she mentioned she ought to head back to Leona's. "She'll be waiting for me, no doubt."

"It was great to see you again, Gloria." John walked her out to the car.

"You too . . . and thanks for the delicious treat." She opened her car door and got in as he walked to his father's old horse cart and untied the mare from the hitching post.

*What a great guy,* she thought wistfully. *Hopefully, he'll find someone special and move on with his life.*

CHAPTER 34

Deacon Ebersol sat at the head of the table, his palms flat against the green-checkered oilcloth. His plump wife, Sallie, sat at the far end reading *Echoes of the Past,* a genealogy book. He reiterated what Leona had told him. "You say Gloria Gingerich is struggling with some life choices?"

"*Jah,* and I'm not sure how to help her." Leona paused to be respectful.

The deacon nodded, his graying eyebrows furrowed. "Well, your friend has nearly reached the end of what's considered her youth. It's high time for her to either be solidly in or out of the church."

Agreeing, Leona said, "I worry she's

already chosen for the world by goin' along with her family, but there are moments she seems betwixt and between." She sighed, hoping she was doing the right thing by sharing this way. "That's why I invited Gloria to come home with me. I do hope it's all right for Gloria to stay awhile with us."

"I understand from Tom that your goal is to win her back permanently," the deacon said.

She nodded. "I hope she'll find what her heart is longing for right here in Colerain, amongst the People."

Deacon Ebersol nodded slowly. "With the Lord's help, perhaps you'll help win her through your meek and gentle spirit."

"That's my earnest prayer."

"Then that's mine, too, Leona." He gave her a gentle smile.

She thanked him for making time for her and said good-bye to Sallie when Tom's mother glanced over her bifocals. The deacon kindly walked Leona to the back porch, where she saw Tom sitting beside a lit lantern.

"Looks like someone wants to see ya home," Deacon said, his eyebrow quirking up as he bid her good-night.

Leona smiled, glad for the surprise of seeing Tom, who rose and walked down the steps with her under a brilliant moon. He reached for her hand. "Feel more settled now?" he asked, the lantern's glow leading the way along with the moon's light as he took her the long way home through the field.

"The Lord God surely chose a patient man to be deacon of our flock."

"He did indeed."

They walked slowly, her hand still clasped in his. "I missed ya while you were gone, Leona." He squeezed her hand gently.

She embraced his thoughtfulness. "It seemed like a long time away. I hope you received my message from Maggie."

"Was mighty glad for it." He looked down at her. "Did you have yourself a *gut* time out there?"

She told him how very tiring the trips to and from Arkansas had been. "But I believe it was the right thing for me to go." She tried to describe the interesting sights she'd enjoyed with Gloria—the sprawling farmland, the rolling hills all around, and the quaint downtown. "There was a perty tearoom, too."

"Are any of her family showing signs of leaning toward the People again?"

She shook her head. "Not that I can tell," she said. "Gloria planned to do baptismal instruction with the HillView deacon, but they left the Amish before she could take more than a few classes. I know that baptism is a sacred act a person must accept without any persuasion. But I have faith that God's at work in Gloria's heart."

"So we'll both keep praying to that end." Tom slipped his arm around her.

"I just hope Orchard John is cautious," she said. "He's havin' coffee with Gloria this evening."

Tom fell silent for a moment. "I guess I shouldn't be surprised, since he's pined for her since the day she left."

She turned to look at Tom. "You know this for sure?"

"It's obvious, isn't it? John puts up a *gut* appearance by spending time with *die Youngie*. But if you've noticed, he rarely pairs up with anyone."

"I can't imagine my cousin going against the ordinance if Gloria doesn't budge and come back to the church." Leona stared up at the star-filled sky and drank in the beauty of the evening. "But love sometimes makes people do peculiar things."

"*Nee*, you have nothing to worry 'bout there. Trust me. John's a dedicated church member."

"I do trust ya," she whispered, and he drew her closer, their strides in unison.

He slowed the pace. "That evening in the clearing, before you left for Arkansas—"

"When it rained on us?" She turned again and patted his arm. "I want to say something about that."

"*Jah?*"

She breathed deeply. "I should've been more sensitive to your worries . . . ya know, before I left to visit Gloria."

Tom shrugged it off. "I wasn't that worried, not about you."

"I mean . . . about Adam."

He paused. "I was more concerned 'bout Arkansas Joe . . . well, you know I don't trust the man. I wasn't sure how it would be for you, staying with his family out there."

They stopped walking altogether. "I used to wonder why God brought Gloria into my life, only to let her go," Leona confessed. "And I regretted her leaving. On one count, though, I'm actually very glad the Gingerich family left."

Tom looked confused. "Really?"

"*Jah,* 'cause you and I had a better chance with Adam gone."

Tom seemed intent on her every word.

"I'm blessed that the Lord planned for us to be together."

Tom put a finger to her lips. "*Ach,* I love you, Leona."

She smiled. "Just wanted you to know."

They turned and walked silently for a

while. Finally, Leona spoke again. "I interrupted you, Tom. You were goin' to say something."

Tom cleared his throat. "*Jah*, that evening in the clearing . . . I'd planned to show you the gift of land my father's offered. It's at the far end of his cornfield, with a view of your Dat's woods and, in the other direction, the neighbor's meadow. There's plenty of room to build a house there and a nice-sized farm."

"Oh, and I spoiled your plans with my fussin' over goin' to Arkansas!"

"That's all behind us now." He stopped walking and faced her. "I'll take ya to see the land when you're able to get away. We can pace off the perimeter, picture our home there."

Leona sighed with happiness. To think, she'd have a brand-new house to live in with her husband and their little ones to come! Not many young brides had such a luxury. "I can hardly wait to see it, Tom. How kind of your father."

"He's awful fond of you, Leona. You must surely know." Tom went on to talk about the blueprint he was having drawn up. "I'd like you to look it over soon."

"I doubt I'm the best person for that, but I do have an opinion on how big our kitchen should be." She laughed softly, and he leaned in to kiss her cheek.

"And our bedroom, too," he said as they turned and continued walking. "Space for all the little ones in cradles . . . someday."

She smiled. "One wee babe at a time, *jah*?"

Tom chuckled, and she had never felt more at home with her truly wonderful husband-to-be.

~~~~~

Even with all the kitchen windows wide open, the house was warm and quiet when Gloria returned. Millie was sitting at the table writing a letter, or so it appeared.

Gloria took a spot across from her. "Is Leona around?"

"She went to see Deacon Ebersol when you left." Millie glanced at the wall clock. "Might've stayed to visit with Tom and the rest of the family."

Noticing Millie's stationery, it crossed Gloria's mind that now might be a good time to write a letter to her grandmother in upstate New York. "Would you happen to have some writing paper to spare? Nothing fancy."

"Here, use this," Millie said, offering some with hummingbirds and flowers along the bottom. "How many sheets do ya need?"

"Two is fine, thanks."

Millie reached into her stationery box and removed the pages.

"I'll wait up for Leona," Gloria said, then rose and headed for the stairs.

*Evidently, both of us need to speak to the deacon. . . .*

Going to the spare room, Gloria was glad for some time to reflect. Back when her mother was Amish, she would encourage their family to evaluate the day prior to going to sleep at night. It was one of Gloria's more pleasant memories of growing up. So she took the time now to consider her rather awkward meeting with Orchard John. Seeing him after such a long time had touched a nerve, though she had tried not to let on.

As had always been her habit before turning fancy, she went to each window and pulled down its dark green shade, then turned on the gas lamp beside the bed. Quickly, she undressed and put on her bathrobe and got cozy for a while before her shower.

She spotted the King James Bible on the dresser and recalled what Benuel had said. *"Gott calls us one by one. . . ."*

"Individually," she whispered. *Community is everything for the Amish, so why did Benuel say it that way?*

She picked up the Bible and opened to Second Corinthians, searching for the verse about being separate from the world. It took a moment to locate it in chapter six, verse seventeen, and she read it twice, realizing this was a command from the Lord himself.

*Must a person be Plain in order to live set apart?* she wondered.

Something in her recoiled, like a punch to her stomach. She thought of praying but was too restless.

Obviously, the latte she'd enjoyed had boosted her energy. She got up and went to the dresser, where she looked into the narrow mirror.

*I need to talk to Leona.* She thought of Naomi Speicher's suggestion to stay around for Preaching this Sunday. Millie's response had been so favorable.

*What if I did stay longer?*

## CHAPTER 35

Nearing her father's house, Leona gasped—the light was still on in the spare room, lantern light visible around the edges of the window shades.

"Are you all right?" Tom asked.

"Gloria's still up. Should I tell her where I've been?"

"Tell her the truth. Gloria's gotta know how unusual it is for someone like her to come back to visit her former church district."

"You're right," Leona agreed. "I just hoped she might be asleep by now."

"Are ya worried your talk with my father might throw a wrench in your plans?"

"Hard to know. She might think I overstepped."

Tom stopped walking again. "I hope you're not tiptoeing on eggshells, nervous that something you say will offend her. Convincing her to return to the Amish ways is ultimately a job for the Lord alone."

She grimaced. "I know you're right."

"You're trying very hard to help *Gott* out . . . maybe too hard."

Lowering her head, she sighed. "I understand what you're sayin'." *Tom knows me so well.*

"Sleep peacefully." He took both her hands in his. "And no frettin', *jah*?"

She promised, glad he'd been honest with her.

Tom walked her to the back steps and waited till she was in the house. When she turned, she saw him headed back across the field, his straw hat glinting like a halo in the light of the moon.

Tom counted his blessings as he walked home, Leona amongst the most treasured. Had he ever felt life was going along this well? Truly, he was mighty thankful.

The thought, however, of his best friend having coffee with Gloria Gingerich disturbed him more than he'd let on to Leona. He sincerely felt sorry for Orchard John, who'd never been able to get Gloria out of his mind . . . or heart. But if Gloria had no intention of joining their church, John could be setting himself up for further heartache.

*Or unnecessary temptation.*

It was odd, really, how closely linked the four of them were—as cousins and friends. *And would-be sweethearts.*

He contemplated John's enduring affection for Gloria, and Leona's for Gloria. Both Leona and her cousin cared deeply about Gloria, and it was a concern.

*What happens when she returns home?* Tom thought.

Yet, looking up at the heavens, he scolded himself. *With God, all things are possible.*

⁕

Gloria was sleeping soundly when Leona peeked in on her, a couple of pages of Mamma's best stationery and a pen beside her on the quilt. She reached down to remove the ballpoint pen and placed it on the dresser, then outened the lantern, which had spread its cheerful glow. She hoped Gloria might have a peaceful rest, although she couldn't help wondering how things had gone with Orchard John.

Closing the door, except for a crack, Leona wandered to her own room, feeling very much like her friend's guardian.

She opened the middle dresser drawer and removed a clean nightgown. It was soft pink in color and had two tiny decorative buttons at the neck opening—her one and only slightly fancy nightdress.

Leona pulled back the sheet and quilt and then put out the gas lamp Mamma had surely lit for her. She knelt beside her bed, her particular habit, and folded her hands to offer the request she'd made a hundred times or more. Yet she believed that the Lord God and heavenly Father knew Gloria's heart—saw her worries and fears—and cared for her enough to want to see her where she belonged. For this night, that was enough to bring Leona serenity.

※

Around midnight, Gloria's phone dinged loudly, signaling a text. Squinting at it—having abandoned her earlier plan to go unplugged—she read her father's text. *When are you heading back?*

*Dad,* she typed back, *I just got here.*

*Leona's home now, so why are you still there?*

She suspected she shouldn't tell him all that was really on her mind.

Her father texted back before she did: *Don't ruin your chance with Darren!*

Was that all this was about? *That's MY concern. Good night, Dad.*

Her father's texts ceased, and she felt a sense of relief, unable to handle more of the same.

Then, just as she was about to click off, another text appeared. *I fear you're being brainwashed.*

It was futile to try to make her point any longer. Gloria deleted the text thread, turned off her phone, and stuffed it under the pillow next to her.

Then, in the darkened room, she realized someone had turned off the lantern after she'd fallen asleep.

*Dear, thoughtful Leona.*

⟋⟍

Early the next morning, after Leona and Gloria had helped clean the house, Gloria offered to work with her to make another wreath or two for market.

"You've already done enough," Leona insisted while they beat throw rugs in the side yard with brooms, lapping them over the clothesline to make the task easier.

"I want to pull my weight."

"But you didn't come here to work, *jah*?" Leona said, reminding her that she'd planned to take time to walk in the countryside and to pray about her future with Darren.

"True, and I will do that." Gloria nodded.

"I also wrote a long letter to my grandmother last night while you were gone."

Leona was surprised.

"I just figured it's time she heard from me, so we can get to know each other before she passes away—not that it will be anytime soon."

*She's really changing . . . connecting with people again,* Leona thought as Gloria described what she remembered of her grandmother. It was clear that writing to her grandmother had revealed things about *Gloria's* struggles and priorities.

"Sounds like the letter you wrote to her helped you."

"It's not the first time that's happened." Gloria began to explain that the first year after moving away from Lancaster County, she'd kept a daily journal. "And all the while I wrote, I pretended I was talking to you, Leona . . . sharing my sadness and pent-up anger and everything in my mind and heart, whatever came pouring out onto the pages. It was one way I managed to cope, missing you and our close friendship."

Leona teared up, hearing this. "Aw, that's really sweet."

"Well, some of it wasn't, let me tell you. My journaling gave me an outlet to vent my frustration, and I wrote as fast as I could some days. Other times, there was a sense of peace as I began to fit in with the new community of the People there. Either way, I tried to get my emotions down on the page, lest they burst forth elsewhere." Gloria flung the next rug over the clothesline and began to slap it with her broom.

Leona waited till she was finished before speaking. "I thought I was alone with my loss when ya left. Strange as this might sound, it helps to know you were going through some of what I experienced." She choked back her tears. "To think, all the months I waited for your letters, you were actually thinkin' of me."

Gloria reached for her, rug and all, and their brooms toppled to the ground as their tears fell freely.

⌘

Tom waved down Orchard John on his way to work early that morning after dropping Danny off at the smithy's. He'd stopped in for coffee at one of the shops along his route and was sitting in the spring wagon when he saw John walking toward his open black buggy, a large cup in his hand. "Hullo!" he called to his friend.

"*Wie geht's*, Tom?" Orchard John came over and stood near his wagon.

"The question is, how are *you* . . . after your visit with Gloria?" Tom asked.

John chuckled. "Well, that meddlesome grapevine 'tis faster than the speed of sound."

Tom said he'd heard it from Leona. "I'm not gonna lose my *gut* pal to the world, I hope." He tried to inject a humorous tone.

John waved his hand at Tom's nonsense, not cracking a smile. A moment passed as he stared at his coffee cup. "Confidentially speaking . . . it's been difficult over the years for me to imagine myself with anyone but Gloria. I've considered it many times."

Hearing this, Tom felt justified in his concern that her being back in town might pose a setback for his friend.

John drank some of his coffee, still sandwiched between Tom's spring wagon and the car next to him. "I'll be right frank with ya. I plan to keep prayin' for her, and, ya know, hoping she . . ." John's voice broke off, and he looked down again.

*He's definitely in too deep.* Tom wished there was a way to reel him back to land before he went plunging over the dam. "You put your toe in the water, and next thing, you'll be drownin'."

"I understand why you're worried."

"You'd say the same if the shoes were on *my* feet." Tom studied him. "You know ya would."

Meeting his gaze, Orchard John nodded.

"True . . . and I'm doin' my best to appreciate it." He turned to go and untie his mare at the hitching post. "Have a *gut* day, Tom!"

"You too." Waving, Tom smiled, but all the rest of the drive to work, he couldn't shake the feeling that Orchard John was already in over his head.

<hr />

Once the rugs were carried indoors and put back in their rightful locations, Gloria insisted on helping make some wreaths, so they went to the screened-in porch and began to sort the materials Gloria had already gathered.

"I don't know if your mother said anything to you, but she mentioned I was welcome to stay around for Preaching," Gloria said. "What would you think?"

"Are you kidding?" Leona loved this. "I think your parents might have something to say about that, though. And what about your job at the diner?"

"I'll figure it out. I need to call Hampton and let him know I'll be back soon."

Leona fretted a bit, wondering if Gloria's employment might be in jeopardy.

"Well, if I do stay for church, can you loan me one of your dresses? I wouldn't want to needlessly offend anyone."

"Of course! The sleeves might be a little short, since you're taller." Leona grinned. She was relieved and more than a little excited about possibly seeing Gloria dressed Plain again.

"Also, your mother said you saw the deacon last evening," Gloria said as she put glue on several dried berries, which she then affixed to the wreath.

"I thought he should know directly from me that you're stayin' with us." She hoped Gloria wouldn't press for more details, and began to tie a bow for the bottom of the wreath.

"Don't wanna be a nuisance."

"How could that be?"

"To be honest, my father's shunning, and the reasons behind it, are so embarrassing to me, Leona. Absolutely humiliating."

"You can't carry that around forever," she said softly, stopping her work to reach to touch Gloria. "Ain't yours to bear."

"But it's there all the same."

Leona wished she could snap her fingers and free her friend of the nagging guilt. *The pride* . . .

And as they worked, she thanked God for Gloria's interest in staying for Sunday. It was another step forward—the biggest, of course, was driving here in the first place.

CHAPTER 36

*G*loria enjoyed browsing in Maggie's Country Store that afternoon. She could overhear Leona telling Maggie that she and Gloria had made some wreaths, and did Maggie want to display them?

"Sure, why not?" Maggie replied. "Unless you think you'll take away from your mother and aunt's trade at the Quarryville farmers market."

"Well, it's *gut* to spread them around a bit, *jah*?" Leona said.

Gloria admired several pretty handmade candles, picking them up and eyeing them closely. She chose a soft blue one for her mother, a souvenir of the trip.

Searching through other items, her conversation with Leona played over in her mind, and she wished she hadn't shared quite so much. Feeling chagrined, she instead focused her attention on the many appealing gift options Maggie had in stock.

Just then, she remembered that this was the day Adam was scheduled to move out of the house, which wouldn't take long, given his few things. She laughed, amused at the idea of her brother and his roommate fending for themselves.

Leona looked over at her, frowning, then smiling. "You all right?" she mouthed.

"I'm fine," Gloria replied, searching through a display of fanciful potpourri sachets, settling on one similar to the gift Orchard John had given her. When she'd made her choices, she told Leona she'd see her at supper and slipped out to the car.

Gloria drove out of the parking lot and headed for the main road. She had felt carefree and tranquil while roaming about the clearing, gathering materials for the wreaths. But it wasn't an option for her to escape there whenever she felt the need for peace. Seeing Orchard John last evening had also brought a sense of calmness, even rightness, but she wasn't going to seek him out for more of the same. It wouldn't be fair to raise his hopes.

Instead, she drove around the area, reliving the troubling years, creeping along past the ministers' homes, which only reminded her of her father's outstanding debts to various farmers here. *Especially Deacon Ebersol.* Since Monday, her idea had grown from a tiny seed to a fully mature plan.

She returned to Leona's parents' house, parking near the *Dawdi Haus* out of respect for their family. Leaving her purchases in the car, she got out and strolled to the barn, wanting to see the new calf again.

"Why am I so restless?" she murmured while observing the new calf eagerly drinking milk from a bucket, making slurping sounds. Sunshine poured into the indoor pen. She enjoyed being around the livestock, watching springtime's new life in a farm setting. She felt closer to God's creation on a farm than anywhere, really.

*Something I would never enjoy again if I marry Darren. . . .*

After a few minutes, Gloria wandered back to the house, but Millie was nowhere in sight. She walked to the front porch steps and sat there thinking perhaps *today* would be a good time to see the deacon. But she guessed Sunday was better for Pete, busy farmer that he was. *Just so I meet with him before I leave,* she told herself.

Random thoughts skittered through her mind, and she watched the clouds drift aimlessly across the sky. *Like my life,* she thought regretfully. *Where do I see myself in ten years . . . twenty? Can I manage being English for the rest of my days?*

She leaned back on the steps and gazed at the fields across the road to the south of Pete's farmhouse. Certainly, she would miss the beauty and harmony of the countryside if she married Darren and moved to town, but weren't there advantages to living in the hub of things?

Yet there was Darren himself. Sure, he was good-looking and charming . . . well-off, too. But he could be impatient and presumptuous. Besides, she wasn't in any hurry to get married.

*Dad's pushy, too,* she realized.

She heard someone whistling and was surprised to see Orchard John walking this way, carrying a book. He waved to her, and she had to smile.

*We just keep running into each other,* she thought. Not that she minded.

"I took a chance you'd be here," he called as he came up the driveway toward the porch. "Got a minute?"

"Sure." She nodded. "You must've finished work early."

"Oh, there's always something to be done at the orchard. And I'll get back to it soon enough." He reached the steps, and she saw that the book in his hand was *Rules of a Godly Life*.

"Mind if I sit, Gloria?"

She shook her head.

He laughed just then. "Right out here in front for everyone and their brother to see." John handed her the book. "I wasn't sure if you still had a copy of this."

She eyed the front cover. "I do, but I left it back home. It's been a long while since I've read it."

"Maybe you could crack it open in your free time while you're here." He glanced over his shoulder at the house. "Is Millie around?"

"Pete's home, but Millie may be out somewhere. I'm just waiting for Leona to return home from work so we can make supper before taking Brownie to Mahlon and Maggie's for a visit."

"Speaking of that dog, where is he?"

"Haven't seen him most of the day."

"Well, what do ya say we find him?" John rose quickly, brushing off the seat of his pants.

"He's likely in the stable. There's a bed for him near the horses." She wondered why John would risk being seen with her. "Are you sure about this?"

"Why not?" His eyes crinkled when he smiled. "We're just two old friends."

"All right, then." Picking up the book, she walked with him to the stable, then around the house, looking in all directions for Brownie. Gloria was fairly certain he wasn't in any danger of being lost, but she didn't mind another opportunity to spend time with John, now that he was here.

Leona's grandfather was sitting on his rocking chair on the back porch. "Hullo there, Gloria." Then he spotted John. "Well, if it isn't my grandson, Orchard Johnny!"

His face turned red at the youthful nickname. He went over and shook hands. "*Wie geht's, Dawdi?*"

"Oh, fair to middlin'." Benuel's eyes darted between them. "Didn't expect to see yous together."

"We're searching for Brownie," Gloria explained. "Have you seen him?"

"Well, he was in the barn with Pete and me just a while ago. I suspect he's fine." He gave them another look. "Come, why don't you pull up a chair." He motioned to two vacant rockers.

Orchard John glanced at Gloria, who nodded. "Maybe Brownie will show up on his own," he suggested, then offered Gloria the chair next to Benuel.

"I daresay it's another day made to order."
Benuel tugged on his black suspenders.
"Mighty nice sittin' here in shirt sleeves."

John sat down, nodding. "*The Farmer's
Almanac* predicts a long, hot summer."

"The weather's in God's hands, so we
never complain," Benuel said with a glance
at Gloria, his gaze taking in her floral skirt
and open-toed sandals. He did a double-take
at the book John had given her.

"Maybe we'll have some rain later," said
John, looking at the sky.

"That'll bring Brownie home right quick,"
Gloria said, enjoying the company. *Better than
sitting alone waiting for Leona . . .*

She realized unexpectedly that once she
left for home, she would most likely have little
contact with Leona. *I'll lose her again.* The
thought was nearly unbearable.

Benuel broke the silence. "Millie said you
were sewin'."

This surprised her. "I offered to help with
her new dress—loved every minute of it."

Benuel bobbed his head. "If ya ask me,
it seems you and your family did the wrong
thing, leavin' the Old Ways behind."

*You're not kidding,* Gloria thought. "And
now it's too late," she said, her hands gripping
the book on her lap.

"*Ach,* if you're on the wrong road, the

sooner ya turn round, the better," Benuel reassured her.

Orchard John nodded his agreement, and Gloria knew she was outnumbered. "Joining any church is supposed to be a result of a person's free will, right?" she asked.

Benuel said it was. "An outcome of following in the Lord's footsteps—His calling."

"Once I made the decision for baptism, it was a joyful thing," Orchard John interjected. "I chose it freely . . . gladly."

"There was a time in Arkansas when I planned to take my baptismal vow," Gloria admitted. "I even started the classes. But when my father left that church, I followed him, just like the rest of my family." What had gotten into her, speaking up like this? Part of her yearned to hear more about Jesus' footsteps, as Benuel had put it, but another part of her was pulling hard away from any further talk in this vein. "I feel torn," she said softly, looking away lest she cry.

"The Holy Spirit nudges earnest souls toward Him," Orchard John said, still rocking in his chair.

There was a faraway look in Benuel's eyes. "I had such a time as a youth—*der Deiwel* tried to keep me from doin' what I knew was right. 'Twas just a little younger than you when I fought with all this, knowing the Lord *Gott* was workin' on my heart."

Such frank talk; Gloria hardly knew how to react. From what Benuel was saying, it seemed that he understood what she was experiencing, even though it had been many decades ago.

"You're not alone, Gloria." Orchard John cast a compassionate look her way. "There are many young people who take their time deciding on baptism."

"It's a vow for life," Benuel said solemnly. "Not to be made flippantly."

She nodded. "I came here to think and get things straightened out in my head," Gloria confessed to them. "For a long time, I've felt like I'm caught between two worlds."

Benuel stopped rocking and folded his gnarled hands in his lap.

"I'm mighty sure our deacon would welcome a visit from you," Orchard John said. "Seems to me it'd be worthwhile. And the book I gave ya is mighty helpful, too."

She patted the book. "Before I leave, I'll reread it."

Just then, Brownie came running through the meadow. He barked playfully when he spotted them, then sniffed his way through the grass in front of Benuel's little porch, almost right up to the porch steps. Without warning, he turned and darted around the side of the house, disappearing once more. "Those pesky little bunnies must be livin' under there again," Benuel observed with a chuckle.

"I'm sure Brownie can take care of that." Orchard John grinned.

Former farm girl though she was, Gloria grimaced at the thought. "Guess it's up to me to stop him, then." Gloria jumped off her chair and hurried around the house, calling for Brownie.

The sun was low in the sky when Gloria drove Leona over to see Samuel, Sadie, and Marianna. Brownie sat on Leona's lap in the front passenger seat, his head and tongue hanging out the open window.

"Your nephew might not remember me," Gloria said.

"Samuel was just about six when ya left."

"Yes, well, Marianna was still a toddler."

"It's awful nice, you wanting to visit my brother's family," Leona told her.

Gloria decided to elaborate more on Orchard John's visit, since Benuel had spilled the beans at supper earlier, saying he'd had an "unlikely couple" drop by today. "Just so you know, your cousin only came by to loan me a book," she said.

"Which one?" Leona asked.

Gloria told her and waited for a dramatic response, but Leona was quiet, and Gloria wondered if she'd known about it prior to John's visit.

She suppressed a smile. *They're doing their best to bring me back into the fold. . . .*

～⌁～

Leona laughed and clapped her hands as, through the kitchen window, she watched her nephew and nieces romp and play with Brownie while Maggie popped corn kernels on the gas burner. Gloria joined Leona at the window to observe the children, too.

"I'm giving Leona the day off tomorrow and Friday so yous can do as ya please," Maggie said, still wearing the nice rust-colored dress and black apron she'd had on earlier at the shop.

"You didn't have to," Gloria was quick to say. "I can entertain myself."

"Well, I *want* to," Maggie replied, shaking the pan. "Yous have a lot to catch up on, I'm sure."

Leona smiled. "You're a dear, Maggie. I couldn't have a more understanding sister-in-law—or boss," she added with a wink.

"You two go on outside with the children," Maggie urged them. "I'll join yous in a jiffy."

Leona and Gloria went out onto the porch, where they leaned on the railing to watch the fun. Gloria pointed and laughed as Brownie chased Marianna round and round a tree, the little girl's light brown pigtails flying.

Pretty soon, Mahlon came from the potting shed with a spongy orange ball that he tossed to Samuel, who threw it to Brownie.

"My father and I taught him to catch and fetch when he was just a pup," Gloria said quietly, her eyes still on the dog.

Leona noticed how subdued she sounded.

Maggie joined them, bringing a large bowl of popcorn and setting it on a small table between the rocking chairs on the porch. "Are yous planning to go to any of the farmers markets while Gloria's in town?"

"We sure are." Gloria gently poked Leona in the ribs, then reached for some popcorn. "I definitely want to go to the one in Quarryville on Saturday, so we can see your mother and Aunt Salome's table."

"What if we stayed to help them for a while?" Leona suggested. "If that's okay with you, Gloria."

"I don't mind one bit." Gloria smiled at her. "Work's my middle name."

*She still has the Amish mindset, for certain.* It was one more thing to be thankful for, yet

Leona couldn't help but feel she and Gloria were running out of time. She thought of Orchard John's surprise visit . . . and the book he'd given Gloria.

*I need all the help I can get!*

## CHAPTER 37

That night Gloria kept thinking about Maggie's children, and how wonderfully happy they were. Oh, their squeals of delight, their contagious laughter . . . and their obvious appreciation for one another. *And their parents.* She could not imagine how any children she might have with Darren, if she married him, would possibly enjoy such a carefree, joy-filled life living at the pace of most English families. The idea bothered her as she brushed her hair. She eyed herself in the small dresser mirror and thought how peculiar she would look Sunday with her hair down to her shoulders, instead of up like all the other young women's. So for fun, she tried to put it into a small bun at the base of her neck, struggling to twist the sides perfectly.

Quickly, she realized it would take more than one attempt to make her hair look respectable for the Lord's Day. *If there's any chance of that!*

Leona knocked at the slightly open door. Her mouth gaped when she saw Gloria in front of the mirror, her hair in a slapdash bun. "Looks like ya need some help."

"Do I ever." *And not just with my hair,* thought Gloria, glad to see her. "Show me what I'm doing wrong."

Leona entered the room. "For one thing, your hair's too short to work into a bun." She began to remove the bobby pins and started over, biting her lip.

"It doesn't have to be perfect—just better than this." Gloria laughed.

Leona continued to pin and twist until at last she stepped back to take a look. "What do ya think?"

Gloria regarded herself in the mirror. "Much better. Now if I could just borrow one of your head scarves for church, I'll be set."

"A dark blue one would be best."

Gloria moved to sit on the bed, where she'd left Orchard John's book.

Leona picked it up and opened to the first

proverb. After a time, she asked, "Any idea why John gave ya this?"

"Well, isn't he hopin' I'll be Plain again?" Gloria told Leona about their visit with Benuel that afternoon. "Your Dawdi and cousin are both working to convert me back to my Anabaptist roots."

"I'm sorry I missed that," Leona said, eyes serious. "How'd it make ya feel?"

"Wonderful, in fact . . . and terrible, too," she admitted. "It's pretty overwhelming. I couldn't be more confused."

Leona's expression turned hopeful. "Ya mean, you're actually giving some thought to what they're saying?"

"This may sound strange, but I guess I had it in my mind that if I *didn't* commit to marrying Darren, I could buy myself some time."

"Time for what?"

Gloria sighed loudly. "Time to figure out what I want, I guess. I thought that I could push off joining church till later in life . . . if I get disheartened with modern life, that is." She sat down on the bed beside Leona. "That way, I wouldn't close the door too quickly on the Amish option."

"In other words," Leona said, "if ya marry Darren, you can't change your mind later."

"Kinda messed up, huh?"

"I'm thrilled that you're actually *considering* it."

Gloria remembered a verse her father had once read during family worship about being either hot or cold toward the Lord God, not lukewarm. He'd read it twice and looked over at her mother, holding her gaze for the longest time. Shortly after that, they'd quit the Hill View Amish church.

*They went cold,* she thought. *Stone cold.*

"Not being Amish doesn't mean I'm not a Christian," Gloria said. "I would still be faithful to my church."

Leona said nothing, and Gloria could only imagine all the things Leona was thinking just now.

"You're my precious friend," Leona said softly. "We were both raised to know what was right and good and pleasing before God."

Gloria bowed her head, fighting back tears. *My sister, I called her . . . she knows me best.* "I guess it boils down to what I can live with and what I can't." She paused. "Thanks for not judging me."

"Ain't my place."

"Well, there may be some who think it is." Gloria wasn't necessarily thinking of Orchard John and Benuel, but the memory of the discussion on the *Dawdi Haus* back porch still lingered. She'd felt quite pressured.

"You can't go wrong following God's bidding," Leona said, reaching again for the book. "John did the right thing in givin' you this . . . if you're ready to read it."

"Part of a divine plan, maybe?"

"I think so." Leona nodded her head. "With all of my heart, I do."

Gloria reached for her hand. "I'm grateful for your prayers all these years."

"Better than stewin', *jah*?"

Oh, how she loved Leona. "You're really something, you know? You really are."

"Remember when we said we'd do anything to live like sisters for the rest of our lives?"

The question rippled through her heart. "I remember."

Later, after Leona left for her room, Gloria went downstairs to shower. After she returned to her room, it was *Rules of a Godly Life* that she opened and read for an hour before turning out the lantern for the night.

Leona offered to line up a driver to take them to Quarryville on Thursday morning, but Gloria insisted on taking her car for the rather short distance. They passed Leona's uncle's vast orchard and savored the beauty of white apple blossoms—the fruitlets would be noticeable once the petals fell away. "Just imagine all the bees in there workin' to pollinate," Leona said as they drove by.

"I can almost hear them buzzing!" Gloria laughed.

Leona was so glad they could spend the day together just out and about.

They poked around at BB's Grocery Outlet, then wandered over to Lapps Family Restaurant for a bite to eat at noon.

That afternoon, just for fun, they stopped in at Good's Store to peruse the bolts of quilting fabric. Gloria admitted to Leona that she hoped to find the time to take up quilting again. "Maybe someday."

⸻

The next day, they strolled on foot together down past the Amish one-room schoolhouse, Leona barefoot and Gloria in her fancy running shoes, recounting their school days.

Later, Gloria suggested they return home to cook supper for Leona's mother. "Let's make a haystack dinner. What do you say?"

"*Gut* idea," Leona readily agreed, knowing how fond her parents were of the dish.

She loved that Gloria seemed so eager to spend time with her and Mamma, especially in the kitchen. It gave her all the more hope that something was happening to move her friend's heart toward the Old Ways. Could it be?

～⋇～

A good part of Saturday morning was spent at the Quarryville farmers market. Leona delighted in tending to Mamma and Aunt Salome's market stand with Gloria at her side. She let herself imagine what it could be like if Gloria were to eventually grasp her need for the People there. What if she and her dear friend could raise their little ones together? What if they could live close by, able to encourage each other through life's hard knocks and rejoice together in the victories along the way?

*Is it possible?* she thought. *Or just wishful thinking?*

Congenial Ada Miller and her daughter, Rebekah, the former schoolteacher, dropped by the table to say hullo, making small talk with Mamma, who was doing a brisk business selling her specialty peanut butter made with marshmallow creme.

Gloria leaned down to coo at the identical twin boys in their double stroller. She touched the babies' dimpled chins. "Aren't they sweet?" she said, looking up at Leona, her eyes sparkling.

Leona agreed, her mind still lost in what-ifs.

She remembered how she and Gloria used to talk about having lots of children. Did Gloria still want a large family? And if so, did Darren have any idea?

Later, after buying hot dogs wrapped in soft pretzels at the market deli, as well as delectable chocolate whoopie pies, they drove back to the house. It was Leona's idea to walk out to the clearing together, enjoying the clement breezes and the many birds flying about. She took pleasure in the thought that her future home with Tom Ebersol would be situated just beyond this knoll of woods.

She took Gloria exploring, the two of them talking all the while, enjoying how far they'd come in reestablishing their friendship. "It's been so much fun havin' ya here, Gloria, a little like revisiting my childhood."

"I know what you mean."

Leona picked a flower. "It also reminded me of my old secret wish . . . seems so silly now."

Gloria laughed. "What *was* it?"

"You never suspected?" Leona held her breath a moment. "I was sure I was born into the wrong family." She paused. "I wanted to belong to yours."

Gloria's mouth gaped. "You're kidding."

"*Nee*, 'tis true. Well, it was then."

Shaking her head slowly, Gloria finally

spoke. "I felt that way, too, at times, growing up. I wanted to be your honest-to-goodness sister, I guess. Your mom is always so sincere."

They laughed together, dismissing it as a phase most youngsters almost certainly went through. But deep in Leona's heart, a piece of that wish was still very much alive.

After evening devotions, Leona found Gloria sitting on the bed reading the book Orchard John had given her. Near the dresser, her suitcase was packed and ready to zip shut. She had told Leona earlier that she'd called Hampton to say how grateful she was for the extra time off, and that she planned to arrive home sometime late Monday, after spending the night somewhere Sunday night. "I hope to be back at work in time for the Tuesday evening shift."

Leona nodded. "I'll be praying for ya."

"Thank you," Gloria said, glancing up at her. "After reading this book, I feel like the thirsty deer mentioned in the Forty-Second Psalm. I just want to know what God has in store for me—not just for the trip, but for afterward, too. Do you ever feel that way?"

*Wonderful,* Leona thought, nodding. *Keep your heart wide open, dear friend.*

Gloria awakened Sunday morning to a powerful sun and a sapphire sky, anxious to get ready for her first Preaching service in years. She leaped out of bed like a calf out of the chute at Arkansas' Fulton County Fair Rodeo, knowing she would need extra time with her unruly hair.

The house was still, at least for now. Pete had surely gone out to the barn already, and Millie was most likely washing up and getting dressed before the breakfast of cold cereal, toast, and coffee. Thinking she ought to wet her hair down before trying to style it, Gloria hurried downstairs in her bathrobe and slippers. After dousing her head in the bathroom sink, she wrapped her thick hair in a towel and went back upstairs.

As she towel dried her hair, Gloria caught herself praying for the courage to do what she felt she must this afternoon when she visited the deacon. *I'll ask Pete if he can take me.* She slipped into Leona's plum-colored dress, making sure to pin all seventeen straight pins in the correct spots—quite an accomplishment.

When she finished, she took time to admire her handiwork in the mirror . . . until it dawned on her how prideful this was. Moving away to the window, she looked over the fields to the north, where Sol Speicher's orchards were in full bloom.

*Help me know Your will . . . guide me, lead me, O Lord,* she prayed for the first time since arriving in Colerain.

earing the navy blue head scarf, Gloria stood on tiptoes at the end of the line of women outside the farmhouse, the temporary house of worship for this Lord's Day. Up ahead, she could see Leona with other women near her age, some married, some even considered *Maidels* by now. Maggie and Millie Speicher were farther back, with the other married women. Gloria had spotted Maggie when they first arrived, her two young daughters at her side, pretty as could be, dressed in matching pale rose-colored dresses and white organdy pinafore-style aprons.

Gloria was struck by the lines divided by gender and age. It was something she'd taken for granted growing up, but now this ritual stood out as markedly as the holy hush that would eventually come over the congregation once they were settled inside, with the men's section facing the women's. All around her, children, young people, and adults wore their Sunday best—the men and boys in their traditional black with white long-sleeved shirts, and the women and girls primarily in the royal blue or the plum Leona had allowed Gloria to borrow today.

Very soon, she was seated with the other unbaptized young women in the back of the congregation. One of the men rose and called out a hymn number from the *Ausbund,* which Gloria held reverently on her lap. *The songs of the Anabaptist martyrs,* she thought. *My own ancestors.* Then the halting voice of the *Vorsinger* cut through the stillness as the appointed man led out with the first few notes before all the People joined in unison.

The congregational singing lasted nearly forty minutes, and once the ministers returned from their customary meeting, the *Abrot,* the first Scripture was read and the first sermon began, an introduction to the second, longer sermon to come. Gloria quickly realized how much she missed the well-padded pews of her church back home—the backless benches were uncomfortably hard, though she wouldn't think of admitting this to Leona or anyone else. It was just something the People had always endured.

One of the ministers read a verse from chapter nine of the Gospel of Luke, verse sixty-two. "'And Jesus said unto him, No man, having put his hand to the plow, and looking back, is fit for the kingdom of God.'"

The words of Christ were convicting, and she felt heartsick. *I haven't followed through, just like my parents,* she thought ruefully. *Each of us has abandoned the Plain life. But I can't keep blaming Dad for that.*

Just in front of her, two teenage girls were passing notes between them, stealing occasional glances.

*Must be something about a boy,* she guessed, wondering if Leona would go to Singing tonight. Of course Gloria would be well on her way home by then. She hadn't decided where she'd spend the night, but she wouldn't push it as hard as she had coming back here, that was certain.

Momentarily, she let herself imagine what might happen if she did stay to attend the Singing. If Orchard John was there, friendly as he was, he might ask her how far she'd read in *Rules of a Godly Life.* Truth be told, she'd felt too miserable to read any further this morning. The devotional readings last night had caused her to cry herself to sleep.

Straining to see her friend, Gloria wished she were up there sitting with Leona. Tears welled up, and she quickly brushed them away. What would the young people there in the last few rows think of her weeping, of all things?

Following the end of the first sermon, the People turned to kneel at the benches where they'd sat. Gloria wished she had a tissue handy, and she dabbed at her nose with the back of her hand till she could reach for her purse.

There, during the silent kneeling prayer, in the quiet depths of her heart, where the seeds of God's Word had long ago been planted, she believed she knew the answer to her deepest yearnings. It was the thing she'd longed for on some level ever since blindly following her parents out of the Hill View Amish church district. But how would she be received by the deacon on the matter? Her father's transgressions clouded her thoughts.

*Deacon Ebersol will be surprised—and, hopefully, pleased—this afternoon,* she thought, eager to set forth her plan.

Gloria breathed a silent prayer as the benediction was offered, then filed out of the service with the other unbaptized youth to wait for the fellowship meal. Leona had been scheduled to help her mother and Aunt Salome on the kitchen committee, so Gloria went to stand alone beneath one of the shade trees, not fitting in with the other young women her age. Several of them had looked twice at her, but it didn't bother Gloria. *The Lord sees my heart.*

Unexpectedly, she noticed Orchard John clear over on the side porch by himself, even though all the other young men his age were congregating near the stable, not far from the galvanized watering tub for the horses. If she wasn't mistaken, he'd seen her, as well, and he bobbed his head toward the road each time he caught her eye.

*Surely not,* she thought but walked over there anyway, going around the side lawn. He walked along the wraparound porch to meet her, then hurried down the front steps.

"Ain't easy to get your attention," he said, falling into step with her. He looked handsome in his black *Mutze* coat and vest.

"We'll be seen together, John. Not such a good idea for you."

He motioned for them to slip out to the road at the end of the sweeping front lawn, out of sight.

"I hoped we might talk again," he said,

smiling at her. "You look mighty Plain today, Gloria. Real nice."

"*Denki,*" she said. "The dress is Leona's."

"And your hair's up, too."

"A challenge, let me tell you."

"You're not the only young woman who's left the Amish, chopped off her hair, and returned."

She looked at him, striking as he was. Should she tell him what she'd experienced during the kneeling prayer—that the minister's sermon had spoken powerfully to her?

His face beamed. "Gloria, I felt a sense of rightness, seein' ya at Preaching. I was real pleased to see ya there. Just wanted you to know."

From the corner of her eye, she spotted Pete Speicher's profile where he was standing behind the house, his straw hat shading his head from the sun. "*Ach,* if we're seen, you'll be in trouble."

"Well, I don't want that. Really just wanted to see you, Gloria . . . to let you know that I think ya really belong here." Then, turning, he said, "I'll go around the side of the house, an' you take the driveway."

She nodded, breathing easier now as she watched him go. But she couldn't help feeling somehow elated that he'd sought her out despite the risk.

Leona gasped when she saw Gloria in her head scarf walking with Orchard John.

"For mercy's sake!" Leona made a dash down the driveway just as Orchard John slipped away and as Gloria switched directions to return this way. Leona noticed Gloria's flushed face and reached for her hand. "You surely have *some* idea of what jeopardy you just put my cousin in," she said as they made their way back to the house.

Gloria inhaled as if out of breath. "I told him that, too. But it was his idea to talk to me. We weren't together long."

"Even so," Leona said softly.

"I hope your father's willing to go with me this afternoon to visit the deacon. There's something I must do before I leave."

"Shouldn't be a problem . . . if Dat can stay awake after the noon meal, that is." Feeling less apprehensive now, Leona laughed a little, ever so curious what Gloria had in mind.

---

"You look downright *ferhoodled*," Tom told Orchard John when he came walking toward the stable.

"*Ach*, I think Cousin Leona spotted me with Gloria," John said, circling back around the barn with him.

"Gloria?" Tom looked over his shoulder

to see Leona and Gloria coming around the opposite side of the house, holding hands.

"I told her how pleased I was to see her in church." John couldn't hide the broad grin that crept across his face.

"You can't let your heart run too far in her direction—she ain't Amish anymore," Tom said, perplexed.

"But I have a strong feelin' she might be inchin' back. . . ."

"Wait, then," Tom cautioned. "Wait till she's safely baptized and solidly in the church."

"*Jah,*" John agreed, but his mind seemed miles away.

Tom moved toward the horses, finding his father's mare and offering a sugar cube from his pocket.

He glanced over beyond the thicket, where Leona and Gloria were still talking rather solemnly near the back porch. He wondered if Orchard John was right about Gloria inching toward the People, if that's what he meant. If so, was it just his heart talking?

## CHAPTER 39

Gloria sat with Leona in the second seat of the family carriage on the ride home, reliving her time with Orchard John after church while they'd walked along the road. She hadn't felt as guilty as she had at the coffee shop, and it surprised her.

Something was changing in her. Was it that tug, that drawing, she'd felt while kneeling at the bench during prayer time?

Now she just had to talk through the things on her mind with the deacon, difficult as it would be. *What will he say?*

On the ride back to the Speichers' farm, she wanted to test the waters with Leona's family. It wasn't her intent to get anyone's hopes up, especially Leona's. After all, there were many hurdles to overcome, namely Gloria's acceptability to the deacon and all the other ministerial brethren.

*And the People themselves . . .*

She sighed. There was something else that continued to nag her, something that could derail everything.

Nevertheless, she wanted Leona and her family to know what she was thinking. Gloria swallowed nervously before voicing it. "I was wondering if you might be willing to take me to see the deacon today, Pete." At his ready nod, she continued. "I'm ready to speak to him about something."

Leona turned toward her, eyes wide with hope.

Gloria's throat suddenly felt dry. *Have I opened a can of worms?* "It's about whether or not I might be able to join church . . . this fall, or even at some later point. That is, if I can pass the requirements."

"Praise be!" Leona reached to hug her.

Benuel responded next. "I wondered if you were getting close to this decision."

"Talking with you and Orchard John definitely helped me sort through some important things," Gloria admitted. "*Denki* for that."

Millie spoke quietly. "You'll be welcome in our home, when you're ready to move your things back." She glanced at Pete, who nodded in agreement.

"But only till wedding season, I daresay," Leona whispered, grinning at her.

"*Ach*, I can't possibly know that yet," Gloria said, uneasy now. "I also have certain things to take care of in Arkansas." She wondered if Pete was surprised at Millie's swift offer of a place to stay. *Not rent free, though,* she thought. *I'd pay my fair share, like at home, as soon as I can find a job.*

Pete was quiet on the topic, although later, as they approached the turn into the driveway, he asked Gloria when she wanted to leave for the deacon's.

"As soon as it suits you," she said, and when Leona said she could handle the chores so he could take Gloria right away, she felt another wave of nerves.

The sunny afternoon was near perfect, a light breeze bringing with it the sound of crickets and cows mooing in the pastureland beyond the road and the rustling of leaves in the trees near the horse fence. The field grasses had inched ever higher since Gloria's arrival a week ago, and it looked like the first cutting of hay was only three or four weeks out. All this and more Gloria noticed as she rode with Pete across the creek and up past her former house to Deacon Ebersol's farm.

Leona's father said precious little as Gloria clutched her purse and embraced the landscape with her gaze, but she found Pete's quiet strength encouraging.

When they arrived, Pete took the lead, escorting her to the deacon's back door, where, together, they waited.

Deacon Ebersol came to the door still wearing his church clothes.

"Hullo, Mose," Pete said. "Gloria here wants a word with ya, if it's no trouble. I'll wait in the buggy."

The kind-faced deacon stepped out to join her on the porch, where they went to sit in hickory rockers just like her own father had made.

Sallie Ebersol came outside almost immediately and offered Gloria a tumbler of homemade root beer.

"*Denki*, but I'm fine."

"I'll have some," the deacon said, waiting for his wife to bring the tumbler to him before saying more. He took a long drink, then wiped his mouth on the back of his hand. "Now, how can I help ya, Gloria?"

He seemed as friendly as she'd remembered, and his calm demeanor gave her a semblance of confidence. "I'd like to take baptismal instruction here this summer . . . if you agree," she began, making herself slow down a bit. "I've been attending a church out in Arkansas, but of course it isn't Amish . . . and my heart is still Plain. What would you want me to do, in order to join church here?"

"Well, this is a surprising turn. Is your family aware of it?"

"Not just yet." The air stuck in her throat.

"I see." He leaned forward. "This must be a recent decision, then."

She shared with him how, even prior to visiting this week and spending time with Leona and others, she'd felt torn about the direction of her life. And now, being here had filled her with a longing to return and make this her home.

"That's all well and *gut*," he said quietly. "The Lord does work in mysterious ways—often different for each of us." Then he inquired about the *Ordnung* of her parents' former community in Arkansas.

"I did get an opportunity to take a few baptismal classes there, but that church district wasn't as traditional or as strict as yours."

"Are you willing to have sessions here with the bishop and the other ministers to prayerfully study the eighteen articles of the Dordrecht Confession of Faith?"

She said she was.

Deacon drew in a breath, his nose making a whistling sound. "I must ask—would you still want to be baptized and join this church fellowship if there were no eligible young men your age?"

His serious gaze met hers, and she realized he'd surely heard the gossip. Most likely, she and Orchard John had been seen together.

She paused for only a short moment. "I believe so."

There was a glimmer of something in the deacon's eyes; he wasn't entirely pleased with her answer. "And if there is such a young man, are you willing to wait till you're a church member to be courted?"

She considered how hard that might prove to be if Orchard John pursued her once she'd broken things off with Darren back home. "Would I be permitted to spend time with someone as a friend, if there *was* such a young man?" She tried not to smile.

"Only in the company of other baptized members."

She had assumed this and felt it was not only fair but for the best. "And will I have a Proving time, following my move back here?"

Suddenly, Deacon Ebersol looked puzzled. "I'll discuss this with the other ministers, considering you were brought up Amish." He looked at her, his brows pushed into nearly one long bushy line above his gentle blue eyes.

"I'll do whatever it takes."

Smiling now, he nodded his head slowly. "Your attitude is one of sincerity, Gloria—a true sign of a humble baptismal candidate."

She didn't thank him, thinking it wouldn't be right.

They talked further about her visit here and what had prompted it. "I've heard you're havin' *gut* fellowship with Leona Speicher."

Gloria smiled. "She's my closest friend."

The deacon leaned forward. "If she wasn't such a dear friend, would we be having this discussion, Gloria?"

Her smile left her face. Goodness, she hadn't been prepared for *this* question. "You mean—"

"Would you be asking 'bout joining church if not for Leona?"

Gloria hesitated. *Probably not,* she thought, unable to think of an acceptable answer, her heart sinking.

The deacon continued. "Also, you said your parents don't know of your hope to be baptized. How do you think they'll respond?"

Gloria bit her lip. "My plan to move here will surely be met with disapproval. Mainly from my father."

"I remember Joe," Deacon Ebersol replied,

his expression concerned. "Are you afraid to tell him?"

She confessed she was, remembering his fierce opposition to her trip here with Leona.

"Why might that be?"

Surprised he would ask, considering he himself had been terribly wronged by her father, she didn't know how to answer. Even though he had every right to, Deacon Ebersol had never pressed charges, instead being patient with her father, never trying to track him down for what he owed.

*Yet here I sit on his porch, a prodigal's daughter, asking to be welcomed back with open arms,* she thought. *What am I thinking?*

Her hands felt warm and clammy. "Our family's no longer Amish, for one thing," she said at last.

Before he could reply, she added, "Excuse me a moment," and reached for her purse. Opening it, she removed the envelope she'd prepared earlier and handed it to him. "I want you to have this."

He frowned, then opened the envelope and removed the check she'd written for partial repayment of her father's debt. Staring at it, his mouth fell open. "What's this?"

Gloria explained and apologized for not offering it sooner.

"From your father, is it?"

She said it was from the tip money she'd saved. "I'm a waitress."

He nodded. "This is mighty generous." He looked again at the check. "However, I cannot accept it."

She was stunned. "I . . . I don't under-stand—"

"Your father's debt is not yours to repay." His eyes were kind as he returned the check for four thousand dollars. "I appreciate your heart in this, Gloria . . . truly, I do."

"But . . ." Gloria stumbled for the right words. "How could I possibly return to live here amongst the People unless I—"

"Gloria," he said, "have ya lived in fear of being judged by others because of your father's indiscretions?"

"How can I *not*?"

His eyes shone with compassion. "I forgave your father long ago for that debt."

Gloria was speechless. "Even so, I don't know how I could hold my head up, unless . . ."

"Perhaps you've forgotten that grace cannot be bought," he said. "It's a *gift*, free for the taking." He smiled. "I do appreciate your willingness to do this. But according to Scripture, the Lord does not delight in sacrifices. He desires a broken spirit . . . and a contrite heart. He will not turn us away." Gloria swallowed as she took this in.

"Do ya still carry bitterness toward your father?"

Slowly, she nodded.

Deacon was quiet again, his eyes squinting. Then he asked, "Have you considered letting go of that burden . . . that resentment?"

"The thought of forgiving my father is next to impossible." Gloria raised her chin to look directly into his ruddy face. "I've felt so ashamed and still do . . . for all those he hurt financially and otherwise." She breathed in the fresh afternoon air. "You see, Deacon, I don't deserve to be treated benevolently here, yet I've been shown nothing but kindness by Leona and her dear parents." She paused. "And now by you."

His face radiated understanding, but what he said next cut her to the quick. "Alas, Gloria, you're not ready to make a decision for the Amish church. You haven't counted the cost." He tugged on his beard. "I believe you're attempting to find some redemption for your father's misdeeds . . . and I doubt you'd be thinkin' of returning if not for Leona. Neither is a sound enough reason to embrace the Plain ways."

She nodded and bowed her head, struggling with the weight of disappointment.

"Most important, are you determined to

follow the Lord God and His ways with a pure and single-minded heart?"

She raised her eyes to meet his. "I want to."

"Wanting and doing are very different." His mouth turned up slightly, then drooped. "Are ya able to stand up to your father's opposition, if it comes to that?"

She did not want to think how that dreadful scene might play out. After a moment, she said, "I'll need all the strength I can gather."

"When we're most weak, *Gott* is strong. None of us can do the hard things on our own."

*Deacon knows my father all too well.*

"Give this some further thought . . . and prayer." He added, "I'll be here, if and when you wish to proceed."

*How can my answers ever ring true for him?* Instead of the relief she'd hoped for from this meeting, she felt crushed in spirit.

"May our heavenly Father go with you, Gloria Gingerich."

"And with you."

When she returned to the carriage, she found Pete dozing, his chin resting on his chest.

*Poor, dear man,* she thought. *This is a day of rest, after all.*

Pete opened his eyes and seemed to read her expression as he straightened and reached for the driving lines.

Tears slid down her cheeks as they rode back toward the house. She understood the reasons for the deacon's hesitation, yet his undeserved act of mercy in refusing her check made her want to join his congregation all the more. Indeed, she felt overwhelmed by Deacon Ebersol's kindness and wisdom.

*But he's right,* she thought. *I haven't counted the cost.*

<hr>

When Pete turned into the driveway, Gloria's eye caught her car parked out behind Benuel's *Dawdi Haus*. It looked exceptionally shiny in the sunlight, perhaps more appealing than ever before.

*Am I really ready to give it up?*

She thanked Leona's father for taking her and offered to help him unhitch, but he waved her on, secure in his own quiet world.

Looking across the serene meadow, she longed to walk barefoot through the long grass, picking wild flowers come summer. Truth-fully, she felt more conflicted now than before she'd left Arkansas. "Help me, O Lord," she whispered heavenward.

She turned to walk back toward the house, still glancing in the direction of the fields and the woods when she heard someone call her name. The intensity, the firmness—

Turning in the direction of the voice, Gloria saw her father sitting on the back stoop in blue jeans and a red T-shirt, as stern faced as she'd ever seen him. "Gloria!" he shouted again.

She felt her breath fade.

*What's* he *doing here?*

## CHAPTER 40

*L*ooks like I got here in the nick of time, considering you're already dressing Plain." Her father rose from the steps as Gloria drew near. "You must have turned off your phone, too." He shook his head. "How's a man supposed to keep in touch with his daughter?"

She took a step backward, suddenly feeling weak. "You came all this way just to talk to me?"

"It's been a long day . . . I took a cab from the airport," he said tersely. "Time to come home, young lady. Your mother and I—"

"Joe?" Pete said behind her, shouldering his way toward him.

Her father mechanically shot out his hand. "Hello again, Pete Speicher."

"It's been a while," Pete said.

Her father nodded, looking less harsh now. "Listen, Pete, I'm here for one purpose alone, and that's to take my daughter home."

Pete turned to Gloria. "What have you decided? Have you changed your mind?"

Gloria remembered the deacon's words and shivered as she observed Leona and her mother standing at the screen door, arms folded. *Waiting for me to respond.*

"Hampton's shorthanded," Joe said, quieter now, but the underlying tone was just as firm. "You'll lose your job if you lollygag any longer."

Pete was still gazing at her—*everyone* was waiting for her to speak. "You're welcome to stay, Gloria," Pete offered.

At last, she found her voice. "I'm already packed, since I'd planned to leave today."

"How was I supposed to know?" Joe shook his head in disgust. "You didn't text me back."

"I'm sorry for this inconvenience, Dad," she said. "We can drive back together."

Glancing at Pete, she forced a smile and walked up the steps toward Leona, who slipped inside with her.

In the kitchen, Leona touched her arm.

"I wish we didn't have to say good-bye. Not like this."

Gloria gave her a hug, then quickly related what the deacon had said. "He doesn't think I'm ready to commit to being Amish." *My motives aren't right. . . .*

"How can that be?" Leona groaned.

"I'll write more about it, okay?"

Leona blinked back tears and nodded sweetly. "You promise?"

"No more silences from me," Gloria reassured her. "I'll write as soon as I return home."

Upstairs, she changed clothes and picked up her suitcase and left Orchard John's book behind, along with Leona's plum church dress and head scarf. Then, taking a last look around the room, she tried to soothe herself.

*No one can take away the new memories I made while here.*

At the back door, Gloria thanked Millie for being such a loving "second mother," showering gratitude on the entire family, including Pete, who stood by offering a compassionate smile. "I have never felt so cared for in all my life," she said, tears threatening.

Openly crying, Leona went to hug Gloria one last time.

Without delay, Pete suggested they bow their heads in thankfulness, and while they stood there, united in prayer, Gloria felt renewed peace in spite of the distressing confrontation—all of this while her father stood outside the window, hands thrust in his pockets, impatiently waiting for her.

When Pete whispered amen, Gloria stepped into the screened-in porch and clicked her key for the trunk. She reached for her luggage and headed out.

Her father held out his hand for her bag and placed it in the trunk while Gloria turned and waved again. Dear Leona waved back, sandwiched there between her parents. "I love you," Gloria called and patted her heart.

Leona looked like she might cry again.

"I'll drive, Dad," Gloria said, heading for the car.

Her father shrugged and went around to the passenger side.

Behind the wheel, Gloria suddenly felt uneasy as her father snapped on his seat belt. Creeping toward the main road, she couldn't bring herself to look back at Leona and her truly caring family.

---

Tom enjoyed the late-afternoon weather, warmer now that the breeze had died down somewhat as clouds covered the sun. Dragonflies would be hovering over the surface of

Little Beaver Creek right about now, attracting brown and rainbow trout. If only he were out fishing on such a day, he thought, taking the shortcut to Pete Speicher's place by way of the main road.

Here lately, it was harder to go indoors before the first bats flew, so unforgettable this springtime weather had been. The season had never seemed more alive to him.

He rounded the bend and blinked twice as he laid eyes on none other than Gloria Gingerich driving toward him in her car—then he spotted Joe in the passenger seat.

Confused, Tom hurried his steps toward the Speichers'. He knew of Gloria's plans to return home today. *But what's Arkansas Joe doing here?*

⌘

Brownie wagged his tail as Tom walked up the back stoop. "Hey, boy," he murmured, bending low to pet him.

Tom knocked on the back door, noticing Millie's vegetable garden over yonder. The asparagus was at least four feet high and all ferned out. He imagined Leona and Millie working side by side in the plot, weeding and hoeing together. Then, thinking ahead to his future with Leona, he pictured her planting and tending a family garden with their own daughters someday.

Leona appeared at the door, her face pink. "There was a confrontation," she told him. "Arkansas Joe was here and insisted Gloria return home with him at once."

"I saw them drivin' away and wondered what was up."

Leona grimaced. "It wasn't supposed to be like this." Her eyes moistened.

Tom held the screen door and led her out to the screened-in porch, where Leona sat down. She began to tell him of Gloria's desire to be baptized.

"Really?" Tom whistled. "*Wunnerbaar-gut, jah?*"

Leona shook her head. "I thought so, too . . . but something went wrong."

"I don't understand."

"I'll tell ya all that I know." Leona sniffled as she described the situation to the best of her ability. "Gloria hasn't told me everything yet. Says she'll write more."

"Are you sayin' she's unprepared to be Amish?"

"Right, but she never explained why."

Tom let it sink in. *It's not like my father to discourage a baptismal candidate. I wonder what's up.*

He could see the disappointment in

Leona's eyes, and his heart was soft toward her. He reached for her and held her near. "Your faith and patience are a testament to us all, my darling."

"Honestly, I don't *feel* very patient," Leona said glumly. Then she mentioned that she likely wouldn't be at the Singing tonight. "It's been such a frustrating day. You understand, *jah*?"

It was clear she needed some time to recover. "I'll leave ya be, then. But the reason I dropped by was to see if next Tuesday morning might be a *gut* day to show you the land my father's giving us."

This brought a light to her eyes. "I'd love to, Tom. And I'm sorry I haven't had time to review the blueprints yet."

"Are ya sure you're all right?"

"It's the Lord's mercy that you happened by just as Gloria left." She had a distant look in her eyes. "Gloria's come so far."

"Well, don't give up hope." He leaned near to kiss her cheek.

She smiled up at him.

"I'll meet you in the clearing, and we'll walk over from there. How's that?"

She gave a quick nod of her pretty head and followed him out to the stoop.

Tom made a beeline for the field and cut across. When he'd passed the stable, he glanced back and saw Leona was still standing there. He waved, his heart breaking for his sweetheart.

He pondered the day's strange happenings as he walked. How could it be that Gloria had *actually* decided to join church, but his father had turned her away? And, of all things, Arkansas Joe had appeared out of nowhere.

*Even so,* Tom thought, *Thy will be done, O Lord.*

## CHAPTER 41

Gloria drove past Sol Speicher's orchard on the way out of town and recalled Orchard John's thoughtful gift. *Leona will know to return the book. . . .*

Her father's voice jolted her. "Once we're home again, your head will clear."

Even so, the deacon's words echoed in her mind. *"You haven't counted the cost."*

New tears welled up, and she wiped her face on her arm, drawing the attention of her father.

"Gloria, surely you know why I showed up."

"Out of concern," she replied, knowing what was expected. "Why else would you travel so far?"

He was silent for a moment. Then he said more gently, "Your mother and I love you, Gloria. You can't question that."

"Well, you have a strange way of showing it."

He frowned. "Caring fathers rescue their daughters."

*No, you're overbearing.* She tried to pinpoint exactly when things had soured between them. Had it been the day he refused to let her stay in Colerain?

Gloria looked over at him accessing Map-Quest on his phone. *There was a time when I admired him.*

He glanced at her, and their eyes locked for a moment.

"Dad, do you remember when I was little, and we used to go on sleigh rides, just you and me? You'd let me sit on your lap and hold the reins. I was so scared the first time. But soon, I was laughing, because I was convinced I had the strongest and most fun-loving Daed ever."

He turned back to his phone again, saying nothing.

"And our summertime walks near the creek . . . remember those? You recognized all the wild flowers by their color and shape . . . you taught me their names."

"We were *Amish* then." He harrumphed. "I'm glad that's all behind us."

"But those are special memories to me," she insisted. "Honestly, they were the best days of my life. We were close then, Dad."

"No one in their right mind returns to a backward way of life after experiencin' the *real* world," he said. "It's ridiculous to think otherwise."

"But, Dad—"

"Don't waste your time reliving the past."

She stared at the road. "There *was* a time . . ." she murmured.

They sped by the farm landscape, neither of them speaking.

*The countryside of my childhood . . .*

Her father's voice sounded husky when he finally said, "Don't worry; I haven't forgotten all of it." He fidgeted a bit. "You once said I was the best father in the whole world."

"I meant it," she whispered, turning south toward Route 222. "But do you also remember the day I announced that I'd made a new friend . . . my first-ever *bescht* friend?"

He sighed loudly, as though suddenly disinterested.

"It was because of your decision to move us from Salem, Arkansas, when I was in sixth grade. *You* made that happen, Dad."

"Listen." His tone was softer now, less obstinate. "I want you to have a secure life, which is why Darren's so ideal for you. He can offer you what I could never give your mother monetarily."

*But I don't love him,* she thought, comparing Darren to Orchard John even now as she was leaving it all behind.

She felt the old anger rising within her, the feeling of being trapped and held against her will.

*"Have you considered letting go of that burden . . . that resentment?"* the deacon had asked so firmly, yet compassionately. *The burden of bitterness toward Dad.*

*Was Deacon Ebersol testing me? All those questions . . .*

He had also asked if she was ready to stand up to her father.

*Apparently not,* she thought, and yet she now understood the deacon's point . . . that her life decisions belonged to her. Her alone. *Becoming Amish is my choice to make,* she thought. *Not my father's, nor my mother's.*

And it was in that moment, something quickened in her. She glimpsed her father and remembered how she'd felt, only hours earlier at Preaching, overwhelming love . . . and a sense of conviction.

With a full heart, she forged ahead. "I realized today that I've been holding a grudge toward you," she admitted.

He actually chuckled. "I doubt you're the only one."

"Dad . . . I forgive you for trying to take me away from the People of Colerain again."

He frowned as if startled.

"And for moving us away three and a half years ago, when I was too young to say otherwise. I'm sorry I wasn't honest about this before, but now it's time I let go of the bitterness."

Her father took a sharp breath and crossed his arms, seemingly disoriented by her frankness. At last, he muttered, "I guess I never realized how much the Plain life meant to you."

"You didn't know how much it meant, because *I* didn't. Not until now."

He shifted and turned to look out the window.

The week with Leona and her family had been so eye-opening—the cheerful hours continued to parade through Gloria's mind. But reconnecting with Leona rose above all the warm memories.

*I was that close to starting something new. Will I always miss the People there?* She thought again of Orchard John, whom she'd left for a second time without even a fond farewell. *And I forgot to say good-bye to Leona's Dawdi Benuel, too.*

Her father was still staring out the window

when he spoke again. "Gloria, you're my only daughter."

She glanced at him, waiting, a lump in her throat. "What is it, Dad?"

He inhaled deeply and gradually released it, his manner tentative. "All those memories you talked about—sure, I remember you meeting little Leona that first day of school. It was around the time I also remember thinking, *My daughter's growing up so fast, I can't keep up. . . .*"

Gloria's eyes were suddenly teary.

"And three years ago, when you wanted to stay . . ." He paused. "I just couldn't imagine . . ." He hesitated, seemingly unable to continue.

"Dad?"

He slapped his leg, as if prodding himself forward or terribly frustrated. "It's just that I couldn't bear the thought of losing my little girl."

She smiled through her tears and reached to touch his arm. "That's not possible, Dad. No matter what."

He clasped her hand, and in that instant, all the years of conflict melted away.

❧

Leona was busy making tuna salad sandwiches later when her mother came down looking quite refreshed, like she'd had at least forty winks. She ambled to the table and sat in her regular spot, fanning herself. "Such a time earlier."

Leona carried over a glass of cold water and set it down in front of her, then sat down to have a sip. "*Denki* for sticking up for Gloria today."

Her mother pulled a face as if to say, *"'Twas nothing, really."*

"And thank you for offering her a place to stay during her Proving, too."

Again, the same face, only with a hint of a smile. Her dear mother was a woman of few words, but it no longer bothered Leona. She remembered her conversations with Gloria. *"Your mother is always so sincere."*

Mamma's eyes were serious as she peered over her glass. "I daresay she needed a family like ours, ain't so?"

Leona nodded. "And so do I."

Her mother's expression was ever so tender.

Leona rose to finish the sandwiches, but Mamma asked her to sit a bit longer.

"*Jah?*" Leona said, lowering herself back down.

Mamma looked into her glass and swirled the water, then met Leona's gaze. "There were occasions when Arkansas Joe and Jeannie lived neighbors to us that I thought you preferred them to your father and me. I knew I couldn't measure up to lively Jeannie. . . . Who could? Guess I thought you'd found what you needed in them." She paused a moment. "It prob'ly sounds odd, but after they left, I believed you might be pining for Jeannie as much as for Gloria."

*I was,* Leona thought sadly. *Till my time in Hill View set me straight.*

Mamma continued. "I even let my imagination run wild, thinkin' that you were angry for not having siblings close to your age. You were so lonely—basically an only child."

"*Nee* . . . not angry, Mamma. *Neimols.*"

"Alas, I should've told you sooner." Her mother paused. "Well . . ." She stopped again, obviously struggling.

"What are you tryin' to say?"

"You couldn't possibly have known, Leona, but—"

"It's all right." She reached out her hand. "Please, tell me."

Her mother breathed a great sigh. "I suffered three miscarriages after you were born. The doctor cautioned me not to have more children. It was partly my age."

"Oh, Mamma." Her heart ached. "I'm grateful for *this* family, the family *God* gave me." Leona paused as she sat there remembering having watched her mother mix dough so carefully and cheerfully, not the way Jeannie always tossed ingredients about, in such a big rush to finish.

It was a crazy thought, but she had to share it. "Did ya know that Jeannie Gingerich hated makin' bread?"

Their eyes met, and her mother tittered unexpectedly. "I suspected there were things that she chafed against." Mamma set her glass down. "Some folk, born Plain or not, resist being fully Amish. And no matter how hard they try, it doesn't seem to take for them. That's why there are always a few young folk who don't choose to be baptized and make Plainness their way of life . . . and faith."

"Deacon Ebersol mentioned to Gloria the importance of commitment . . . and I encouraged her to think on that very thing here lately."

"There's no better wisdom than that." Mamma's eyes shimmered with tears.

*I've observed kindness and mercy in Dat and Mamma all my life,* Leona thought, *but somehow, I missed it till now.*

※

Later, after Leona helped her father in the barn, grooming their driving horse, she strolled back toward the house. Brownie was waiting for her, whining on the back stoop.

"What's a-matter?" She sat beside him on the step. "You hankerin' for something?" She nuzzled him, then got up and called him into the porch. Going to the pantry, she opened the lid on the plastic bin of doggie treats and gave him two. "There, now. That should make ya feel better."

He thumped his tail appreciatively. "If only a simple treat would help me," she said, thinking of Gloria.

When her father came in, they all sat at the table, where Mamma had slices of snitz pie on small plates for each of them, leftovers from the common meal. Prior to partaking of the pie, Dat opened his big German *Biewel* for evening devotions.

"S'pose Gloria and Joe will take turns drivin'," Leona said, a lump in her throat. "Sure hope they'll stay the night somewhere to rest."

Mamma folded her hands on the table while Dat located the Scripture reading, and the three of them sat quietly, surrounded by the glow of the gas lamp overhead.

Her father broke the silence, reading an encouraging psalm. He repeated the final two verses, "'They that sow in tears shall reap in joy. He that goeth forth and weepeth, bearing precious seed, shall doubtless come again with rejoicing, bringing his sheaves with him.'"

Mamma nodded. "We daresn't give up on Gloria," she said softly before they bowed their heads together in prayer.

## CHAPTER 42

*F*reed from their stanchions, the host family's dairy cows moved through the grazing land opposite the large bank barn as Tom arrived at Singing to drop off his courting-age sisters. They seemed to know for certain they were getting rides home from each of their beaus, so he wasn't staying for long. *Just long enough . . .*

The sun cast extended shadows as he got out of his buggy. Even though the People did not revert to "fast time," as the English did, Tom loved the light at the end of the day.

After tying up his horse, he walked around the back of the barn to the grassy ramp and entered by way of the haymow. The wood floor had been swept clean for the large assembly tonight, and tables were set up in a straight line with benches on either side.

*Will Danny propose to his sweetheart tonight?* he wondered, observing his sisters milling about with Linda Miller and other young women their age. Tom waved to several of his male cousins, but it was Orchard John he was looking for.

When he spotted John, Tom hurried to relay the news that Gloria had left for home that afternoon as planned. He did not mention the fact that her father had shown up and caused some trouble at Pete and Millie's.

"So what do ya think will happen now?" John asked dolefully.

Tom shook his head. "Leona's awful disappointed."

"*Jah* . . . I can sympathize." John rubbed the back of his neck. He added that he'd come to Singing for the sake of fellowship. "Just don't want to be alone. Nothin' more."

"Well, do ya wanna stay or go an' get some coffee with me?"

John glanced over to where the young women were gathering. "Where's Leona? Is she too upset to sing tonight? Don't see her here."

"She's not comin'."

So John agreed to ride with him, since he'd come on foot. "*Denki* for the suggestion."

"Thought you might need a *gut* friend." Tom led the way out of the hayloft and down around to the carriage.

※

Sitting in her room, Leona stared out at the fading sky, thinking about the Singing, wishing she'd gone. She prayed softly, not the Amish rote prayers she had been taught, but as if God were her *friend.*

*I'm blessed with so much,* she realized anew. *I have my family and Tom and his family . . . and Gloria's ongoing friendship. I have a feeling we'll always be close from now on,* she thought, hoping.

There was a distant rustling in the driveway outside, and it wondered her, if only for a moment. She thought of the verses her father had chosen for the reading earlier, and she pondered the coming months, all of the preparations ahead with Tom. Oh, she must keep her mind on that, and she was looking forward to seeing the blueprints for the house—their eventual home.

*We have lots to do,* she thought, looking forward to making bed quilts and using all of her hope-chest items to help furnish the house Tom was so eager to build.

Going over to the spare room, she noticed a cluster of bills on the dresser with a note.

*Thanks for everything, Leona. Here's the money I promised to help with your trip out to Arkansas, remember? I also jotted down my mailing address so that you have that and my cell phone number. We can keep in touch either way, okay?*
                    *Your friend for always,*
                    *Gloria Gingerich*

Leona returned to her room and reached for her devotional book, *Streams in the Desert,* trying to set her mind on other things. She was thinking about getting ready for bed early tonight; it might do her good. That had always helped in the past when she was feeling blue.

As she opened her dresser drawer to get her nightgown, Leona detected the sound of the back door opening downstairs. *Maybe Dawdi Benuel wants a piece of pie,* she thought, smiling. And Mamma might want another piece, too. After all, it had been a difficult day all around—going from a rather miraculous sort of afternoon to this.

There were footsteps in the kitchen, and voices. She didn't try to listen, but someone had come quite late to visit.

Feeling fidgety herself, Leona left her room and headed for the opposite end of the hall to look out front, thinking she might spot a carriage, perhaps relatives dropping by for an after-supper dessert and some fellowship.

She wondered what Tom was doing tonight. Was he finishing up chores in the barn, talking with his deacon-father as he liked to do?

"Leona," she heard her mother calling from the foot of the stairs. "Someone's here for you."

"I'll be right there," she said, hurrying to her room to see if her hair was all *schtruwwlich,* which it was. She smoothed the loose ends and tucked them beneath her *Kapp,* which had also gone topsy-turvy. She straightened it, just in case it might be Tom checking up on her, kind as he was.

Then, mystified, Leona made her way downstairs.

Gloria was standing just inside the back door, her suitcase at her side. "Your Mamma says her offer still stands. Okay with you?"

"You're back?" Leona pressed her hands to her cheeks. "Oh, Gloria!"

Gloria patted herself all around. "Well, I'm not a ghost, if that's what you think."

"Oh you!" Leona went to her and hugged the stuffing out of her.

"I'm back to stay," Gloria said, reaching for her suitcase.

Leona was flabbergasted. Seeing her again after mere hours had stretched into what seemed like weeks, she was dying to ask what precipitated her return.

Leona waved her forward. "Come upstairs right quick and tell me everything."

"Well, let me start with my car—I handed over my keys to my father," Gloria said, following her upstairs to the spare room. "Once home, he'll sell it for me."

*An enormous step,* thought Leona, ever so grateful Gloria had stood up for herself. This was just unbelievable!

"Also, my dad felt bad about coming on so strong earlier, here with all of you," Gloria told her. "He wanted me to apologize."

Sitting on the bed, Leona listened as her friend recounted the miles she'd driven and the long talk she'd had with her father. Gloria had also called her mother to say she was putting everything on the line for what she wanted to do—what God was nudging her to do—for the rest of her life. "Mom's disappointed that I'm not coming home with Dad, but she seemed to understand when I shared my heart," Gloria said. "She'll ship the few personal items I requested." She glanced around the tidy room. "I won't clutter up your guestroom." Tears sprang to her eyes. "You and your family . . . I just don't know what I would've done without all of you. I wish I could explain how peaceful I feel now."

Leona was tempted to pinch herself. "I can only imagine, since you've made your choice."

Nodding, Gloria admitted, "It's strange, but I'm not even tense about calling Darren tomorrow." She shared that she disliked the idea of ending their relationship over the phone. "But I see no better option."

"Surely he won't make things difficult."

Gloria shrugged. "Either way, I'm settled on my course."

"I hope it's all right that I told Tom you'd left when he stopped by earlier. I thought you were gone for good, but he was happy to hear you'd spoken to his father today 'bout possibly joining church."

"Well, that's on hold for now," she said. "I just pray it'll be possible . . . someday. The biggest hurdle is to prove to the deacon that I'm here for the rest of my life . . . with the right motives."

"*Ach*, it's a dream come true for me." Leona smiled, amazed to think that Gloria had turned around and driven right back here.

"Dad and I stopped to have coffee in

Clayton, Maryland, and I kept mulling over what Deacon Ebersol had asked me: What would I do if my family objected? And you know what? That question actually gave me the courage to tell my dad that I really didn't want to go back to Arkansas. So I let him know that my heart is here, with you and the People."

"And Orchard John, too?"

Gloria dipped her head. "Once I'm baptized—if the ministers accept me—I'll know better about your cousin."

Leona reached to hug her and suppressed a little squeal. Oh, what a day this had turned out to be!

Following breakfast the next morning, Leona and her mother worked together to get the first load of laundry out on the line while Gloria went to the clearing to make her phone call to Darren Brockett. She'd called Hampton the evening before while having coffee with her father, so she guessed he would pave the way for her call to Darren today. Leona hoped the breakup wouldn't be too stressful for either of them.

Leona and Mamma headed for the house, setting down their wicker baskets to wait for the second big load. Mamma asked if she'd sit and have some iced tea with her, and Leona chose peppermint.

"I'll have the same." Mamma seemed to want to slow down the morning to put things into perspective, reciting the helpful psalm that Dat had read last night before Gloria's surprise return.

When Leona came to the table with the iced tea, Mamma smiled all of a sudden and said quietly, "That was quite something, you bringin' Gloria back to the fold, dear."

Leona drank in her words. "Truly, it was the Lord's doing," she said. "And it's kinda funny . . . because I thought bringing her home again was my dearest wish, Mamma." She stopped again, hoping her mother might fully understand what was in her heart. "But I was wrong."

"Oh?" Mamma's eyes probed hers, questioning.

Leona tried to keep her tears in check as a newfound understanding seemed to pass between them. "In many ways, it was Gloria who brought *me* back . . . to you, Mamma."

Her mother took a sip of tea, eyes glistening as she shyly averted them. "You couldn't have known it, Leona, but that was *my* dearest wish."

Leona's tears slipped down her cheeks. She felt ever so amazed . . . and blessed.

As planned, Leona met Tom after breakfast Tuesday morning. Their walk over to his father's land couldn't have been lovelier, and Tom seemed to especially enjoy holding her hand again, since they'd missed their usual date after the Sunday night Singing.

When Leona first laid eyes on the lot for their future home, she noticed the view they would have of the green hills in the distance, and her father's own woods . . . as well as Mose Ebersol's meadow, dotted with black-eyed Susans and hollyhocks.

"It's ever so perty," she said. "Tranquil, too."

They strolled along the border, still hand in hand, Leona ever so happy to be by Tom's side.

Later, in his mother's kitchen, Tom rolled out the blueprint, and together they decided on having four bedrooms on the second story and one large one on the main floor for guests. "That way, when we're too old to climb stairs," he joked, "we'll have a place to lay our heads."

Leona added her two cents as he'd requested, maintaining she wanted a kitchen similar in size to Ada Miller's. "And with custom-made cupboards, too," she hinted. "Is that possible?"

Not long ago, Mamma had asked for wedding gift ideas, and Leona had decided on a set of pretty dishes with a delicate rose-and-vine motif—service for twenty as a starter set. Someday, as their family grew, she would need more place settings.

"There's plenty of room for our children to play," Tom said when they returned outside to walk back toward the clearing.

"I trust we'll have lots of little boys and girls," she said, never wanting her children to feel as lonely as she had growing up.

Tom stopped walking, and in that very private haven, he cupped her face in his hands and kissed her on the lips for the first time. "I love ya, sweetheart, ever so much."

She could scarcely speak after the tender moment, and reaching up, she hugged his neck, yearning to be his bride.

CHAPTER 43

*G*loria was relieved when several boxes arrived from Arkansas. "Mom came through for me!" she said, getting a kick out of how thrilled Leona was to help find places for everything, saying she wanted Gloria to feel absolutely at home there.

Pete, too, seemed energized when he stumbled onto "a great deal" on a used hope chest, which he sanded down and redid for her in a light oak stain, making Gloria feel even more like part of the family.

And, just as Deacon Ebersol had aptly instructed, Gloria spent time praying that her reasons for joining church be right and pleasing in God's sight. Along with being asked to work for Ada Miller as a mother's helper now that school was out, Gloria busied herself in her free time, sewing dresses and aprons, too, working on her Amish wardrobe in hopes this church district would accept her once she had the courage to speak again to the deacon.

❦

June was cherry-picking time at Uncle Sol's orchard. Leona, Gloria, and Mamma worked closely together, enjoying the companionship all the more as each day passed. Sweet cherries were ripe now and ideal for jam making, and in another week or so, pie cherries would be ready to pick, as well. Leona's mouth watered at the thought of the delicious eating ahead, including the black raspberries coming in late June. By mid-July, juicy Redhaven peaches would be ready, and oh, the joy of canning and baking, especially with Gloria!

When the official start of summer came, Leona measured her days in chores and part-time work at Maggie's store. *Lots of work frolics ahead,* she thought, excited to attend them with Maggie, Mamma, and Aunt Salome, as she did each summer. But it was Gloria who brought that special spark to their gatherings.

At the shop, out of earshot of customers, Maggie occasionally made veiled remarks about Gloria's being in limbo. But one day

Maggie went so far as to ask if Gloria might not be someone Leona would like to have as a wedding attendant.

Leona was quiet as she pondered this. "I'd always thought she would be in my wedding, but that was back when she and I were teenagers. She's still not gone to see the deacon again, so I just don't know."

"You must have other girls in mind," Maggie said as she counted the coins in the register.

"Anna and Miriam, of course . . . Tom's courting-age sisters."

Maggie smiled, looking up. "I'd wondered if ya might not choose one or both of them, since you don't have sisters of your own."

"Well, if a bride could have a sister-in-law as an attendant, you'd definitely be one. I mean that, Maggie."

"Ain't you sweet!"

Leona went to the window to look out. "Between you and me, if Gloria was actually baptized this September, she would be eligible to be one of my attendants."

Maggie returned the change to the register drawer, the various coins clattering into their respective slots. "I guess you'll have to wait an' see, *jah?*"

"Maybe she just needs some encouragement," Leona said, thinking that perhaps she could put a bug in Tom's ear to have the deacon seek out Gloria. *Just maybe.*

⊰⊱

The following weekend, while Leona and Tom were dining out, he asked what she would think of having a double wedding with Danny and his fiancée, Linda Miller.

"They're engaged?"

Tom grinned. "They've kept it quiet, observing the Old Ways."

"Not like us." She smiled. "I think most folk know . . . or suspect, at least."

He winked at her, and she dipped her head, blushing.

Later, when their meals arrived, Leona asked who would sign for Danny during the wedding service. "Or will he read lips?"

"Maybe the bride'll sign," Tom said, chuckling. "If I know them, they'll figure something out. Linda's a creative one, that's for certain. Not sure just who's gonna wear the pants in that family."

"Well, bein' that she's related to the bishop . . . I see what you're sayin'."

They shared a discreet laugh, and Leona thought about Tom's suggestion. "I do like the idea of a double wedding. And if you and I are married a few minutes before Danny, he could still be your wedding attendant. What do ya think of that?"

"Now you're talkin'!" He reached across the table for her hand and held it for a moment.

Tom named off a few of the teenage fellows he'd considered to be in charge of the road horses the day of the wedding—their *Hostlers*. And then, pausing a moment, he said he'd like to ask Orchard John to be one of his two male attendants. "Would that bother ya?"

"John's my cousin—it's perfectly fine."

Nothing was said about Orchard John's impatience to start spending time with Gloria, once she got things squared away with the deacon. Tom had mentioned this to Leona before, so she knew it was surely in the back of his mind. "By the way," she said, "I'm thinkin' Gloria's ready to talk to your father again about church. But honestly, she seems either bashful or just plain terrified."

Tom seemed to understand what she was asking. "I'll see what I can do."

Leona hoped she wasn't stepping out of bounds, but a nod from the deacon might just be the push Gloria needed.

~~⁓⟩⟨⁓~~

It was a beautiful Lord's Day afternoon, an off-Sunday from Preaching, and Gloria had been told by Leona at breakfast that the deacon wanted to see her.

A bit anxious, Gloria walked through the long field to knock on his door, being met by the deacon himself sitting out on the porch, munching on some pretzels in a bag. He motioned for her to join him and handed the bag over to her when she was seated.

"I'm glad you got my message," he said, nodding his head. "Have you given some thought to what we talked 'bout before?"

"I've talked to my parents," she said. *And counted the cost in more ways than one.* She considered her conversation with her dad and mom, and with Hampton, who had been sorry to lose her good waitressing help, and Darren's surprisingly agreeable response, too.

Deacon led her through a series of questions, many like those before, but with a few new ones. She answered each one thoughtfully, confidently.

And she sensed he was building up to the clincher: "Have you forgiven your father?" She was prepared for that, but then he surprised her by saying, "His check arrived the other day."

Gloria nodded, relieved.

"Do you know 'bout that?"

She told him the truth: that while she and her father had stopped for coffee on the drive home, Gloria had urged him to make things right with those whom he had cheated.

"And apparently he has, although I'd forgiven his debt years ago," Deacon said.

Knowing the minister, he would put the money in the alms fund for anyone in need amongst the People. It was one of the things about Deacon Ebersol—and this community—that Gloria respected so much.

Then came the final question. "Did you return primarily for your friendship with Leona?"

"In many ways, yes."

His eyes widened.

"From what I've experienced through the years, Amish society is about community," she said. "We're linked together by family and lifelong friendships, and it's this tradition that weaves us together, encouraging one another in the Old Ways as a people set apart. We're loyal to our family and friends," she said, meaning it. "And sometimes we *return* for the same reason—relationship is the tie that binds us in unity with God."

The deacon nodded thoughtfully, a slight glint in his eye. "If you'd said no," he replied now, smiling, "I would have worried."

She hid her own smile. *A trick question.*

The deacon rose, and she stood with him, returning the remaining pretzels. "I'll give you further information about your Proving." He extended his callused hand. "*Willkumm heem,* Gloria."

❧

Gloria tried to stand still on the wooden kitchen bench that evening while Leona pinned her hem for the new dark green cape dress, but she was ever so keyed up and eager to share her conversation with the deacon that day.

All the same, she was completely surprised when Millie mentioned that Pete and the deacon had put their heads together at a farm auction the other day. "Mose asked if we'd be willin' to be your overseers till your Proving's done."

Leona jerked around with a straight pin in her hand, poking Gloria in the leg. "*Ach,* sorry!"

"I'm okay," Gloria assured her, even though Leona looked dismayed when the pinprick had drawn blood. "I couldn't imagine a better match."

"Me neither," Millie agreed.

Gloria was conscious of the summertime sounds just out the back screen door—crickets twittered heartily, and hoot owls supplied the bass line for a hundred-bird chorus.

"Just think, you'll get to visit with Orchard

John from time to time when he's over here for supper and board games," Leona said as she dabbed a wet tissue at Gloria's leg. "Maybe Tom and I can double-date with ya, since we're both church members. What 'bout that?"

Gloria glanced at Millie. "Do you think that would be all right with the brethren?"

"As long as you're in the company of other church members, you should be fine." Millie made a motion as if to zip her lips, a twinkle in her eyes.

"Now you're talkin'!" Gloria said, which caused Leona and her mother to dissolve into laughter.

"There—your hem's marked." Leona got up from her knees, and Gloria hopped down from the bench.

"*Denki*, now I just need to make the apron." She went over and planted a kiss on Millie's cheek. "That's for bein' so *wunnerbaar*."

Millie looked like she might faint. Come to think of it, so did Leona.

"I mean it," Gloria said, "with all of my heart." And she flounced off to hang up her new dress, pleased to have been given a second chance, not to mention a second mother.

*And a sister!*

The following Saturday evening, Pete and Millie wasted no time in inviting Orchard John for a supper of chicken and dumplings, topped off by Gloria's cherry cobbler, which turned out better than any other time she'd made it. Pete contributed the homemade ice cream, and Benuel told his laugh-out-loud tales, making for a very merry time around the Speicher table.

Afterward, the six of them played a rousing game of Dutch Blitz. Gloria couldn't stop smiling, appreciating how Pete, Millie, and Benuel were chaperoning the evening—the first of many to come, she suspected from the look of admiration on John's handsome face. *Or is it love?*

When it was time for John to leave, he asked if he might speak to Gloria out on the back porch, and Pete agreed after taking time to light a lantern and hand it to him.

"I want to win your heart," John told her when they'd sat down just outside the back door.

"You did that years ago," Gloria said, meaning every word yet mindful of the restrictions on their relationship. "If things hadn't been so complicated, I would've been baptized in a heartbeat. If I'd had the gumption, I would've returned sooner."

Sitting there with her first beau felt so

familiar and normal, a reminder of the best year of her life.

John's eyes held her gaze. "Would ya consider letting me court ya, once you're baptized?"

She remembered what Deacon Ebersol had said about her Proving—that she must remain within its guidelines. "I'm not baptized yet, but if I were, my answer would certainly be yes." She paused. "Well, *jah.*"

John brightened all the more. "You've given me the gift of hope."

"There's always that." Gloria nodded. "Perhaps I've given more hope than I should've at this point."

He started to reach for her hand, then caught himself. "Just so ya know, I'll be counting the days and weeks."

She smiled and wished she could let him know how very happy he made her, but that day would come. *Surely it will . . . in the Lord's good timing.*

# Epilogue

*onnect the dots backward*, I thought as the baptismal candidates—most of them younger than Gloria—reverently filed into Preacher Miller's spruced-up home on Sunday, September 20, that very fall. If any detail at all had been altered in the steps that had brought Gloria to this sacred moment— if Joe Gingerich had chosen a different state to move to after his dustup in Salem, or if Gloria had fallen in love with anyone other than Orchard John, or even if Mamma had given birth to a second daughter—Gloria might not be kneeling before the bishop.

During the holy hush of the ceremony, I found myself holding my breath as Gloria vowed to turn her back on the world, self, and the devil, pledging to gladly submit to

Jesus Christ her Savior and the *Ordnung* of the church in Colerain for all the days of her life.

*Home for good,* I thought, attempting to suppress my jubilation.

Not only had I circled the date on my bedroom calendar, I'd drawn short little rays around it. *"Joyful strokes of thanksgiving,"* I'd told Gloria when she came in dressed in royal blue and her newly made white organdy apron this morning. My humble friend, my sister, looked almost saintly.

Deacon Ebersol stood before the baptismal candidates and poured a bit of water from a cup into Bishop Mast's hands, which rested on Gloria's auburn hair. As he released the water, it trickled down over her head. "I baptize you in the name of the Father, the Son, and the Holy Spirit. Amen."

When Gloria and the other baptismal candidates rose and received the handshake from the bishop and the holy kiss from his wife, Gloria's eyes caught mine.

Inwardly, where no one but the Lord knew how desperately I'd yearned for this day, I was rejoicing with every ounce of my being.

Bishop Mast informed Gloria and the newly baptized youth that they were no longer sojourners and strangers, but *members* of this blessed and godly fellowship.

*Thanks be to the Lord,* I prayed silently,

grateful that Gloria had at last become my true sister in the family of God. She would also be at my side on my wedding day come the second Thursday in November.

The only thing missing was Gloria's family. Privately, before breakfast, Gloria had shared with me that having *my* parents, Dawdi Benuel, and me witness her baptism, along with Orchard John and his family, was enough. And judging from the glow on her freckled face as she filed out of the congregation just now with the other *Youngie*, I believed her. With all of my heart, I did.

# Author's Note

Creating stories set in Amish farmland has sustained my writer-heart in countless ways. It has taught me the importance of meticulous research and demonstrated to me just how universal some themes really are: At its core, each story is about lifting the spirit and stirring the heart, something that means readers from all ages and walks of life can connect to this cloistered and rather misunderstood group of people.

In this novel, Hill View, Arkansas, is a fictitious place based on the actual city of Ozark, a location my husband and I enjoyed visiting last fall while vacationing. Unlike the fictional Hill View, however, there is no Amish settlement in Ozark, though the town offers many other charms.

For his kindness and unfailing wisdom,

thanks to my longtime editor and friend, David Horton. For directing my writing to mine the depths and find the sparkle, thank you to Rochelle Glöege and her expert editorial team—Helen Motter, Ann Parrish, Cheri Hanson, Sharon Hodge, and Jolene Steffer. And for fine-tuning bits and pieces of the manuscript, my appreciation goes to Barbara Birch. I also appreciate my niece Lizzie Birch's enthusiasm for the game Dutch Blitz!

Special gratitude to each of my research assistants, including Hank and Ruth Hershberger, Erik Wesner (Amish America), and the unnamed Amish and Mennonites who kindly read my first drafts. To the Young Center for Anabaptist and Pietist Studies at Elizabethtown College, the Lancaster Mennonite Historical Society, and the good folk at Kauffman's Farm Market, thank you. And to my partners in prayer, crucial to my writing endeavors: I am daily grateful for each of you.

And last, thanks to my wonderful husband, David Lewis, my first editor and brainstorming partner, salad-maker extraordinaire, and dearest prayer partner. And to our grown children, Julie, Janie, and Jonathan, and granddaughter, Ariel, thank you for being my biggest fans ever . . . and the dearest legacy I could ever have.

*Soli Deo Gloria!*

**Beverly Lewis**, born in the heart of Pennsylvania Dutch country, is the *New York Times* bestselling author of more than ninety books. Her stories have been published in twelve languages worldwide. A keen interest in her mother's Plain heritage has inspired Beverly to write many Amish-related novels, beginning with *The Shunning*, which has sold more than one million copies and is an Original Hallmark Channel movie. In 2007 *The Brethren* was honored with a Christy Award.

Beverly has been interviewed by both national and international media, including *Time* magazine, the Associated Press, and the BBC. She lives with her husband, David, in Colorado.

Visit her website at www.beverlylewis.com or www.facebook.com/officialbeverlylewis for more information.

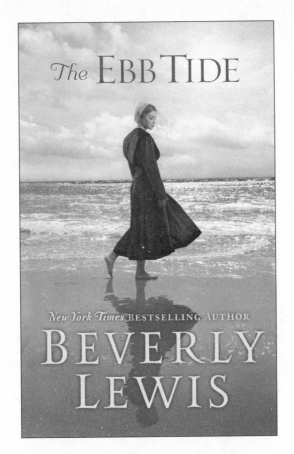

# The Ebb Tide

## The Next Novel From Beverly Lewis

### AVAILABLE APRIL 4, 2017

# ⬦BETHANYHOUSE

 Stay up to date on your favorite books and authors with our free e-newsletters. Sign up today at bethanyhouse.com.

 Find us on Facebook. facebook.com/bethanyhousepublishers

 Free exclusive resources for your book group! bethanyhouse.com/anopenbook

an open book

# Sign up for Beverly's newsletter!

Keep up to date with news on Beverly's upcoming book releases, signings, and other events by signing up for her email list at beverlylewis.com/engage/newsletter

# More From Beverly Lewis

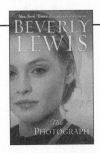

Old Order Amishwoman Eva Esch feels powerfully drawn to the charming stranger from Ohio. Will the forbidden photograph he carries lead to love or heartache?

*The Photograph*

# You May Also Enjoy . . .

A young widow with two children travels to her uncle's ranch in Montana seeking a fresh start. There, she encounters a suitor from her past, and her brother-in-law catches up to her—desperate to bring her back to New York.

*A Love Transformed* by Tracie Peterson
SAPPHIRE BRIDES #3

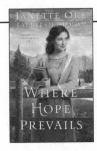

Beth Thatcher returns to Coal Valley, where a second schoolteacher has been appointed who openly rejects God. As she struggles with how to respond, she and Jarrick face new challenges in their relationship.

*Where Hope Prevails* by Janette Oke and Laurel Oke Logan
RETURN TO THE CANADIAN WEST #3

## BETHANYHOUSE

Stay up to date on your favorite books and authors with our free e-newsletters. Sign up today at bethanyhouse.com.

Find us on Facebook. facebook.com/bethanyhousepublishers

Free exclusive resources for your book group! bethanyhouse.com/anopenbook

an open book